Flashing across his viewscreen, an iridescent image was Jeremy Thorpe's first glimpse of the Vegans, the mysterious infiltrators of Earth's galactic sector, bent upon a seemingly mindless determination to eliminate the men of Earth.

That first glimpse was very nearly his last when Jeremy's ship *Quest* was almost instantly plunged into the cehrer of a holocaust of heat-beams and fragmentation bombs.

Jeremy and the two other survivors of *Quest* escaped with their lives only to find themselves stranded on the shores of a Vega-occupied planet. And in order to survive they had to discover that the key to Vega lay in the strange magic of a race that seemed to consist entirely of the opposite sex.

**Turn this book over for
second complete novel**

Also by John Rackham:

WE, THE VENUSIANS (M-127)

DANGER
FROM
VEGA

by

JOHN RACKHAM

ACE BOOKS, INC.
1120 Avenue of the Americas
New York, N.Y. 10036

I

THE TEN-SECOND ALARM had come and gone. Every one of the twenty-man crew braced himself and shivered as S.S. *Quest* slipped from the dark security of Pauli-space into the chill hazards of real space-time. There was that vertiginous moment of rainbow pinwheels and implosion, and then no time to dwell on it as they went into rapid and hard-eyed ready-up for anything that might happen.

Lieutenant Jeremy Thorpe knew his motions as well as and probably better than the rest. After five incredible years of this he had exceeded the average survival statistics so many times he had forgotten to count the multiples long ago. Space-suited only to his waist, his nimble fingers tripped and set and adjusted the controls before him. Suit-up was the order, but he was alone in the bow-torpedo control blister, and you could manipulate controls just that little bit faster without the armored gloves of a suit. And speed counted. Fire-and-aim controls—on. Detector-and-range screens—on. Outside viewscreen—on. Tubes loaded and ready—the three lower spots on his board winked into life to tell him that three crewmen were closed up and standing by to reload as he fired. Blister-space tight and sealed. Everything checked.

He touched a button, heard the quick-fire chatter of other stations, waited for a gap, and reported. "Bow-torp station to control, check!"

"Control to bow-torps, thank you. Maintain alert!" That was Captain Warnes, and that "maintain alert" was repeated, grim and meticulous, with his every acknowledgement. It was the leitmotif of the whole ship. Be on your toes. The first sign you see of anything that even looks like an enemy, lash out with everything you have, as fast as you can. A policy of desperation, hammered into men who knew that any second now might be their last. Thorpe listened to the chatter. After-torps; belly torps; forward beamers . . . the tale of aggressive armament rattled in the speaker as *Quest* hung in the vastness and spun lazily on a precessional twist. A quarter of a million miles away in any of six directions, other ships were doing the same, and still more ships beyond. Two dozen ships flung out into a tenuous globe in a near-hopeless attempt to contain that area of space where the earthside war-computers had calculated the Vegans were most likely to break out next time.

"Calculated!" He tasted the word in his thoughts and smiled without mirth. Educated guesswork was all. The war-comps guessed right about six or seven times in ten. Not good, but it was the best that could be got. Failing the guess-work, nobody *knew* anything about the Vegans that was helpful. Thorpe recalled what his father had told him, five years ago.

"They flash into the here and now out of nowhere. Bunched. Big shining ships, like chrome-plated eggs. They throw fragmentation-bombs at you. They fry you with heat-beams. They can stop on a pinhead, and lash into speed so fast you wonder how the ships stand it, never mind the crews.

6

They make rings round you, cut you to ribbons, and then—snap—they're gone again!" Five years ago, when he was only a newly-graduated youth, valiantly looking forward to "doing his bit" in Space Service against the Vegans in a murderous war that had then been going on for ten years. And now, after all that time, nobody knew anything more than that. Nothing that was helpful, at any rate.

A crackling tension held the ship, the strained silence of men who waited because there wasn't anything to do. Men who didn't know what to hope for. If the war-comps had guessed on the nose, a cluster of Vegans would materialize within the globe of ships, and then they would lash out with all their weapons. They would blast some of the shining ones, perhaps all of them. But some of the Solarian ships would die, too, because the Vegans were fast, and deadly. If the comps were away off this time, nothing would happen, and they would complete a waiting period, then jump back into Pauli-space and go back to base. To do it all over again soon. But the odds were more that the guess would be part accurate, that the enemy would emerge within hitting range of just one, or two, of the waiting ships.

Jeremy Thorpe grinned mirthlessly again. Then it would be every man for himself, with the chances of survival extremely remote. What the fragmentation-bombs left unripped, the heat-beams finished off in fused lumps. And, if by some miracle you did survive, chances of being picked up were so small as to be not worth thinking about. The spaces involved were too big, and fuel-capacity too limited to permit a lengthy search for bits of human driftwood.

He scanned his detectors by habit. His eye fell on two pictures, stuck there between a pair of gauges. Pin-ups. Two laughing, bright-eyed women. Color 3-D snaps that he had taken himself, on the white sand beach of a lake, long ago. Two lovelies, their scanty monokinis leaving no doubt as to their ebullient charms. Curious shipmates had asked him, had tried to raise a snigger about them, had eyed them with frank interest. But only once, each.

His retort, flat and straight, was always: "One's my mother, the other's my sister. Care to guess which is which?"

Nobody ever asked twice. Friendly envy and curiosity withdrew in a sense of embarrassment. Suggestive remarks somehow didn't seem right about a fellow's mother and sister. And Jeremy Thorpe had thereby concreted the impression that he was an unfriendly, unsociable sort. Which was true. It was also true about the photographs, in one way. In another way it wasn't. He took his gaze away from the lifelike pictures, pushing away the sore memories they evoked, and stared at the outside viewscreen.

Very few men of his acquaintance cared to look space full in the eye. That immense black-velvet out there, laced with fragile rainbows of ionization and studded with jewels that flamed in every imaginable color, was too vast and icily impersonal for them. They preferred to rely on their detectors and alarms, to preserve the illusion of security by means of steel walls and solid things to the touch. But Jeremy Thorpe liked to look at space. It was the one thing before which he could feel humble and impressed.

Most ironic of all, he was probably the only man present who need not have been. Fifteen years of insane war had laid its hand on social rules. If you were of the right age-group and reasonably fit, you had to be somebody very special to evade the net of conscription. He grinned again; it was almost a sneer now. He could have dodged it. And honorably, too. But he had chosen otherwise. He had wanted to be here.

Alarms screamed at him suddenly, shattering the musings into shards. He crouched over his screens instantly, fingers alert. There! Five bright spots in a cluster, and close. By God, they were close. Two of them leaped into motion even as he looked, moving so fast they drew thin green lines of fire on the target-scope, so fast that his insides heaved in sympathy with the g-forces involved. Twisting his DF controls frantically to keep them in view, he wristed down to launch one anti-matter torpedo at a spot ten degrees ahead on one of those lines, spun to focus on the other. It stopped, held still for a breath. Part of him wondered, for the thousandth time, how the hell they could do that. Power-gauges sagged and rose again as the beamers sucked energy and spat it at those shining things.

The *Quest* lurched and bucked as Captain Warnes tried to dodge what was being thrown at him yet remain within range. Thorpe twisted his scope grimly, holding that spot, waiting for it to jump. Which way? All at once it was off, a thin green line, leaping from dead-still into incredible speed. He tracked it, aimed well ahead, and wristed down again, bracing himself against the straining heaves of the ship. Two torpedoes gone. No sense in watching to see if they would hit. That took time. He shifted his scopes again to find more, his brain refusing the equation which said that five Vegans to one Solarian spelled certain destruction.

He caught another, and hesitated for just a breath at its odd behavior in the screen. Then he realized. This one was jumping, but almost straight towards the *Quest*. He flashed a glance to the outside screens, and saw what very few Earthmen had ever seen and lived to tell. There, a disc of shimmering silver, growing visibly with its velocity. And it stopped, virtually within its own length. He spun the DF madly, wristed down to let loose ravening death on a tail of ion-fire, and again. Then he stared at the viewscreen again, saw the shining thing hang there. Splashes of fire coruscated from it as *Quest*'s beamers stabbed out. The chrome-plate ovoid grew a ring of black holes suddenly, pockmarks which spat fire, and Thorpe grunted as the *Quest* lumbered sideways to evade the death that had been thrown. The gleaming image slid from the screen. He snatched a glance at his wide-range detector, just in time to see one green trail disappear in a fuzz of light. One down. They could be hit, if you were lucky.

His eyes were drawn back, fascinated, to the viewscreen. *Quest* rolled and heaved and the shining thing slid back on to the screen again, the ring of black ports now shut. Getting ready to jump, he guessed, and felt fury at the way the thing had dared to come so close, defying the worst the Earth ships could do. Then he yelled and was dazzled as the gleaming thing suddenly sprang apart in a hell of bright fire, a swelling globe of incandescence. The torpedoes had struck. Blinded, he twisted away from the screen, and *Quest* lurched, in an upwards leap. In that second he knew they'd been hit. Even as the straps snapped him back into his seat the stricken ship leaped again, harder, and the reverberation of impact echoed through the hull. Another buck-jump, and his head flailed against something steel-hard. Sparks flared and died in his head. Barely conscious, he fumbled to do up his suit all the way, struggled with the helmet, dragged it down, heard it click into place, and the ship seemed to spin and shiver and then dive into darkness, taking him down, too.

Down into a dream, a strange dream in which he was privileged to stand remote and watch himself doing the things he had done . . . A time when he had not been Jeremy Thorpe at all, but someone else. Gerald Corde. The afternoon of graduation day. He and the real Jeremy Thorpe, together in the study they had shared for two years. And there was one other, smaller and older than the two twenty-year-old six-footers who looked so much alike, but not in the least overpowered by them. Vice-Admiral Corde was accustomed to dominate any gathering of which he was part. He did so now, arrow-erect and formidable in his uniform.

"Good grades, Gerald," he said, and as he spoke you knew that "Whip" was the only possible nickname for him. "Just as I had expected. Counted on it. Best in the school!"

"Not quite, Dad. Jeremy nosed in ahead of me, as he always does."

"Fractionally," the old man dismissed it with a shrug. "No offense, young man, but it's Gerald's grades I'm interested in. I've gambled on you, son, and it paid off. I knew it would."

"I don't follow, Dad. What's this all about? Something special? I suspected something of the kind when I saw you in the crowd. Never expected you to be able to make it."

"Had to bend a regulation or two, at that. I haven't a lot of time, so listen. You've been expecting to go straight into Space Service from school, haven't you?"

"Doesn't everybody? I mean, that's the law now, isn't it?"

"Except for special cases. Very special cases. Like you!"

"Me?" Gerald sank into a chair, stared in bewilderment at Jeremy, who shrugged his lack of understanding, too. The old man permitted a chill smile to disturb his hard features.

"You're my son. The only son I have left. Since your mother died I've had to be mother and father to all of you. And, God help me, I haven't done too well at it. Andy and Jim were both hell-bent to follow in my footsteps. I let them. I was proud to have them in uniform. Now—they're both dead. I was a fool!" It was the nearest Gerald had ever heard his father come to admitting an error, and he marveled at it. "It's not going to happen to you, Gerald. I've made up my mind on that. It's not for you!"

"What?" Gerald was stunned. All his life had been spent in the smell and shadow of the Service. He had taken it for granted that he would wear the black-and-gold with sunbursts, and see space. The old man must be crazy. "You can't say that! I'm eligible now."

"I can pull strings. I have done. It was all arranged long ago. You've heard of Venus Special Research Center? United Earth set it up, about three years ago, to skim off the cream of our youth, the potential geniuses, the brains and resources we need, and keep them safe. Son, this war is bleeding us of our best and we are getting nowhere. Nowhere! Sheer guts and courage aren't going to get us anywhere, ever, in this business. We need brains, inspiration, new weapons, something to give us an edge. The Vegans— this is strictly within these four walls, mind—have us beat all ends up. It is sheer inertia and ignorance that keeps us going."

"You mean we haven't a chance?"

"Just that. We know almost nothing about the enemy, except that he can match us ship for ship, weapon for weapon, and fly rings round us in actual combat. We've known it for years. We haven't made it public, for obvious reasons. But we can't go on much longer. We're squeezing our resources, making them last, but we can't squeeze manpower much more. And we are fighting blind, like a punch-drunk blind boxer trying to beat a swarm of midgets with spears."

"I find that hard to believe." Jeremy Thorpe spoke timidly, his uncertain voice coming oddly from his big frame. Vice-Admiral Corde slanted a hard eye at him.

"It's true enough. Gerald knows most of it already, or he's not as smart as his grades seem to indicate. But we haven't publicized the true state of our plight simply because —as you've just said—it's hard to take. We humans have a built-in tradition of believing ourselves capable of overcoming anything in the long run. But we haven't got a long run, this time."

"Skip that!" Gerald was terse. "You're hoarding genius. All right. But what's that to do with me?"

"When Jim died, and I realized you were all I had left"— the harsh old voice cracked just a trifle—"I made up my mind you weren't going to be sacrificed on the juggernaut like the rest. I had to figure out how. I did it by making sure you had the very best schooling there was, by encouraging you to develop as fast and as far as possible. It wasn't such a gamble, at that. My side of the family isn't exactly half-witted, and your mother was a brilliant woman, God rest her soul. Then I originated the notion of a reserve of brain-power, and saw to it that the idea grew. I pushed it. I yanked every damned string I had, and they were plenty. I may not have been much of a father to you, Gerald, and I haven't seen as much of you as I ought, but I never let up on that aim. I was determined to save you from the bloody war machine out there!" The last words were a snarl.

More calmly, he went on. "Two years ago I saw the scheme come to fruit. And I put your name down as one potential candidate—on condition that you did well enough in your studies. That was the gamble. And you did, and I'm proud of you."

"Now just a minute!" Gerald leaped to his feet, the violence that was part of his impulsive nature breaking through. "Didn't it occur to you that I had some say in this?"

"You're my son. You'll do as I say!"

"You can't have it both ways. If I'm in uniform, I'm under your orders. If not, not. And be damned to your scheme!"

The old man got to his feet, squared his shoulders, set his jaw and bent a hard eye on his son.

"You'll do it!" he snapped. "You'll obey orders, damn you! It's all arranged. Here!" He slid a hand into his tunic, brought out a folder and slapped it on the table. "All the documents. Reservations for the shuttleship to Venus. Full clearances. You'll be on that ship tomorrow, hear me? If you try to defy my orders I'll ruin you. If you try anything so insane as to enlist"—he smiled a vicious smile—"but you won't. You're a smart lad, my son, and no fool!"

"Why you—!" Gerald had never had any deep affection for his father, had not seen enough of him for it to develop. But he had known a certain degree of respect. Now it was swept away in a rage so intense, and so futile, that he was robbed of speech.

"Cool down and think about it," the old man advised. "At your age I know there's glamor about a uniform. But there's damn-all glamor out there. It's a gamble, with the odds against you, and sudden death when you lose. We aren't *fighting* the Vegans. We're fly-swatting them, and missing most of the time." His hard old eyes took on a distant look. "They flash out of nowhere. They can stop on a pinhead, jump into acceleration that would mash us. They throw fragmentation-bombs, fry us with heat-beams, cut us to ribbons, and then—snap—they're gone again!"

"Can't we do anything?" That was Jeremy again, shrill now.

"We can't. Yet. It's up to brainy ones like Gerald here, and the finest scientific resources we can lay hands on, to pull something out of the bag to give us the edge."

"You realize"—Gerald was bitter—"that everyone will think that you contrived this? That I'm a dodger, so labeled, because of you? D'you think I'm going to like that?"

"Who cares what anybody else thinks? You be on that ship tomorrow. And that's about all. My time's tight. Goodbye. I don't imagine I'll be able to see you for a year or

13

two, but I'll be in touch. Venus Directorate will keep me informed. I'm counting on you to show 'em!"

And with a flourish he capped himself and strode out of the quiet study, away down the corridor, leaving a desolation in his wake. Jeremy went to the table to finger the folder, his face a chaos of uncertainty.

"Was it right, what he said about the hopelessness of the war?"

"Eh? Oh, sure, it's right enough." Gerald muttered. "If you'd spent all your vacations as I have, milling around officer's quarters, or being shooed away from some high echelon meeting in a hotel suite, you'd know. You hear things, things you're not meant to hear or understand. Sure the war is tough. I can't give you precise figures, but we're taking a hell of a pasting, by all accounts."

"You knew, and you still want to enlist?"

"Ever since I was old enough to have an opinion of my own it's been the automatic future for me. Andy, and Jim, and Dad—and me, in my turn. Call it a family tradition, if you like. And now that old coot with his yap, yap, yap— who the hell does he think he is, telling me what to do?"

Gerald glared at the shut door, seeing again his father strut away, boiling with impotent rage, and then he turned to Jeremy. And his rage died as he noticed something remarkable. To a casual observer the two youths were very alike, both big, brawny, blond and more than passably good-looking. To anyone prepared to look closer, however, there were subtle differences in the stance, the line of a chin or eye. Where Gerald was volatile, quick in thought and intention, Jeremy was passive and inclined to wait. His was the face of the intellectual introvert, ready to ponder the details and arrive at the measured solution. At any other time his expression was one of brooding calm, but now it was a confusion of emotions. Gerald saw him clutching that precious folder, saw him shake with some inner turmoil.

"Hey!" he said. "What's up? No need for you to get upset, old son, over *my* family quarrels!"

"It's so damned unfair!" Jeremy turned on him, his face pale with unusual vehemence. "You get this . . ." he shook

14

the folder, "a passport to safety, just because your father is a Vice-Admiral and can pull strings. There's nobody to pull strings for me. My family scraped the bottom of the barrel to be able to maintain me here this long. And now, tomorrow, I have to be swept into the damned military machine whether I like it or not—and I don't—where as you, who *want* to join up, will be excused!"

"That's the way it goes. That's life!"

"Is that all you can say? Life? It's a criminal mockery. You're the military type. You'd love it. But no—you get let off!"

For a moment Gerald was taken aback by his friend's near-hysteria. He had never seen Jeremy like this before. The thought flashed through his mind that Jeremy was scared, had probably been dreading this for some time, but had kept it to himself. He felt resentment, too, at the implication that it was in some way his fault. But the words he might have said were stillborn as an utterly fantastic idea burst into his mind. He stared, seeing Jeremy still clutching that precious collection of documents, and let the idea run, leaping for the conclusion and scorning the possible obstacles in between. Why not? The question shouted so loudly in his mind that he marveled that Jeremy couldn't hear it.

"Passport!" he babbled. "Why not? You've got it in your hand. Why not hang on to it?"

"Eh? What are you talking about?"

"The folder. You have it in your hand. Why not keep it? Who's to know?" The inspiration was so urgent that he shook with the effort to be rational. Going close to Jeremy he said, "What's to stop you marching out of here tomorrow, taking a cab to the shuttle field, and presenting those papers in my place? Who's to know, or care? Here, let me see them just a minute!" He took the folder from Jeremy's limp grasp and shook out the contents on to the table, stirring them with a quick finger. "Just as I thought. Flight reservation, seat number, baggage clearance, authorizations— but not a thing about identification. Whoever is carrying this is Gerald Cord. Get it? You, in my place!"

For a further three breaths the confusion raged on Jeremy's face, but then it cleared and was calm. The fine mind had been presented with a problem, and now tackled it in habitual fashion.

"It would never work, Jerry. Too many snags."

"All right. You name 'em, I'll shoot 'em down. Come on!"

"I might run into your father."

"Forget it. The old man wasn't kidding when he said he had a tight schedule. I was surprised he was able to make it here at all today. There's a war on, brother. I'll bet you he's airborne right now, and spaceborne in hours from now. Forget him. Next?"

"What about your part, as me?"

"What about it? I know the drill. Proceed from here to your State Induction Center with reasonable speed by first available transport . . ."

"I meant—about the rest of the school. You'll be seen!"

"Be your age!" Gerald scorned. "How many kids in the school know us to speak to—a dozen? And who's to care?"

Jeremy frowned, half-closing his eyes. "But what about—after you are in? Remember what your father said. And he is a Vice-Admiral!"

"But he won't give a damn, even if it ever came to his ears, about one Jeremy Thorpe, crewman trainee. Jerry, it can't miss!" Gerald snapped his fingers in triumph. "And it's better this way. Think. I'm in. It's what I want, what I intend to get, and I'm the type, as you said. The old man can kid himself about my grades, but you know better than anyone that they aren't as good as yours. And I'm not the 'potter-about-in-a-lab' type, at all. You know that. Lord knows we've done enough aptitude tests to make it clear. My talent, such as it is, is speed, fast decisions, and mechanical know-how. You're the 'abstract theory' one. Brother—it's perfect!"

"Are you really keen to get into the Service, Jerry? After all you know about it?"

"You find that puzzling?" Gerald laughed. "I've got my own reasons; I won't bother you with them now. Don't matter, anyway. It's all fixed. As of tomorrow, we swap places, you and me. . . ."

"What? What?"

Jeremy tossed the folder back on to the table and sighed. "I knew it was too good. And I missed the obvious thing. Jerry, you said you know the drill. We all do. Induction Center, tests and check-ups, assignments to training camps—and they they give you two weeks leave, starting at once, because it might well be the last you'll ever have—" He let the sentence dwindle into silence. Gerald froze, then turned, walked to his chair and sank into it.

"Hell!" he mumbled. "Hell and damnation! Leave—I never gave it a thought. I've never had a home to go to, never bothered to consider—"

"There's my mother," Jeremy said, very quitely. "And my kid sister, too. They know I'm due home. I wrote and told them." The silence in the study grew and thickened. Gerald raged internally. It was such a good scheme. It had a justice, a rightness about it. He just couldn't imagine Jeremy in a military environment, jumping to it, reacting on the hop. It would be murder! But he had a home and family. Gerald had no way of assessing such values. In all his life he had known only the hard-faced Admiral as a father, remote, and the impersonal care or orderlies and hotel staff. But his mind, violently impatient as always, flew at the problem, beat at it.

"I'm sorry." Jeremy sounded dull in defeat. "I wish it could have been possible. It was such a good idea. . . ."

"Just a minute!" Gerald lifted his head, clutching desperately at a faint hope. "Your mother's looking for you to come home by Saturday, day after tomorrow? And she'll be disappointed, hurt maybe, if I turned up in your place, wouldn't she?"

"It's out of the question. She would never understand!"

"Oh yes she might, if you wrote a letter and I took it with me. If you wrote and explained. Look, which do you think she would rather have, you on leave for two weeks and then—bam!—into Space Service? Or you not coming home for a long while, but tucked safe and secure on Venus? Well? Is it so hard to figure?"

"I don't know." Jeremy hesitated. But he did know. The

17

answer was too obvious to miss. After some hesitation and shuffling he surrendered and took out a pad and pen. Gerald was on fire with victory. To get into the Service after all, and to put one over on the old man—he wasn't sure which element was more tasty, but he liked the sensation.

"Get writing, brother," he urged. "Make it good!"

The dream began to break up, to go out of focus, to whirl into a fractured unreality in which the magnification closed in and settled on that pen, on the paper, scratching laboriously away. Scratching—

II

THE SCRATCHING SOUND was in his right ear, irritatingly. He stirred, and cringed as the top of his head came off. Keeping absolutely still, he waited for it to settle back into place. Helmet. He felt the seal-ring at his neck, felt the hard curve against his forehead. His helmet was too small for his head, which was ridiculous. His head was a low-pressure can through which a tenuous gaseous ache swirled and curled. The scratching came again, was a strained and ragged voice.

"This is Captain Warnes. I ask again, can anyone else hear me? Anyone? If you hear this, report—please!"

Suit-radio. He ventured a movement, discovered that in some inexplicable fashion he was upside-down, retched at the wave of pain that came with the finding, and wriggled his chin to move the talk-switch. The first try brought nothing, second try a croak, and on the third attempt he said, "Lieutenant Thorpe hearing you, sir."

"Thank God. One more. Anybody else? Report—please!"

There came nothing but the low hum of carrier-waves and intermittent crackling. He wriggled tentatively. He was upside-down. And the torpedo-control compartment was in utter blackness, not even secondary battery-lights showing. He thrust away that significance and struggled to move his cumbersome arms enough to switch on the suit-lights that were fitted to each cuff. Then, by their tenuous beams, he tried to get himself oriented.

"I'm going to assume that there are only the five of us," Warnes said, sounding as if he were stretched to the limit but determined to keep on. "I'll call the roll, just to make sure. Lieutenant Thorpe, you seem to be next senior to me. Bow-torpedoes, I think. Gladden, power-deck crew. Hadley, you're starboard aft beamer-crew. Skoda, radio-man. For the last time, is there anybody else?" The only answer was an indifferent wash of static.

"Very well. We are five. We still live. I'll hear your reports, in sequence, and let's see if we can get a picture of some kind. Thorpe?"

"Total blackout here, sir. So far as I can make out by my suit-lights, and the tension in my suit, the space is tight. Not holed. But that's all."

"And you yourself?"

"I've had a clout on the head. Knocked me out for a bit. But I'm all right otherwise, I think."

"Thank you. Hadley, I'll hear you now."

"I'm fit, sir," the voice was a thick growl with a suspicion of brogue in it. "Shook up a bit, but nothing to bother about. Blackout, as Mr. Thorpe just said. I've checked around a bit. Far as I can tell, the whole after-section is hanging in rags. Flapping in the breeze. Do I check some more, sir?"

"Yes. Be careful now. Thank you. Skoda?"

A shaky, rather high-pitched voice made a false start then settled down to say. "All black here too, sir. The shack is a bloody mess. Weebly and Lieutenant Juno—all chewed up. Equipment is smashed all to hell."

"And you, yourself?"

"Can't use my right arm, sir. Sorry—"

"All right. Don't worry about it. Gladden, let's hear from you."

There was a harsh roar of static, at once, over which Thorpe could just hear the unsteady voice saying "Tech-sergeant Gladden reporting. The power-deck is a mess of bomb-fragments. No survivors, only me. And not me for very much longer."

"What the hell does that mean?"

"Radiation, sir. The space is blue with it. Bomb-fragment shattered the pile-shielding all to pieces. She shut herself off, automatically. That's why where's no power on. But the damage is done now."

"Take your anti-radiation capsules!"

"Too late for that, sir. And they won't cope with this density anyway. Stupid—"

"Gladden!" Warnes shouted. "Don't give up, man!"

"Was going to say, sir, it's stupid. The drive is O.K. by the look of it. I can override the automatic quite easily. But if I do the whole bloody ship will be as hot as this space in about thirty seconds. Stupid. We're all dead, one way or the other."

"That will do!" Warnes snapped. "We're not dead yet. Attention all. We're in a hell of a mess, no sense in trying to minimize that. But we are not dead yet. Mr. Thorpe—Hadley—you two seem to be capable of movement. I suggest you do what you can to check lifeboats. You too, Skoda, if you can manage with one arm. If there's only one boat intact, there's a chance. Gladden!"

"Forget it, sir." The roar of interference came as Gladden opened his talk-switch. I'm staying right here. I've had it and I know it. If you want the power on for anything, just say. But don't leave it too long, I haven't much time!" Thorpe was already on the move, groping for the bleeder-valve that would discharge the compartment pressure. A small omission came to his mind.

"Captain Warnes," he said, "how about you, sir? Are you all right?"

"Never mind about me."

"We've a right to know, sir. There are only five of us." He found the valve, and felt his suit pop as the pressure dwindled on the outside. The hatch-lock moved under his hand and swung open to show stars.

"Right?" Warnes grunted. "What right has any one of

us, in a situation like this? Gladden is right. We're all dead, only we won't admit it. We keep on trying, in futility. I'm smashed, Lieutenant. Damned control-module tore away from the bulkhead and has me trapped from the waist down. I can't feel a thing, yet. Never had time to get into a suit, but I managed to reach the helmet, which is how I'm talking to you now. But don't write me off. We need all the wits we have. How about those damned boats? And how does she look, from outside?"

Thorpe had snagged his lifeline on a ring-bolt and was now drifting away from the hull, squirming to spin himself so that he could see. The big dark was all round him, blazing with glorious jewels of fire. Back there on the end of the slim line, the *Quest* looked pathetically small, a toy cast adrift in vastness. It spun helplessly as he watched and saw where one bomb had struck flush on the transverse bulkhead which separated the control-deck from the drive-space. The gaping wound was black and ragged-edged. All that side of the ship was in ruin. He saw the star-limbed midget that had to be Hadley on a similar errand. He saw the stern, and Hadley had called it exactly. Hanging in rags. Flapping in the breeze, if there had been any breeze. But the drive-and-steer tubes seemed unhurt, thrusting through the wreckage like fingers of a steely hand. The slow spin of the ship began to wind him back and he took a handgrip on the line, jerking gently.

"Not worth bothering to check on any of the midship boats," he reported. "Or the after-section. It's a mess. Forward end looks hopeful. I am moving that way now."

"Confirm." Hadley growled. "I'll make my way forward too, see if I can give Skoda a hand."

Minutes later the three of them were clustered round the blister that held the forward port lifeboat. Thorpe reported.

"This one seems O.K., sir. We'll come and help you out . . ."

"Take it and blast off!" Warnes interrupted, his voice crackling with urgency and pain. "You can't do anything for me. No suit, and you can't get in here without bleeding

21

the compartment. I haven't long, anyway. Good luck, Lieutenant, and you other two. . . ."

"We can't just shove off and leave you!" Thorpe was aghast at the suggestion. He tried to see Captain Warnes in his mind, to see him half-crushed and dying, and the picture would not come.

"For God's sake, go!" Warnes shouted. "I'm finished, I tell you! I have a capsule. Carried it ever since I first blasted off. A quick death. I've taken it. A man has a right to some dignity in his last moments. Go, damn you!" The voice cut off with a click. Thorpe felt sick, mentally and physically. His head banged like an empty can. He was slimy with sweat and condensation. Nausea hovered in his gullet. Around him the beautiful stars blazed in sublime indifference. And fifteen men were dead, a ship was dead, they were all dead, in everything but name. Warped and ruptured metal, lifeless gadgetry, and the unthinking enormity of space—and three feeble human bodies dared to hope.

"Pointless to man the pod," Hadley growled. "What would we do after, wait? And for what? Who's going to come for us? Where can we go?"

"There's got to be something!" Thorpe muttered.

"We're a week away from anywhere, even in Pauli," Skoda mumbled. "We can't hope to reach anything, not in a pod."

"If the ship's drive still works, as Gladden said—"

"It's O.K." Gladden's voice came over the sudden hailstorm of static as he cut in. "I've checked round. I have only to throw the manual reset and you have the lot, steering-jets, ion-drive, Pauli—everything—"

"And a bellyful of curies!" Hadley snarled. "A fat lot of good that is, to us!"

"Hold it!" Thorpe snapped, snatching at a stray idea. "We have first class shielding, too, right here!" and he thumped his armored hand on the hull. "This is designed to shield the crew from external radiation. No reason why it won't work the other way round."

"But somebody's got to be in there, to operate—"

"Oh no! Remember the module construction theory?" It was a basic in everybody's training. All ships were so designed, compartmented, so that in emergency the ship could be conned, flown, and fought, from any sector. There were multi-point plugs and multi-core cables in all sections, just for such a case.

"By remote," he declared. "We can do it from out here, from the pod! Come on, give me a hand to hook up. Skoda, you cable-up the pod. Hadley, with me. The bow-torp space was intact when I left it. We can cross-link from there!"

Shuffling and scrambling over the foreshortened horizon of the hull in sudden hope, they forgot their fears and discomforts, shaking and fumbling in their urge to be quick, cursing the thumb-fingered clumsiness of their suits. Massive cables were plugged in and they got back to the lifeboat, to scramble in alongside Skoda. Thorpe chinned his talk-switch, offering a silent prayer.

"Gladden! You hear me? Still there?"

He winced as the storm of static came again, hurting his ears. "What d'you want?" Gladden sounded lightheaded, uncaring. "Thought you'd gone a long time ago. Waiting for? You want to come in here? Pretty! All blue and mauve, everything sparkling like diamonds . . ." The disjointed mumble faded out below the static roar. Thorpe felt imminent panic, the urge to scream. Gladden had gone over the edge, that was obvious. He was crazy. And they were all stuck with it. He cast a feverish glance round the dim blue glare of the confined lifeboat space. Two hulking shadowy forms loomed, staring sightlessly at him through obscure face-plates. They said nothing. They were leaving it to him. *My God!* he thought, *I'm senior. I'm in charge!* The knowledge dragged him back from the breaking-point, made his wits churn.

Gladden had gone crazy. No blaming him, at that, but what to do? It was pointless to try to break in on him, even if he could have achieved anything by the doing. Ten seconds in that radiation sleet and he'd be all through. A crazy man. Humor him. Why not?

"Gladden!" he tried to be loud and firm without quaver. "You hear me? It's pretty down there?"

23

"Beautiful. Like fairy-land. Everything shining. Shining!"

"Gladden. I bet it would shine ten times as bright, if you made that switch, re-set the trip, made the drive hot. Eh? Wouldn't that be good?"

Thorpe waited, holding his breath, feeling the cold sweat collect in beads and dribble down his face. That damned roar was getting louder. He heard Gladden mumble something, couldn't tell what. Then the hailstorm roar surged into a sudden and deafening tattoo, a scream—and then a silence that echoed. The life-boat's dim blue glare flickered and became bright. In the same instant the awkwardly twisted sense of "down" being a bit sideways went away. Everything seemed to orient properly. The far fringe of his mind told him the pseudo-gravity unit must have been jarred out of phase in the strike, but was now bedded and functioning normally. Hadley's thick growl sounded in his ear.

"We ought to say Amen, sir. Begod, he was a man!"

"That's true. He's given us a chance. And we'd better not waste it." Thorpe rallied himself into action, anything rather than contemplate the hell of hard radiation that was sleeting through the guts of the *Quest*, just the other side of the hull. "Are we tight? All right, the first thing to do is half-suit. Skoda, I want a look at that arm, see if we can do anything for it." He started to unclip his helmet. Skoda protested.

"The hell with that. Let's get going somewhere!"

"That's what I intend to do. And you're our radio-man, the only one we have. We need you to tell us where. Look, I can fly this thing, with luck, but I need you to plot and set course. Now shut up and get that suit down. Hadley, lend a hand. . . ." The lifeboat was not meant for luxury. The crewman nickname for it, "pod," was scathingly accurate. In essence, not more than an armored metal tube, the lower third of it was taken up by a miniature ion-drive operating from minimum storage-batteries. The upper section was crammed with a simplified module read-out of the controls, and a remote-access to the ship's masters. What was left of space between was devoted to hooked harness and bulkhead lockers containing the bare essentials for survival.

Four men could cram into a pod, if they had to. Now, with only three, but bulking huge in space suits, the room to move was at a minimum. Thorpe got his hand and arms free, reached for Skoda.

"I'll try not to hurt anything. Hadley, be checking round; see what we have in the way of grub and water. And medical. Now then—" He took Skoda's arm and palpated it gently through the sweat-sodden cotton union suit that was all of any of them ever wore in action. On a stray thought he said to Hadley, "Look out for anti-rad capsules, too. We'll need those right away."

"I thought you said the hull would shield us." Skoda quavered, his face gauntly white and corpse-like in the blue glare.

"So it will, but we're on the outside now, and there's space-radiation to think of. The pod ought to keep off most of it, but we can't take any chances." His fingers traveled swiftly, his whole attention given to what he could feel, his dragging weariness and throbbing head ignored. Skoda, as he could see now, was a dark, shock-haired Italianate type, with high cheekbones and cavernous eyes. The harsh light made him look ghastly.

"I can't feel anything broken—ah!" He had reached the upper arm, and from the way the man cringed as he tried to help, the answer became obvious. "Dislocation is all, I think. And I've done this before, thank the Lord. Hadley, I'll need you to brace. Damn this pod, there isn't enough room to turn round. Now, you hold on to him. That's it. Let me get set. Skoda—this will hurt like hell, but only for a moment, so set your teeth. Ready!" He shuffled his shoulders solidly against a bulging locker, took a firm hold. In that moment everything seemed to blue and go out of focus, like a scene from a nightmare. He sucked in a breath, shook his head, and made the effort. Skoda bit down on a groan —and it was done.

"Right. All over. You take a breath or two and then get busy on that board; see what you can make of it. What's your score, Hadley?"

"Not very bright, sir. Plenty of food-paste tubes, but not

much water. Four bulbs is all I can find. About enough for twenty-four hours and a bit. For what good that is."

"About what I'd expected," he muttered. "We're lucky there are any stores at all. The whole lifeboat idea is just a token gesture. I never heard of anybody being rescued from one. Space is just too damn big!"

"There's a medical kit, sir. If you'll hold still I might be able to do something for that head of yours."

"Eh? Oh, never mind that now. It's not serious."

"Take a look for yourself!" Hadley lifted the lid of the box to let Thorpe see himself in the mirror there. He couldn't recognize that spectacle as himself at all. The blue glare made it worse, of course, but even allowing for that, he was a sight. Blood had flowed freely from a dark gash over his right eye, had spread itself all down one side of his face, across his mouth, and was flaking away now. His eyes were black-ringed and too bright by far, and he shone with greasy sweat. He tried to grin, looked at Hadley, and saw a big craggy face, equally grimy and greasy, staring at him.

"Christ!" he mumbled. "We're a sight for sore eyes. All right, see what you can do, but don't worry too much. It looks worse than it is."

He settled against the bulkhead in a crouch to let Hadley loom over him. At the first clumsy dab of cleansing antiseptic jelly, he shut his eyes and fought against the pain-arrows. Strangely, it was easier to bear this sharply localized agony than to fight off the overall drag of ache that had suffused him so far. Then, in seconds, the anesthetic in the paste was doing its work, the pain went away, and he felt light, like a feather.

"That's cleaner than it was. I'll be stitching it now, sir—"

"Nothing much on board," Skoda called, craning back over his shoulder. "The memory banks don't recognize a thing, by these readings. I'll try analysis." Thorpe shut his eyes again. It was eerie to be able to "hear" the screw-needle biting into his scalp and yet not feel it. Skoda's news was bad, but no more than he would have expected. They were too far away from any system known to them for it to register on their limited scanners. That figured. The jump

26

from base to rendezvous had taken almost a week in Pauli-drive. So the only thing left was analysis. Feed the data into the ship's computer and hope it would identify something reasonably close as being sufficiently Earth-type to offer chance of planet-fall. That was hope stretched to gossamer fineness. Hadley lurched back.

"Best I can do, sir. Here, you'd better take an anti-rad capsule. Skoda, one for you." Thorpe scrambled erect again, cinched the waistbelt of his suit and stretched to lie along-side the radio-man where he could see the control-console.

"Any luck?"

"Coming through now, what there is of it. God knows what that radiation is doing to the electronics in there, sir, but I'm getting a solid string of negatives so far. Not a bloody thing. No, wait, there's one!" Skoda's fingers flew to recall and hold one cluster of data. Thorpe scanned the reading, knowing enough to recognize it as barely within the permissible parameters. "If it isn't a mocker, it's a chance. An outside chance. By this, it's a small sun, GO type, plan-ets doubtful—and it's forty-eight hours away, near enough exactly."

"Nothing else?"

"Not a ghost of anything. What do we do, sir?"

Again the load came back on his shoulders. Senior. In charge. Make a decision, Jeremy Thorpe. You have two other men depending on you. You have water, life's essential, for twenty-four hours only. You have a crippled ship, alive with boiling radiation. And one dubiously possible sun-system two days away. If everything works the way it should. Some choice!

"What else can we do?" he growled. "Check that read-ing again and firm it up for course and jump. Hadley, let's make sure everything's lashed down tight, and let me see that medical box again, will you?" He lifted the lid and fingered the contents, hoping to find what he was looking for. He lifted out a small foil-wrapped package.

"We'll use these," he said. "Knock-out pills. As soon as we've made the jump—" They couldn't see the crossed-finger thought in his mind, for which he was profoundly thankful.

The P-drive was a delicate thing, not meant to be bathed in savage radiation, "We'll take a little water, food, and one of these each. Twenty-four hour coma—"

"One of us ought to keep watch," Hadley protested.

"For what?" he snapped. "And why? What can we do to anybody we might run into?" In theory, one kept watch while in Pauli because there were rare times when the nearby presence of power-generators registered through the field, and you could snap out into real space-time and engage. But now?

"It's the only way to make the water last out. All right? Buckle up the harness, and stand by." They struggled, fumbling past and around each other, until they were trussed in the hammock-like harness that served in lieu of acceleration-couches. Thorpe squirmed to get his face and arms turned towards the controls. They were small and crude, nothing as efficient as those inboard, but they would have to serve. A dizzy sense of unreality swept over him again; clusters of needles and gauge-lights swam before his eyes. Vomit lurked at the back of his throat, jerking his stomach. He swallowed once, made himself steady, and gripped the controls.

His tentative touch brought an instant shudder rumbling through the hull. That much still worked, anyway. He tried again, watching the wheeling star-patterns, stilling them, sending them creeping back at an angle, striving to get his sensors and the course-computer's requirements into line with each other. The target-scope shifted and blurred as he glared at it. He squeezed his eyes tight shut, tried again. Gently. Just a nudge. The green-fire cross hairs wandered perversely all round the center. Sweat ran from the end of his nose. He itched. His arms felt like lead.

"Oh, come ON!" he mumbled, nudging the levers again, seeing the cross hairs shiver and creep towards each other. And match. He slammed a switch home to lock on. Now—if only the P-drive were still functioning. He gripped with both hands and twisted, slipped the notch and rammed home—the real universe dissolved in a rainbow pinwheel, bringing vertigo, the wrench of implosion—the spectrum spun, ran in on itself and dwindled rapidly into infra-red blackness, taking him with it.

III

THE DREAM CAUGHT HIM as he fell, but this time it was disjointed and fragmentary. Bits and pieces jostled for audience. Jeremy Thorpe—Gerald Corde. Five years. Five incredible, nerve-numbing years in which he had gradually come to accept himself as Jeremy Thorpe all the time, not just when someone else was about. It had been difficult in the beginning, in training. Camp Cochise was a rugged, ruthlessly efficient place. No time for frills or tactful introductions. You were there for three months, and every minute of every day had to count, because you had a lot to learn.

Without knowing it, he had grown accustomed to a certain measure of respect as the son of his father. At Cochise there was none of that. He was just one more unit in the machine. Crewman trainee Thorpe, who had to learn the basic structure and function of every part of the whole range of ship-types that were being slapped together rapidly in other parts of the country. Earth had gone into deep space too early, been dragged into it before there was time to refine, to invent and develop all it would need. There was a merciless man-eating war on. The need was to establish half a dozen basic designs and then produce them, in great quantity. With crews to fit. So you learned all about everything, to start with. On performance, you specialized in one department until you could function efficiently, even if you were four days away from your last sleep, staggering with fatigue, and next door to unconsciousness from wounds.

It had been done. Every one of the instructors had done it, and had survived. Survivors were rare, and precious; they were merciless autocrats, respecting only the hard rules of Space-Regulations. The dream gave him a flash of that first day, of Camp Commandant Boltz addressing them.

"You are all one hundred percent fit and reasonably intelligent. You would not be here otherwise. There are other training camps for the less able. This is Cochise. So you will *not* drop down dead during training. You may feel like it at times, but you won't do it—" From seven in the morning until seven at night, continuously on the jump apart from grudged breaks for meals. Every day for six days. Every Sunday, that mythical day of rest, came performance tests and gradings, to see whether you were with it or not.

But "substitute-Thorpe" had expected it to be rugged. He had almost enjoyed the contest, applying himself to the task with all the gusto of keen youth. Until the Sunday afternoon of the fifth week, when malicious fate had struck a very close blow indeed.

"Trainee Thorpe to report to Commandant's office—now!" He went, on the run and in tense wonder, trying to recall what he had done wrong.

"At ease, Thorpe." Boltz was lean, colorless, a gray acid-drop of a man who looked as if he had a permanent grudge against life, and unrelenting indigestion. He grimaced now, trying to look pleasant. "I have your grades here, mister. Excellent results. Commended! I am recommending you be transferred to O.T.C. right away. Service needs men like you. That's all. Dismiss!" But the trainee stood fast. Boltz looked up, elevating his brows.

"Well?"

"No, sir!"

"What the hell does that mean, mister?"

"I don't want to go to O.T.C., sir."

"Are you questioning my judgment, Thorpe? Your aggregate performance grades show you a seven point lead over the next best man. Best grades I've seen. You're officer material!"

"No, sir. I mean, just as you say, sir, but I would rather finish as crew, sir."

"Are you refusing to obey an order, mister?" Boltz made it sound as if he hoped this was the case, by way of excellent entertainment.

"No, sir. Space Regs; Section Five, sub-section advancement and promotion—no man to be upgraded unless personal application made and by his agreement, or by direct nomination in the exigency of battle or other such emergency. I don't want to be upgraded, sir." He clamped his lips on that. He could have said more, but the regulations on insolence were wide and all embracing. He did not want extra fatigues for insolence. But even more he did not want to be jumped to O.T.C. That would bring him just that much more dangerously near contact with his father, and the disaster that would inevitably follow such a meeting. Boltz snorted. His watery eye took on a vicious gleam. But he was blocked by the very regulations he held sacrosanct. And he knew it.

"Very well, Thorpe. So be it. I'll just say this. You're a fool! I won't go so far as to call you a traitor, but I'm thinking it. Get out!"

If training camp had previously been rugged, it now became as near pure hell as the combined instruction body could make it. The word got round. A smart guy. Somebody who could have had accelerated advancement, but didn't want it. The word drifted down to the trainee level. Within a day, he had not one friend in the whole of Cochise. But now regulations worked on his behalf. There were strict limits to what they could throw at him. And he was just fit enough, smart enough, and bullheaded enough, to take everything they could throw and beat it. In a perverse way, he enjoyed this challenge. He completed training with the highest grade-scores ever logged at Cochise, the general detestation and envy of everyone present, and a red-ink memo on his papers to say he was a troublemaker and arrogant, but to be considered for soon-as-possible advancement to higher rating.

"I want you to see this, mister." Boltz had sent for him

just to let him read the citation. "You try—just try—to duck out from under this notice, and you'll be in for a court-martial. Understood?"

The dream fragmented again, giving him snap highlights. Four years and four ships. He had taken fantastic chances, had volunteered to make one wherever there was an action vacancy. He'd been shot at, had shaken hands with death again and again. S.S. *Lloyd*, her entire bow-section blasted away by a near-miss in a minor fracas one-and-a-half "lights" from outbase 61 Cygni, Fort Carne. With only half a crew and all of them shivering in shock, *Lloyd* had made it back to Carne. Crewman Thorpe cited for resource and heroism, recommended acting temporary sub-lieutenant, volunteered to fill a berth on the next ship out.

S.S. *Caroline*, hit three times and her whole after-end a fused mass, managed to limp back to base with ion-jets squirting fire in all directions, steering like a scow in a gale. Confirmed sub-lieutenant Thorpe now. And volunteering again. For a moment the dream personage stood away, outside the play, and studied this perverse figure, this death-seeking young man. And then the whole dream wavered, went dark, and he was conscious of an ache and a most desperate thirst.

He pried his eyelids open to a ghastly blue glare, tried to swallow, and his mouth was full of the ashes of an old camp-fire. The faint banshee wail of the P-drive scraped at his nerves. He twisted stiffly to scan the interior of the pod, memory dredging back. The blue-glare hiccupped. He squirmed in his harness to get a look at the control-panel, focusing with difficulty on the miniature gauge-complex. The P-drive automatic showed a half-traverse. Halfway there, wherever "there" was. But the rest of the instruments, which should have been sleepily steady, were kicking and jittering in intermittent instability. He could feel the buck-jumping through the harness-straps. Imagination made him see the arrays of solid-state electronics in the *Quest*'s innards, visualizing their sparking and glowing in the deadly rain of gamma rays, neutrons and mesons. He imagined those delicate micro-circuits fusing and peeling, shedding molecules, frying together into new and weird combinations; he shivered.

He saw the inert, hanging forms of his fellow-fugitives, and fumbled his wrist-lights to glow, to peer into the face-plates of each helmet. They looked dead. Why did he feel sick? Was it just the bash on the head, or could it be something more? Radiation, maybe. He groaned and creaked and fumbled his way to open a bulkhead cabinet. Medicine chest. Waterbulbs. Foodtubes. He shook the bulbs, one at a time. One empty, one half-full, two full ones. It looked as if Hadley and Skoda had made do with the minimum before putting themselves to sleep. He pushed the half-empty bulb-end into his mouth and squeezed, and its moistness was heaven. That, and the second one too, never got as far as his throat, the wetness being immediately absorbed by the desert-sand tissues of his mouth. A third grudging squeeze gave him just enough to provoke a swallow that went down like brick fragments.

He held a foodtube close, peered at it. "Roast chicken with spiced ham, champignons and Burgundy sauce"—that was a laugh. His faced creaked as he tried to grin. It would taste like lumpy library paste. They all did. He gagged on the gooey mess which left a fine film all over his tongue, and chased it away with another squeeze of water. His sense of smell and taste came back, a mixed blessing. He was now aware of the stink of stale sweat, the tang of collodion from his head-wound, hot oil—and a rubbery kind of undertone that was his suit. Nausea leaped in him and he clamped his mouth shut desperately until it passed.

After a while he managed another mouthful of the paste and one more mouthwash. He could still feel the juddering through his harness. His mind kept wanting to speculate, fearfully, on how much longer the ship's mechanisms could be expected to hold up. Retreating from that, he picked up fragments of his dream and mused on them. He had no room to complain. He had begged for this. But it wasn't suicide. There was a deeper, more crucial motive behind it. He'd explained it, once. Now who was that he had told it all to? His headache came back violently as he tried to remember. Not that it mattered, not now. The blue glare died, flared again. On the board the gauges went wild for a breathless second. Shivering again, he stared at the two lolling forms alongside him, and wanted for an insane moment to wake them and scream at them. It was all useless. The ship was falling apart.

A glint of light caught his eye, from a crumpled piece of foil. It had held a half dozen coma-pills. Now there were only two left. Hadley and Skoda must have taken two each. But the trip was half over now. He grasped one, fumbled it into his mouth, took a taste of water, was about to luxuriate in the rest of the contents of the bulb when he remembered the anti-rad capsules he ought to take. He got out two, gulped them, sucked down the last of the waterbulb's precious drops, tossed it back into the cabinet and began to zip up his suit. That was pointless, but long habit had drilled it into his reflexes. They trained you like that. Quasi-hypnotic drills, constant repetitions, everything simplified down to mnemonic codes, endless tapes playing to pillow-speakers all night, repeat, repeat, repeat—until the skills and responses became instinctive. As he strained to pull his helmet forward over his head he felt something angular in the external breast-pocket of his suit. He remembered it as soon as it was in his gloved hand.

A pin-up pair. Two beautiful blonde ladies, one honey-gold, the other butter-fair, like perfect dolls resting in his hands. Long ago he had bathed those pictures in inert polymer, to preserve them from damage. He grinned at the fairest one.

"I told you," he said, with careful clarity because his tongue seemed to be strangely thick, "told you it wasn't suicide. Had a purpose. A big reason." It had all made sense to him at the time. Not any more. He was wrong. He had been wrong all the time. The blue glare faded as the drug began to affect him. He let the pictures fall, dragged down on his helmet, felt it click into place. Jeremy Thorpe, about to die. He giggled as he realized it was the wrong one. Not Jeremy Thorpe. *He* was safe under the cloud-cover of Venus. A genius. He would think of something.

34

"Not your fault, old man," he mumbled. "My idea. You wrote the letter for me. I did all the rest. Not your fault. Good letter—did the trick—".

Reality went far away, became a blurred backdrop of sound and indeterminate blue. Blue sky. Sunny day. The big overland bus swooping and purring along the highway, rocking gently on its air-cushion. Padded seats. All women and old men. That had struck him with acute force, had given him a new focus on the war. Pretty soon now there would be no males left except old men and boys. Then what? The dream blurred and he was looking into blue eyes and green. Mrs. Thorpe, Jeremy's incredibly young-looking mother, and his "kid" sister Mary, who was a luscious nineteen. They had been very kind and good to him. They had helped him to understand just how desperate the war was. They knew, even if Vice-Admiral Corde firmly believed the truth was being kept from civilians.

They knew. Mary had said, "All I'm waiting for is the day when they break down and have to admit that women can fight a ship just as good as any men. I'll be there!"

That had shocked him into a trap. She had sprung it.

"If it's such a terrible life, so dangerous, why are you so keen to get in? Your father tried to stop you. You've even impersonated our Jeremy, just to get into Space. Why?"

To him it was very simple.

"Look!" he said. "The Vegans got us with our pants down, clobbered all our best ships and best men. So the High Command said we'll hoard our brains, our geniuses, keep them safe, and let only expendable people go out and get killed. And that's all wrong! If we're ever going to get a line on what makes the Vegans tick, we've got to get smart and intelligent people out there, to see what happens at first hand. People like me!"

It had sounded conceited at the time. It still did. But he knew he was right. Earth knew pitifully little about the Vegans, didn't even know for sure that they were from Vega. That was just a guess. Man had leaped into space with a new drive, had made starfalls on Procyon, 61 Cygni, Sirius, Altair, all within the fifteen light-year range of the first generation of engines. And then the mystery enemy had struck without warning or mercy. Postmortems and guesswork placed their point of origin as "possibly" Vega. Later deadly contacts had confirmed that. So they were Vegans, as a best guess.

But the rest of their information was pitifully meagre. Precious scraps of wreckage bought with blood and death showed that the crews were human, or humanoid, and that the ship-drive systems were virtually the same as Earth's. But that was all. If the Vegans communicated, it was not by any method that Earth instruments could detect. And no one had the vestige of a clue as to how those ships could whip about at such speed as they did, without smearing the crews into jelly. Nor would they ever know, he thought, so long as the best brains sat at home and deliberated about it.

The dream began to blur and tear now, got all mixed up with the knife-edge severity of his training.

"Your control-space is holed, what do you do, Thorpe?"

"Emergency, your manual fire-control is jammed, what do you do?"

"You have a total power-black, what do you do, Mr. Thorpe?"

"What do you do next, Mr. Thorpe? Thorpe? Mister Thorpe ...!"

IV

A SAVAGE HAND shook him violently. A demonic voice howled at him. "Mr. Thorpe! Mr. Thorpe—for God's sake, wake up, sir!"

He screwed his eyes open to a blue glare that stuttered, to Hadley's beefy face contorted into frantic anxiety, and Skoda's haggard stare.

"Uh! What?"

"Thank the Lord! We're less than ten seconds from break-out, sir. If we hold up that long." The pod shuddered to give point to his words.

"Suit-up!" the command was automatic and unthinking. He shrugged his own suit into place where Hadley had undone it to rouse him, snapped the helmet over his head and twisted to glance at the control-board. The P-drive traverse hung on the thin line of completion. He put his gloved grip on the ion-drive levers and set his teeth. Last gasp. A veritable straw! If the machinery held up, if they were delivered safely into real space—what then? The banshee wail snapped off. There came the familiar dizzy-spin rainbows, the fractional moment of implosion and nausea and then the soundless thump of transition. Three pathetically small screens lit into life and movement, one for Skoda to read and discover what they had found, one to steer by, and one to let them see outside where the stars wheeled and spun to the random toppling of the ship.

That toppling was his concern, something he could deal with. He eased the controls, felt the shuddering response, saw the spinning star-spots slow their movement, and then a great flaring fireball came to fill the screen with dazzling light.

"We're close!" he muttered. "Too damned close for comfort. Skoda, get your data on that as fast as you can, before we get too close to back off." He stabilized the spin so that the sun was just clear of the screen, and watched as Skoda twirled his controls to scoop information for the computers. He could guess at the significance of the results which showed, and they were not comforting, but he waited grimly for the expert reading.

"Unless the comp is crazy," Skoda mattered, "this is a freak system. There's only the one planet. See, sir? These other echoes are ghosts. Dust masses at the orbital balance-points. Sun-dogs!"

"And the planet itself?"

"I'm just getting the analysis on that now. There! It looks all right, sir! Within a percent for mass, gravity, surface

37

temperature and general spectrum. And we're practically on top of it!"

"Give me a fix. Let's see if we can get a good look at it." Skoda put a shimmering pair of cross hairs on to the steering-scope for him, away up in the right quadrant. He nudged his controls again, sensing the heavy sluggishness of the dead ship but thankful for any response at all, and the cross hairs crept until they stood, waveringly, full center.

"There she is!" Hadley's helmet clicked against his as the big man stared at the blue-and-gold ball in the viewer. "Looks pretty, doesn't it?"

"Anything would look pretty right now," Thorpe said. "We have yet to get down there in one piece. If anybody knows any prayers, this is a good time. Skoda, keep a sharp eye out for local rocketry, satellites, things like that. Hadley, I could do with a drink. Break out the last of the water. We have about fifteen minutes before we need worry too much." He touched the main drive, felt the first thunder of it, and eased it gently into half-power. This part was easy, so long as he could see his objective. All that was called for was a light touch occasionally on the tangentials to keep that image in view. The hard part was to come.

He flipped back his helmet again and sucked at the water-bulb Hadley handed him. In his mind he was trying to get the overall picture.

"How d'you reckon our chances, sir?"

"Depends on the drive, Hadley. If that holds up we have a chance, but not much. No sense in kidding ourselves. We're living on borrowed time as it is."

"But if the drive and the power hold out, we can land, can't we?"

"We can try, but it's going to be guesswork all the way. Our best bet is to make a passing orbit or two and see if we can spot an ocean to fall into."

"If you say so, sir." Hadley grunted, but his heavy face showed bewilderment. Thorpe sighed.

"Look, the ship is designed to land tail-first, preferably with a con from the ground, but not necessarily. Tail-first because that's where the main drive is. And for that we need astern-viewers, and those we haven't got. Damn it, man, we haven't any stern. You know that!"

"Christ! I forgot all about that. Then we'll have to back down blind, and chance it?"

"That's right. That's why I said we need an ocean to fall into." He had the vision clear, now. The black teardrop bulk of the *Quest*, with her stern structure in ruins, and this frail little pod stuck into her bows like a pear with the stem at the wrong end.

"Can't we kick the pod loose and land in it?" Skoda wondered, and Hadley grunted instant disagreement.

"You ought to know better than that. These things don't have that kind of power, not to make planet-fall. Enough to steer a bit and make a rendezvous, is all. D'you suppose there's anybody down there, sir?"

Thorpe had been trying hard not to think that same thing. It would be the outside ironical limit for them to have survived so far only to fall into a Vegan base. Skoda craned his head round.

"I was wondering about that too, sir. Should I make a signal?"

"No! This place is none of ours, we know that. And we can't chance the opposite, that it's Vegan."

"But the Vegans don't have radio, sir!"

"You don't know that, mister. If there's anybody down there, let them sing out to us, first!"

The planet began to loom large in the viewer and Skoda reported the first faint impingings of ionosphere. They buckled their helmets into place again, saw to their shock-harness, and Thorpe settled himself to the tricky part of the business. Main-drive off. Delicate touches on the forward jets, spilling wavering streams of fire-cloud over the viewer-picture. Gently, to make allowances for the sluggish responses of the ship, to get her into a looping orbit, not too close. Hearing the shrill scream of tortured upper atmosphere, now. Must be getting hot with friction. Snatch a glance at the viewer, at the sensors, at the speed, distance, the radar soundings. Is anyone down there? What sort of intelligent life could develop on a single planet sharing a sun with nothing more than a few ghostly dust-clouds? Pray for a big stretch of open water.

"I'm getting something on the shortwave, sir!" Skoda's voice shrilled in his ear. "Can't make anything of it, but it's something!"

"See if you can identify the type of transmission, speech or code."

"Looks like speech. No way of telling except by the look of it, not with my bloody helmet on. Should I take a chance, and listen?"

"All right, but be quick. And don't talk back unless I say!" Skoda flipped his helmet back, and at once Thorpe could hear the rapid gabble of an alien voice, distorted as it came from the panel-speaker through Skoda's helmet microphone.

"That's people!" Hadley grunted. "People like us!"

"So are the Vegans, so far as we know." The gabble cut off as Skoda pulled his helmet forward and down again, shutting out the sound.

"What d'you reckon, sir? I never heard anything like that before, but it sounded like speech. Human talk, I mean. We're losing the signal now. It'll be gone in a minute!"

"We'll be going round again, in any case." Thorpe scanned his instruments hastily. "We have to make a fast decision on this. There's only us three, and this could be life or death. I'm going to have all the grief I need just taking her down. We could use help from the ground, if there is any. Or we could be sticking our necks into a trap. I can't decide that for all of us. I'm not competent. All I can say is this: we will be dead lucky if we get down there, water or not, in one piece. We can't be much worse off whichever way it is. I vote we give them a hail, but it's up to you two to say what you think."

"What can we lose?" Hadley growled. "Give 'em a shout, Skoda!"

Off came the helmet again, but this time the radio-man had closed his talk-switch and they had no idea what he was actually saying. Thorpe had no eyes to spare now, as the *Quest* was dipping into a closer spin. He touched the controls delicately, trying to strike a middle course between fast and slow, snatching a glance every other second at the panorama unreeling below. They were into the sunset side now, and it was dark down there, but that did not mean too much. At this distance, something over a thousand miles, it would have to be an enormous light to show enough to be picked up by their little screen. The picture was almost black, so he couldn't be sure, but he fancied the read-out itself was beginning to fail. Skoda was fiddling with something inside his helmet. All at once his voice came, with different overtones and an echo.

"Got the mike out of my helmet, sir. You ought to hear this. Mush all over the dial, but nothing clear enough to pull in, so I reckon it's not worth the trouble of trying to raise them. Probably all asleep or minding their own business."

"I'm shrinking our orbit," Thorpe decided. "Can you get a directional on that speech, if we get it again?"

"Should do. It was a good strong signal."

"All right. Do that and let me have it for a beacon. It will help as a guide when I flip her over. Otherwise we're blind!" He was nudging the forward jets steadily as he spoke, watching the dark down there, alert for the first sign of a limb of light. When it came, his fears were confirmed. The screen carried a ragged picture, rippling and tearing across.

"Beginning to break up," he muttered. "Lord knows how everything has held on so long. . . ."

"Got it!" Skoda cried, and they could all hear the gabble again, very faint but quite clear. The radio-man made quick movements and now the steer-scope held a pinpoint of green that perpetually swelled and burst into an outrush of ripples. Thorpe juggled his jets until that green point sat in the dead center of his screen, and then leaned on the retarding levers. The viewer-picture dissolved into a shimmering mass of ion-fire as they slowed and fell deeper into the planetary atmosphere.

"Hello! Hello!" Skoda called. "This is Spaceship *Quest*, of Earth. We are in distress, and landing. Do you read?"

The gabble halted abruptly. The pod's fabric wailed with the scream of the ship's dying dive through atmosphere. The viewscreen was virtually useless now, its picture torn into incoherent slashes and fragments. There was only that green spot, now steady. All at once it resumed its swelling, and a shrill voice came from the speaker.

"You are of Earth? Say again, please. You are of Earth?" The accent was like nothing he had ever heard before, but the words were unmistakable.

"God save us!" Hadley growled. "They speak English. Talk to them again, Skoda. Tell them we need help!"

"No! Hold it, Skoda. There isn't a damned thing they can do to help us now. We're on our way down, like it or not. All I have is that radio-signal to line up on. I'm heading straight for it now. I intend to hold that as long as I dare, and then flip end-for-end and try to back down on to it. How will it read, from astern?"

"Same as now, sir, only weaker. But we can't land smack on top of their transmitter!"

"What else can we do? See for yourself, the viewer's shot. I can't see a thing!" Skoda's gloved hand reached across in front of his face to thump a fist on the screen mounting and fiddle with the setting. For one crazy second the picture steadied, showed the white cotton-fluff of cloud masses, and below them the long sweep and curve of a land mass. And green-blue ocean. Then the picture failed altogether and the screen went black.

"Aim to the left, to the left!" Skoda urged. "That was a sea down there. The transmitter will be on land, almost for sure. You saw it?"

"I saw!" Thorpe growled. "You know what you're saying?" He snatched a frantic glance at the radar-altitude reading. It was sliding slowly below the three hundred mark. "You expect me to turn this thing over, blind, and then aim to the left? Are you crazy?" All the same, there was precious little else he could do. The protest of ruptured air was a solid shudder now and the forward jets were useless in checking such a headlong fall. Two hundred and still falling. The green spot was steady.

"Here we go!" he muttered, and leaned on the tangential triggers. The spot slid straight down off the scope, leaving it blank. There was no sensation of turning, or movement of any kind apart from the now-frantic shudder of the air-shock outside. He glared at the blank scope. "Oh come on!" he breathed, easing off on the sideways thrust. And there it was, slipping in at the top of the screen. Fast. Too fast! He kicked over the jets on the check side, saw the spot halt its mad rush and weave unsteadily towards the center. It held. He moved his hands, clumsy in their gloves, and took hold of the main-drive levers again, bearing down on them. The gut-crushing drag of deceleration hit him instantly.

Then, sickeningly, the drag came off for a second, leaving him to surge upwards under the pull of his harness. And then on again as the ship's unit coughed back into life. The gauges kicked madly then settled. One-fifty and still falling. The hideous pressure of weight blurred his vision, but he bore down on the levers ruthlessly, praying that the drive would keep on firing. One hundred . . . and still falling fast. Again the drive coughed, kicked out and came on again, jerking them up and down like helpless puppets. Then it began to stammer in stunning hammer blows, making it impossible to know what was happening. He clung to the levers, dragging them as far down as he could, wrenching helplessly in the surges of his harness. The gauges were meaningless now.

"Hang—on!" he yelled. "I'm—going—to—kick—the pod—away—from—the ship!" almost biting his tongue as he snapped to and fro. He made a grab for the red release handle, missed it, tried again, got a savage grip, and heaved. It resisted him. He heaved again, almost blacking out with the effort. And it came away. There was an almighty crash as the bottom of the pod surged to meet them. The blue glare snapped off, came on again at reduced intensity. The control-board became steady. There was a picture now, of sunny sky and clouds. And just the hiss of air past the skin of the pod.

We're still falling, he thought, and reset the controls as fast as he could, then bore down on the drive once more. This time it was different song as the pod's batteries labored to pit a feeble stream of ion-thrust against the powerful pull of a planet. Once more that foreign gabble sounded in his ears, and the scope showed a stream of ripples from somewhere off its outer rim.

"Skoda!" he snapped. "Get your helmet on, man. We're going to hit dirt any minute! Hadley? You ready?"

There was no answer, and a quick glance showed him Hadley's face, dim within the confines of his helmet, but lifeless and with blood streaming from his nose. And the drag was bad now, as the puny drive gathered strength, struggling to check the pod's fall. It wasn't designed to run at this rate for long. He braced himself for the shock to come, prayed it would be soon, before the batteries were completely drained. There came a crash that dwarfed everything that had gone before. He screamed as the harness bit into his chest and shoulders and then ripped away from its moorings. There was bright agony in his feet, his legs, as he hit the metal floor of the pod and slumped in a breathless heap.

But then, amazingly, he was not dead! He moved cautiously, lifted and turned his head. It grated, but moved. His arms moved too. And his legs. There was a strange see-saw motion about everything. He stumbled over something in the dark, remembered his wrist-lights, flicked them on, and saw Skoda's face staring whitely at him through his visor. Those eyes blinked.

"You all right, Skoda?"

"Damned if I know, sir. What the hell happened?"

"I don't know. We seem to be down, if nothing else. Is it me, or is this damned thing rocking up and down?"

"I can feel that too. Hey! We must be in the sea, after all!"

"I suppose we are. We haven't an instrument left. No power, either. There's only one way to find out. We'll have to open the hatch. Hold it. Let's look at Hadley, first." Skoda managed to stand up and groan, then came to crouch over the inert suit where Hadley lay. Thorpe fumbled to get the helmet free and lift it back. Blood ran slowly down Hadley's face from his nose. That didn't mean a thing at this moment. Blood takes time to congeal. You can't feel a pulse through armored gloves, nor can you hear breathing when you have only radio-contact with someone else in another suit. He slid the helmet back again and said,

"Hold your breath, Skoda; see if we can hear him breathing."

It was a waste of time. There were too many interrupting noises from the suits, and their own hammering heartbeats. By chance his hand fell on the outer pocket which held the two 3-D snapshots. Glossy surface! He set Hadley's helmet back again, held the surface of one of the pictures close by his mouth, then snatched it up to peer. It was clouded.

"Fair enough!" he snapped the helmet snugly into place again. "He's alive. Let's hope he's only knocked out."

"You know why we couldn't hear him, sir? Didn't have his talk-switch closed. I reckon we're both a bit punch-drunk, just now. I know I am. What with being clobbered by Vegans, jumping in Pauli in a red-hot ship, smashing down on a planet like this—and they were talking English. You reckon we died, sir, and this is all some sort of hell?"

"If it is, we're all in it together. Look, we seem to be floating, if we are floating, right way up. That means we must be about halfway under water. So, when we burst that hatch open, this thing is going to flood and go down pretty sharpish!"

"Christ! There seems to be no end to our troubles!"

"But this one isn't all that bad. That's why I mentioned it, just to warn you. The pod will flood, and sink, but we've nothing to worry about so long as our suits hold and we don't get in a panic. All right? Fortunately the door opens inboard. Now, the first thing we do is to shove old Hadley out, and then we follow. If we drag him over to the side, you can launch him as soon as ready. Then you follow, and I'll be right on your heels. Right?" He struggled across to the hatch, took hold of the locking-wheel, and set his feet as best he could. One hearty twist and the door flailed open, sending him sprawling and a great rush of water tumbled him over into helplessness. Floundering, he struggled up to give Skoda a hand, but it was impossible to shove Hadley's inert bulk against the spouting water. In a matter of seconds they were chest deep and then lifting. And the flow seemed to dwindle. But the hatch was down there, out of sight.

"Punch-drunk is right!" he growled. "We're a pair of fools. Now is the time to duck out, while the internal air-pressure in holding the water back. Ready? Down you go now!"

Skoda's helmet disappeared beneath the surface, taking Hadley's with it, and then, after a moment or two, the radio-man's voice, thankfully, "It's all right, sir. Nothing to it. And it's sunny out here. Marvelous!"

Thorpe grunted to himself, bent his knees and saw the waterline rise up in his helmet-visor, plunging him into green murk. He felt for the hatch, ducked through and kicked out into a bright glare that was almost painful. Waves lapped on a level with his nose, set blurring dribbles down his visor, through which he could see two rounded bobbing helmet-tops. And beyond them, a long way off, the dull smudge of land! He flailed round clumsily, saw the cylindrical end of the pod bobbing drunkenly in the gentle swell. No sign of the ship. They tried to hoist up in the water, but with little success.

"How the hell d'you reckon we're supposed to swim in these things?" he wondered.

And Skoda's voice came, chirpily enough, "I reckon I could manage, if I knew which way to point."

"That's the easiest part. There's land right behind you!" He saw Skoda's helmet bounce as he flailed round, and began bobbing himself again, trying to see further over the waves. All at once there was a splash of something surfacing close by him, and in the same instant something clamped on his back and an arm circled his neck, constricting powerfully into the soft flexible folds of the throat of his suit. Before his startled eyes a face rose out of the water and stared at him. A human face. A woman's face, a woman with blue-green cling-curl hair, silvery green eyes, and a

46

complexion like warm ivory. She would have been attractive, had her expression not been so militantly hostile. As he stared at her in stricken amazement she stood up in the water like a seal, revealing a black strap at her throat. He saw her hand arc over and pluck out from behind her head a long gleaming blade. The constricting arm left his neck, but the blade point came close, aimed under his chin, and held there, quite steady, quite deadly.

V

HARSH IN HIS EAR he heard Skoda's sudden gasp of surprise. He kept as still as he could in the gently heaving water. "We have company, and they don't seem any too friendly!"

"Has yours got seaweed hair and fisheyes, sir?"

"And a damned great knife, yes. I reckon we had better go quietly, unless they mean to drown us right here. I wish we could talk to them, but I daren't move."

"You'd have to crack your helmet seal to do that, anyway, sir, and you'd go down like a stone. What d'you reckon they want, anyway?"

"Just capture, I think. Mine could have filleted me long ago, if she wanted to." He caught sight of more heads bobbing in the water. "There's enough of 'em to eat us. Couple of dozen, at least!" And not a friendly face among them, he realized, as several pairs of silvery green eyes came to peer at him and swish away again. Mermaids! And quite pretty, if it weren't for the unbroken hostility in every gaze. He felt a grasp and tug at his wrists, and then the splash of a little bow-wave as he began to move.

"I'm being towed," he announced. "To shore, I think. I hope!" He squinted as far sideways as he could, peering through the drift of water on his visor until he could be sure that they were collecting Hadley, too.

"Got me, too. Gawd, I hope they're not cannibals!"

Thorpe grinned, feeling slightly hysterical from reaction. He wondered how many more kinds of death were going to come and gibber at him before he finally succumbed to one of them. The shore line drew closer and he could see treetops. Great fronded trees, they were, like palms. And then a yellow sand beach sloping gently upwards to the tree cover. Beneath the trees, in shade, there seemed to be a whole horde of people waiting. The constant spill of sea-water over his visor made accurate seeing impossible, but they looked kin to the mermaids who were towing him. His booted feet struck bottom, tossing him face-forward. He stumbled, found footing, and felt the imperious tug of bonds on his wrists hurrying him through the small surf.

Now, as the glass ran dry, he could see properly, could see Skoda's lumbering figure being impelled up the sand just as he was, away to his left. And he could see the pu-tative mermaids, that they were human enough to have legs and feet just like other women. They were completely human, being naked but for hip-hugging belted harness and the neckstrap with the long knife. This was common garb for all of them that he could see, including the host who scurried down the sand to greet their fellows. And they were all, without exception, female. A fine, long-limbed, vig-orously fit-looking bunch, he decided, as they dragged him unceremoniously up the slope and into the shade of the trees. He could see them jabbering at each other, but heard nothing but a distant murmur. There seemed to be some difficulty. He screwed his head round inside his helmet enough to see that Hadley was lagging, that they were hav-ing to drag him bodily. Six of them had clapped ropes on his suit and were heaving strongly. Such energy and de-termination made him sweat as he realized just how help-less he was.

"Skoda!" he said, tried to keep his tone light. "I don't know about you, but it's my guess that they don't much care for us."

"Bunch of naked savages! I expect they think we're some new kind of fish they've caught."

"Hold on! Don't write them off too quick. They must have seen us come down. We must have made a hell of a racket. But they don't seem scared, and that argues against them being all that savage. Almost as if they had seen spacemen before." As he spoke he was being hustled along a narrow game-trail between the tall trees, two shapely women hauling on the ropes which held his wrists. Their short, blue-green hair, springing up in a dense cluster of curls as it dried, was not unattractive. He wondered what the men would be like, and why these women were so immediately and violently hostile. It could hardly be a routine thing to have a spaceship crash-land off their beach!

All at once the trail delivered them into a great open space, a clearing so big that he could only guess at its true size. A village. A large one, too. And not huts, as he had thought at first glance, but houses—by the arrayed hundreds—houses laid out in orderly fashion, with unusual outlines and alien methods of timbering. The houses disgorged people in swarms until the clearing was alive with them. There must have been a great chatter and shouting out there, but his helmet reduced it all to an indistinct mumble. He saw it in snatches as he was hauled along—staggering now from sheer fatigue—to what looked to be a huge hole in the ground. Then he was on the brink and stumbling down the steep sides of a square-cut amphitheater, down to the hard packed earth of its floor. And there the women on the ropes gave him a last tug to send him sprawling, and by the time he had struggled to his knees the fastenings were undone and they had backed away to a safe distance.

He scrubbed at his visor with the cuff of his suit, to rub off the dried smears of saltwater. He saw Skoda sitting up, only feet away. And the inert huddle of Hadley. He glanced up and around. The edges of the amphitheater were some ten or twelve feet above him, the whole thing about fifty yards square where they lay. It had the feel of an arena, or a sacrificial pit. He hoped he was wrong, but

49

when he craned his head again, he saw that ranged along the rim above—were women. And they were on the alert, some with long spear-like weapons and others with unmistakable longbows.

"We seem to be well and truly in for it," he said. "Those ladies up there look capable."

"Reckon it would be all right to up-helmet, sir? My suit-unit has just about run out. I can smell my own stink."

"Me too. We'll have to chance it. Got to, in any case. I want to have another look at Hadley. That dragging can't have done him any good."

Thorpe lifted his gloved hands and fumbled at the catch of his helmet, keeping a sharp eye on the sentries above, but they made no overt move. It was a delight to feel the cool clean air on his face and in his nostrils. And to hear the buzz and murmur of life. For the first minute after his helmet went back he did nothing but sit and breathe, great thankful lung-fulls of fresh scented air scouring away the slimy pond-water taste of long confinement. He felt better, more optimistic with every breath. The silent watchers made no move, showed no surprise, either. And that was significant. No strangers to spacesuits, evidently. Thus hardly savages.

He got to his feet, threw back the rest of his suit down to waist level and cinched it there, letting the helmet and sleeves dangle at his back. Skoda had moved too, was similarly half-suited. He looked grimy and more haggard than ever, but alive and alert. They converged on Hadley.

"What the hell d'you reckon we've struck, sir?"

"No idea, but they've offered us no harm, yet. We'll just have to wait and see." Hadley was still unconscious, but breathing strongly. The blood had dried on his face and chin and he looked a ghastly sight, but so did they all. Thorpe checked as far as he could, unfastening the suit to feel for possible injuries.

"Seems all right," he muttered. "Just knocked out, far as I can see. That's not surprising, the way the ship went crazy at the end. It's a miracle we're here at all. Let's be thankful for that, if nothing else."

"Not much else to be glad about," Skoda said. "I want to get this damn suit off, but I don't know. I'd feel sort of helpless without it."

"I know what you mean. But we might as well. After all, those knives of theirs would make short work of rubberized canvas and plastic. And apart from the radio-unit there's nothing any good any more in the suits. The air and moisture units are flat. Come on!" He set the example of standing and unfastening his belt-cinch. It was true. He felt uneasily defenseless as he stepped out of the suit and stood clad in nothing more than a cotton union suit, now dark-stained and foul from long confinement. But the sense of freedom was almost worth it. A few moments later they had peeled Hadley, too.

"Now what?" Skoda wondered. "You reckon they're civilized enough to feed their prisoners?" From some unseen resource his lean and wiry personality had acquired an angry desperation. Standing erect he made a trumpet of his palms and shouted up, "Hey! What about something to eat, then? The service is lousy here!"

It moved them. Thorpe saw two of the women make signs and call to each other. They came together for a rapid interchange of words, then one went away, vanishing from sight beyond the edge. That edge, he saw now, was efficiently straight, and the sloping sides were not smooth, but in regular steps. A terrace. So this *was* an amphitheater, after all. The earth under his feet felt rock-hard, but he could see no signs of stains, or blood, or anything like that. Any village, he thought, must have a center, a focal point where the elders and rulers could meet and make decisions, or where the ceremonies took place. If there were any here. He dug back in his mind for what little he had absorbed of sociology theory and human groupings. Hadley groaned suddenly, and they both knelt by him at once. The big man stirred, opened his eyes.

"Easy now," Thorpe warned. "So far as I could tell you're not badly hurt, but you keep still and check up on yourself while I tell you what's happened." Hadley kept still as

51

he listened, only his eyes moving. Then he grunted and stirred cautiously, managed to sit up.

"I'm all right. I fell like the Kilkenny dancers have been using their clogs on me, but I can use my arms and legs. What's all that about fish-women with green hair?"

"See for yourself!" Thorpe thumbed a gesture to the guardians up there on the rim and the Irishman bunched his big face into folds as he peered up into the bright sunshine. At that moment there came a faint chatter of voices, and movement at one corner of the prison-square rim. They saw faces appear, and then a delicate-stepping procession of women bearing trays and baskets. But ahead of them came two with hard faces, each with a drawn bow and a straight arrow nocked and ready. Their gestures were eloquent. The three men backed off to the far side of the floor and watched as the baskets and trays were set down and left. Thorpe assumed that the stuff was food and drink and ignored it for the moment. He was far more interested in the women who had brought it. In face and figure they were like their war-like sisters, but they were dressed. Three of them, in skirts and jackets of some patterned woven stuff with a silk-like sheen. The skirt was a simple wrap-round, falling inches short of the knee and caught on the right hip with strap and buckle. An undoubted buckle, in glinting metal. And the jacket was sleeveless, short, open in front and caught under the breasts with yet another strap and buckle. But most important of all, in a slit-pocket at either side of the jacket stood the haft of a short knife or dagger. The effect was startling, a clash between decorative adornment and savage readiness for combat. Buckles argued a skill with metals. Weave and color spoke of sophistication. But the daggers told of constant readiness for danger. And where were the men?"

"How do we know this stuff is fit to eat?" Skoda demanded. "It looks all right, but I'd just as soon my hair didn't turn green."

"We'll just have to chance it. At least the crockery is clean." Thorpe took up a stumpy ceramic pot and examined it curiously. It was light and glazed and symmetrical enough to have been spun on a wheel. A great two-handed pitcher matched it exactly. It was brimming with a pale amber fluid. He poured out for them, his mouth watering in anticipation. The taste—he rolled it on his tongue and frowned —was difficult to place.

"It's a ferment of some kind. More like lager than anything else. We'd better go easy on it until we've something solid to hold it down."

"Settles the dust, anyway," Hadley declared as he emptied his pot. "Begod, that's a civilized drink, which is more than I ever expected to taste again. What's the red things, Skoda?"

They sampled with care, but eagerly. One basket held a cluster of meat-joints that tasted like tough chicken but the bones were angled like no creature any of them could name. There were offerings of dried fish as small as sardines, but tasteless. And fruits of all shapes and colors, many of them bursting with juice. Confidence and hope grew with every nourishing swallow. Thorpe glanced from time to time at the silent watchers up there, his mind seething with questions. The sun was high now, and hot, with no shade in the pit.

"I'm going to try talking to them," he said, and put palms to his mouth to shout, "Hello! We are from Earth. We want to talk to you. We come in peace!" That last phrase sounded supremely ridiculous but he had to say it. The watchers stirred, chattered at each other, and he stared suddenly at Skoda. The radio-man stared back wide-eyed.

"That's the same kind of jabber we heard in the radio!"

"You think so too? If only we had a radio now . . ."

"We have!" Skoda dived for his discarded suit, grabbed the helmet. "I noticed, when we were in the pod, that that transmission was broad-band and almost the same wavelength as these. We couldn't hear because we were shielded inside the pod and the suits. But now—" He had the suit-unit out and in his hand. No bigger than his palm, it comprised sender, receiver, loudspeaker and microphone, and isotope batteries, all in the minimum of space. The "hear" button was a projecting rod that was automatically held down all the time the unit was in place. Skoda depressed it now with a thumb and the gabble came.

"Same stuff. And close!"

Thorpe dived for his own unit and Hadley's. When ready he drew a careful breath, then closed the "send" switch.

"Hello. We are of Earth. We spoke to you before. Now we are landing and being held prisoner. Do you hear me?"

"You are of Earth?" It was that same oddly-accented voice again. "You speak like Earth, but how do we know this is not a trick of the Shining Ones?"

Thorpe let the switch close, stared at his companions. "That *must* mean the Vegans. Their silvery ships. Got to be. This is where we have to be careful not to ball it all up. Hold it!" He opened the switch again. "Wait. We will speak to you again in a little while." He let his hand fall to his knee and frowned. There was too much to grasp, all at once. The spoken English was bad enough, was a staggering thought all by itself.

"Do you recall enough of the course settings to give a rough guess whereabouts we are?" he asked Skoda, and the radio-man passed a shaking hand over his black hair as he scowled in thought.

"Rough would be right. Rendezvous was fourteen 'lights' from Cygni, bearing four degrees away from Second Quadrant. And we jumped two more 'lights' from there, at least, to hit this place. Best I can do."

"Fair enough. I just wanted to clear it in my mind that we can't possibly be anywhere near a human base, or settlement of any kind. You'd agree on that?"

"Can't be any doubt about it, sir. And I see what you mean. How do they come to know our language?"

"Yes. That smells, to me. That voice talked about a trick of the Shining Ones. Strikes me that there might be a bit of trickery on the other side, too. We're a hell of a long way from any known friends." There came a sudden clamor of voices up there on the rim and they looked up to see a procession of figures coming down the ramp once more. Longbows led the way, but this time there was a vigilant crowd at their heels, a squad of women stripped for action and carrying coiled ropes. The three Earthmen stood, and drew together in instinctive readiness.

"Never a man among them!" Hadley mumbled. "How the blazes d'you suppose they breed? By parthenogenesis?"

"You got it wrong, but I know what you mean. I don't think it matters just now. I don't like the look of those ropes."

"Do we have a crack at them, sir?"

"Wouldn't be much sense in that. There's a score of arrows looking right at us. We might as well go quietly." The longbows moved to either side, and the rope-carriers advanced, stern-faced and determined. Two of them held long strips of cloth. Thorpe stood still as his arms were seized, and a strip of fabric was bound tightly about his eyes, blinding him. Then the ropes went on, knotted with swift and efficient jerks. His thin-soled slippers told him when he had moved from the packed-earth floor to the up-climbing ridges of the ramp. On and up, obeying the insistent drag of the ropes, and then on to level surface again. A surf-rustle of many voices in hushed whispers. Hurrying. The coolness of sudden shade to tell him that he was among the trees again. And then nothing but the steady tramp, the shock of uneven surfaces under his feet, the occasional stumble and going on. And on, until he lost count of distance. A mile, at least, and probably much more. His legs began to ache and protest but the tugging ropes gave him no quarter. And there was no speech among his captors.

His mind fastened on that odd fact, added it to others, and tried to build the collection into some kind of sense. Blindfolded but not assaulted. Led hastily, even roughly, but not driven or lashed. And in silence. As if these people were afraid he might see or hear something they wanted kept from him. It added up to a confusing mixture of fear, suspicion and anxiety. One thing was abundantly plain. They could have killed him at any time. But it had not happened. Therefore there was hope, no matter how scanty.

Without warning, the march came to an end. The rope-ties jerked him to a standstill. Panting, he felt fingers at the knots, and then the clamping grip of bare hands on his wrists and arms. Now he was led onwards again, but more slowly, with care. His toes bumped against steps, and he began to climb. Wooden steps, by the feel, but solid and firm. Then a cool floor, possibly of stone. And the sense of being within a building, a big one. A strangely pungent smell, one that tickled memories and made him wonder, when he had identified it. Ozone? He heard the grunt and shuffle of others by his side, the gentle slap of leather-shod feet. Then a voice, an old but steady voice, in tones of quiet command. The murmur of many voices in hushed response. His arms were released. He stood quite still, sensing that his immediate captors had withdrawn. The imperious old voice spoke again, in a measured cadence of syllables out of which one sound came distinctly, the one word "Hathar!", accenting the final syllable.

"I am Hathar! You say you are of Earth. How may I believe you?" It was not the same voice, but it was the same alien accent, speaking almost perfect English. Thorpe heard a grunted gasp to left and right of him, and guessed that it was his companions, equally dumbfounded. He found his voice.

"We are of Earth. We don't understand what you mean by proof. What kind of proof do you want? And who are you, anyway? How is it that you speak our language?"

"He who speaks, that one with hair of straw and a wound in his head, how came you by that mark?"

"An injury." Thorpe frowned but answered as simply as he could. "Our ship was struck. I hit my head on something. Does it matter?"

"The wound will be examined. You will keep still. Do not try to resist, or you will die, instantly." His nerves wound up to a snapping-point as cool fingers touched his head, pressing ungently, probing the gash, stirring twinges of pain through his scalp and head. Then they went away, and there was a sudden flow of quiet syllables, all meaningless to him but spoken in a calm feminine voice.

"What did they do to you?" Hadley growled, over to his right.

"Nothing much. A bit rough, but it could have been worse. I hope they're satisfied . . ."

"The wound is slight," the old voice announced, "and has broken the skin only. It should heal soon. It is a point in your favor that the other two show no such marks. I am now giving orders that your garments be removed. Do not resist!"

"What the hell!" Skoda fumed. "You'd think we had a plague or something!" Again the fingers were cool and efficient, brisk but not needlessly rough. And again there was a brief discussion in that meaningless tongue.

"You say you are of Earth. Tell me how you came here."

Thorpe kept his patience, trying to guess what the thinking was behind the question. Again he made his words as simple as possible.

"We were in a battle with the Shining Ones. Many of their ships, and many of ours. We were hit and damaged. By good fortune we were able to make our ship carry us this far before it destroyed itself."

"Your ship plunged into the sea. You escaped from it in a smaller vessel. Both will be examined to see whether you speak truth."

"Just a minute!" His mind reeled before the implications of her ready acceptance of ships from space, but one fact burned above all. "Be careful how you handle that wreck. You know about spaceships?"

"We know a great deal. What would you tell us?"

"That ship is rotten with radiation. The drive-unit was running unshielded for forty-eight hours . . ."

"For two days?" The old voice lost a degree of its calm. "How can that be? You would be dead!"

"We were on the outside of the hull. In a lifeboat. That was the second vessel you mentioned."

"It is being brought ashore now. It will be examined. I will think of what you have said about radiation. How far is Earth from here?"

The unexpected question shook him for a moment. "I'm not sure," he muttered. "We were in a battle, you understand. But it must be, at least, as far as a beam of light

57

might travel between the time a child is born and when it is old enough to be called a man. Twenty light-years."

"So far? We have made many estimates. That is one of them. One more question. You spoke to us from your ship. And then again when the Shalla had you safe. The first time I understand, for you had instruments, just as we have. But how could you speak by radio, with nothing but your hands, as you did the second time?"

The insanity had doubled and redoubled on itself so many times that there was no more room for wonder in his mind. He still held the miniature suit-radio in his right hand. He raised it now, making the movement slow, and pressed the "hear" button. Immediately the silence was filled with that rapid gabble, sounding small and metallic from the little speaker.

"Ah!" It was a great gasp of wonder, and told him that there must be at least a dozen people present. He released the button, bringing silence.

"I wish to see that wonder," the old voice shook now. "You will permit this?"

That's a change, he thought. He held out his hand, felt the unit being taken, waited a moment, then said, "The lump on the back . . . press it to listen." A moment or two more and he heard the speaker start up again, and again that gasp of wonder.

"Enough!" the old voice declared. "Let them see! They are Earthmen!"

VI

"I AM HATHAR!" she said, and there was a frosty twinkle in her eyes as she added, "In your tongue that is High Priestess. I am sorry we had to treat you with suspicion.

It was justified, but there will be no more of it. You are welcome."

The three men blinked in the warm light, mellow and golden, that flooded from great lanterns hanging high in the roof. As Thorpe had guessed, this was a big room, as big as a church. The simile was provoked by her words and underlined by the atmosphere of stateliness and peace. Filling three-quarters of a circle, there was an array of seats, all in richly carved dark wood. The floor bore an inlay of green stones against grey. The walls soared high to a vaulted roof crisscrossed with beams shadow-dark above the hanging lanterns. And there was a silent, watchful audience of young women, barefoot, skirted and jacketed in white, and each with a keen blade held righthanded and ready.

The old woman herself sat on what was virtually a throne, a great high-backed chair standing at the apex of a low pyramid of steps. The wall at her back was draped with a mighty curtain richly worked in a symbolic design that combined circles, curves and slashes of vivid color in a way that was almost mobile. She was old. Thorpe saw that at once. But not in any way senile. Her face was lined rather than wrinkled, and her head was held high over a broad collar of winking jewels. Her hair was pale, a green that was close to silver, and long enough to be caught back from her face with a silver band about her forehead. Like the rest, she wore the sleeveless jacket with the twin dagger-pockets, but hers was studded with gems and embroidered against the white.

He met her quizzical gaze, and then looked away to the two who stood below her on the steps at either side. Again the color here was pure white with slashes of embroidered color. And there was frank curiosity mingled with wonder on these two faces.

"I thank you for your welcome," he said. "There are so many things I don't understand I hardly know where to begin. May I speak freely?" He cast a meaningful glance at the watching audience.

"We are all the handmaids of Hathar," she said. "We speak and understand your tongue, as part of our religion.

The Shalla do not, but they obey and respect us. You may speak in safety, here."

The word "safety" struck the very note he was most conscious of, as if this were a land at war and ridden with suspicion.

"First things first," he said. "You speak of the Shining Ones, those we call Vegans, because we believe they come from a star we know as Vega. I ask you now—what is your relationship to them?"

The old face hardened into stern lines. He heard a rustle from the mute audience and could feel the sudden tension.

"They enslave us," she said harshly. "They force us to build and repair their ships, to provide them with food and fuel and other needs. We have no love for them!"

"They force you to do these things?"

"They order us, and we obey, because each one carries a small thing, a weapon that spits fire. Should one be so foolish as to rebel"—she made a pointing-finger gesture and a hissing sound—"that one dies. If the work is not done well, they come and take one in five, and they die. And the rest work harder, because it is a terrible thing to be burned to death."

Hadley cleard his throat harshly. "Would you tell us now, ma'am, just what kind of things these Shining Ones are?"

The hooded silver-green eyes swiveled to him, to burn as she said, "They are men. Like you!"

Thorpe could almost feel the hate radiating from her and the quiet gathering, could almost taste it.

"If they are—just like us, then how do you know we are —all right? That we are safe?"

"You speak the Earth tongue, and fluently. Your ship did not shine. You used hathari, that which you call radio, which the Shining Ones hate and destroy. And you do not bear the mark of Satan!"

His face must have shown his bafflement for she made a gesture and went on, "All Shining Ones bear a silver disc— here," and she put a finger to her brow, between her eyes. "You have a mark, a wound, but it is not in the right place. These others bear no mark at all."

"That's something to be glad of, anyway."

"It is something. Perhaps enough. But you are still men!"

He became abruptly and awkwardly conscious of his nakedness in front of this silent group of female observers. That their gaze was cold and suspicious didn't help much. "We are hardly in a fit state to be seen," he mumbled. "You said something about a welcome. Are you going to leave us standing naked, or can we have the chance to clean up a bit, and dress, maybe, before we go any further with our talk?"

"Certainly!" She raised her hands, clapped them gently, and the silent circle of women bowed and rustled away. To the attendant girl on her right she said, "Shanne, take them to the pool. See that they have what they need, and then bring them to my chamber. Varis, we must send the word immediately to our sisters over the sea. Come!"

The girl named Shanne made them a tight smile and led them away to one side of the throne, into a narrow passageway and out into the open sunlight again, to where a chuckling stream straggled down over rocks and gathered in a clear pool edged with white stone. The water was cool, and they hardly had time to duck under before she came back with armfuls of fleecy cloth and a pitcher of syrupy green liquid which made an excellent lather.

"This beats anything I've every heard of," Skoda declared as he splashed and spluttered himself clean. "Look at her!" The girl had taken up his suit-radio from where he had laid it on the poolside and was now holding it to her ear with an expression close to rapture. "It's crazy! They've got radio of their own. We heard it, didn't we? So why should she want to listen to that? I mean, it's only talk. And it can't be important news. We're the important news, right now."

"That's what she's listening to," Hadley rumbled, rubbing the green stuff into his hair. "I'll bet the airwaves are burning right now with the full account. We're the local heroes, I bet you!"

"We're more likely to be martyrs if the Vegans catch

that broadcast," Thorpe suggested, but Skoda snorted his disagreement.

"I told you," he said. "They don't *have* radio, or we'd have picked up their signals long ago!"

"You know . . ." Thorpe was struck with sudden inspiration, "that could be the answer to a lot of things. If these people have radio, and have had it a long time—and the Vegans don't, as they would know—and we show up all equipped with portable models: that's what must have saved our skins, after all!"

"What d'you reckon on the Vegans now, sir? That mark she was talking about, that they stick on a man's head?"

"I don't know what to make of it. It sounds like some kind of operation on the brain, a lobotomy perhaps. I hope we never get to find out the hard way, that's all!"

"You hold still a minute, sir, and I'll have another look at your head, see how it's getting on." Thorpe submitted patiently to Hadley's inspection, then gave voice to something that had been irking him for some time.

"Let's get one thing straight, right now. Here we are, three of us together and all mother naked. We've lost our ship and just about everything else we have that's of any use, except what wits we have. We seem to have fallen in lucky so far, but we can't count on that being permanent. I'm trying to get to the point of saying—let's drop the rank and position stuff. My name's Jeremy. What's yours, Hadley?"

"My well-meaning parents had me christened Padraic, sir —sorry, I forgot. I'll answer to Paddy, if you say it loud enough."

"That's fine!" Thorpe grinned. Skoda managed a shaky grin too.

"Anybody calls me Nikolai I'll never forgive 'em. Just Nick will do. I reckon we'll be dead lucky if we ever get back to uniforms again, at that. Or wages!"

"Speaking of uniforms, I hope they intend to provide us with clothing of some kind. I don't fancy spending the rest of my time parading naked in front of a horde of goggling women!" He waded to the edge of the pool. "Miss Shanne!"

She put down the suit-radio, grasped a dagger, and went two fast steps away from him, all in one breath, then said, "You require something?"

"Something to wear, if it's possible."

"These," she indicated three white wrap-skirts on the grass, "are all we have." He nodded, made the best of it, and heaved himself out to begin drying on a square of fleece. She backed off more.

"No need to be scared of me," he said, irritated by her attitude.

"You are a man!"

"Is that a crime?"

"The man who touches me, dies with me. I have so sworn!" Her tone left no room for comment. Eventually, when they were clean, dry and skirted, she led them by another passage to a heavy door studded with metal and bearing a symbol in gold, a zigzag flash with a vertical through it. The door let them into a small room hushed with drapes and thick with carpet. The old priestess sat at a table, listening to a steady drone of speech from an ornately carved box. Thorpe noted the symbol again. The old woman shut off the sound.

"Sit!" she commanded, as Shanne brought stools. "Now you look more as we have imagined Earth people to be. In a moment Varis will bring drink for you, better than you had of the Shalla." She sounded like somebody trying to be gracious. She had shed her jeweled clothes and was now in plain white, but the daggers were still there, on either side of her breasts. Shanne circled the table to sit by her side. The other two men shuffled and waited, ill at ease, by the stools. Somebody had to make the first move. Thorpe sighed, pushed a stool close to the table and sat.

"You're very kind," he said. The other two sat. Varis came with a jug and goblets, to pour rosy wine. "I've a thousand questions, but one most of all. How is it that you speak our language so well?"

"The speech of the gods?" She swirled the wine in her glass. "It is sacred to us, to the daughters of Hathari. It has taught us much. Our sun has only one planet, this which we call Lodor. Our day is slightly shorter than yours, our year longer, our orbit eccentric. In our winter the sun grows smaller, in summer larger. We have land areas about our equator, seas at the poles. We have cities, villages, islands. This now, where you are, is an island, called Shallon. The people are the Shalla. You have seen them. All this we know and can tell you, because of Earth and the voices from the void."

"By radio?"

"We call it Hathar. When our history was young we were a contented folk. We harvested the land, we sailed our seas, and we had simple skills. And we spoke with one voice, because we had learned, so long ago that no records tell the date, how to talk with each other at a distance. By radio. By hathari. We knew how to make small lightning and tame it to our will."

"The symbol! The lightning tamed?"

"Exactly. This is sacred to us. So it has grown, over many generations. A religion, with shrines and devices with which we speak one to another."

"My old grandfather was a bit of a philosopher," Hadley rumbled. "He told me more than once that half the troubles of our world came just because we had so many different languages. And it's true. How the devil can you deal with a man when you don't know what he's talking about. Sure, this must be a wonderful world, if they've had the radio all that time!"

"It *was!*" the old woman's voice sharpened. "It became even more wonderful on the day, a century ago, that we first heard murmurings and music, from a mysterious source. A great wonder, it was. And a fear too, at first!"

"Are you trying to tell us," Skoda spluttered, "that you received radio signals from Earth? More than fifteen light-years away?"

"What's wrong with that?" Thorpe demanded.

"Wrong? It's impossible! Man, you'd need an antenna a mile long, and amplification to make your hair curl, and a detector so sensitive—and filters and strainers—nah! This I have got to see before I believe!"

"All right, leave it for now. Go on, Mother Hathar."

"Have I shown you a marvel? Think then how much more wonderful it was for us when we realized that this was only the work of people like ourselves, not mysterious, but real. We listened. We learned to understand the speech. We learned much, many wonderful things."

"Did you try to talk back?" Skoda demanded.

"Many times, but we were unsuccessful. However, we learned much. We of Hathar learned. We passed on much to the ordinary people. We gained a fame, respect and reputation for wisdom, one we hardly deserved. We became proud. And we were punished for that!" The chill in her voice made Thorpe shiver.

"For thirty years we had listened, and interpreted to others, the voices from the void. The gods spoke to us, and we spoke to the people. The days came when we learned that the Earth-gods planned to journey through the void in great ships. We hoped they would come here. We prayed for that. And then, one day, the Shining Ones came. There in our skies were the glorious ships. And we, the priesthood of Hathar, proclaimed to all the people that the Earth-gods were come at last. We commanded the people to give a great welcome to the Earth people."

"Oh no!" Thorpe groaned, seeing the obvious and terrible truth.

"Oh, but yes!" she said, icily deliberate. "I was a babe-in-arms at the time, not old enough to understand, but I have heard the story many times since. We have five major cities, all on a seafront because we were, we are, a sea-loving people. And five shining ships came down. Landed. From them came men, tall and handsome in glittering raiment, each with a shining band about his brow. They said nothing, those men, but they smiled much. And our men were curious to see the insides of those wonderful ships."

"That's natural," Hadley rumbled. "We'd be the same."

"The men went in. The Shining Ones welcomed them, but turned away all women. Only our men, by the hundreds. And when they came out again, they were men no longer. Satan had taken them."

"Satan?"

The old eyes flashed at Thorpe. "Before, we never had need to personify evil. This was a happy world. But when the Shining Ones came, we needed a word, and we took that one, from your speech."

"All right!" Thorpe sucked in a breath to steady himself. "We're now getting close to it. The Shining Ones did something to your men, but let me ask this. Were they men, these Shining Ones? What I'm getting at is, did they do it, or were they just repeating something that had been done to them? Do you know about disease, how it can spread from those who have it to others who haven't? That kind of thing?"

"Why do you ask this?"

"Because you speak of Shining Ones, and we talk about Vegans, but are we talking about the enemy himself—or just his slaves?"

The room went thick with silence, and then the three women began to mutter among themselves. Varis and Shanne had gone pale. The old woman was scowling in thought. Thorpe interrupted them with a question.

"Tell me this, then. You say when the men came out, your men, they were changed, had become evil. How? What was the difference?"

"I can tell you," the old woman muttered, "because I have seen. These children have not. Also my mother told me this, about her husband, my father, and my older brother, her son. They look the same, except for the metal disc on the head, that you have already heard of. But their eyes are dull and dead, and they do not speak with each other, only to the women, to order them like work animals. And they are strangers to us."

A mellow-toned bell began to sound in the distance and the three rose hurriedly.

"It is the hour for sunset devotions. We must go. Stay here. We will return soon."

They went away, leaving the three men to wonder.

VII

"THAT DIDN'T GET us very far," Thorpe sighed, then struggled against a huge yawn of weariness. "My guess is that the Vegans, whoever they are, are just as far out of our sight as before. The Shining Ones sound like puppets."

"That radio throws me," Skoda confessed. "By the time any signals of ours got this far they'd be scrambled, attenuated, distorted all to hell. If they can detect that and smooth it, they've got something I want to see."

"Some hope of that!" Hadley growled. "The way they think about men, I reckon we're lucky to be alive!"

Varis came ducking through the drapes to bow and say, "Mother Hathar sends excuses, and I am to show you to the room set for you. Come." The followed her along quiet passages and short flights of steps until they heard a mumble of speech and the smell of ozone was very plain.

"That's electrical discharge," Skoda declared. "Their radio-room must be close. I'd like to take a look."

Varis inclined her head. "It is permitted. Mother Hathar said so. You come this way." She made a sharp right turn into a room so high-vaulted the apex was lost in shadow. There were rows of jars, a maze of glittering wires and coils, and a girl sitting by a central bench before a carved box like the one in the old woman's room. She moved a hand to make silence, stood and bent her head in submissive attitude.

"The Earthmen wish to see and examine the secrets of hathari," Varis said. "You will show them whatever they ask."

"And tell her not to fear," Thorpe suggested. "Tell her we are not going to do her any harm." Varis made what was virtually a shrug.

"I can tell her, but I cannot command fear to depart. Molleen can see that you are men!"

"Molleen!" Hadley exclaimed, before Thorpe could protest about the unfairness of the insistence on their maleness. "Now there's a fine sweet name for a girl. No girl with a name like that would ever be afraid of me, surely?" And there was a surprising gentleness in his manner as he went forward with his hand out. The girl paled. For a moment she stood rigid, then she came round her table to meet the Irishman, to stand distant, to look up at him. Thorpe could see, now, that she was about eighteen or nineteen, into the first bountiful blush of womanhood. She wore the same sterile white jacket but had no dagger. A six-inch wide strip of gauze, extending from a white silden cord about her waist, bore the embroidered symbol of hathari, and it shimmered with her agitation.

"There now," Hadley reached and took her hand, very gently, as if unaware that she was quivering, "it's been a long time since I saw a prettier girl than you, my dear. A long time. And we're good friends, aren't we? Nick is a good friend too. He'll want you to tell him all about this wonderful contraption you have here, and mind you explain it to him nice and simple, now, because he's none too bright. Will you do that?" Watching, Thorpe saw the girl's face flutter into a smile and wide-eyed wonder. She shifted her gaze to Skoda, who grinned. And her smile grew, became a pretty thing.

"Nick," he murmured, "we'd better locate our chambers first, then Varis can bring you back here to potter on your own, without us. We would only be in the way among this lot." Varis led them on, not too far, into a small room with four couches, one in each corner. And in the middle of the stone floor were three familiar objects carefully laid out.

"Our suits!" Skoda cried. "That's a bit of luck. Or a kind thought on somebody's part. Now, if only it hasn't fallen out—" he turned the flat and flexible shapes over eagerly, recognized his own and pounced, to stand up again holding a flat-folded pack. "Always carry a little kit of tools," he announced. "I feel a lot happier about that radio-room now. Which door was it?" Varis turned and pointed, indicating the crest of the arch over the door.

"That way is inward. The hathari is central to the shrine, you see? That way," she indicated the opposite door, which had a stout wooden bolt across it, "leads outside, to the gardens. These doorways connect with other sleeping chambers." She went away, Skoda following excitedly. Thorpe stooped to turn his suit over and retrieve the two pictures from the pocket. There was nothing else of value. He had discovered that the skirt-garment had a small inner pocket at the waistband. He slid the pictures into it and sat down on one of the bunks.

"Nothing monastic about this, anyway," he commented, feeling the firm resilience of a mattress of some kind. "I'm about ready for this. It has been some time since any of us slept easily."

"You're right, there." Hadley stretched himself out and sighed with the bliss of it. "I'll need no rocking this night."

For all his weariness, however, Thorpe felt sleep eluding his eyelids. There were too many questions nagging his mind. After what seemed an age he stirred and sat up, to see that the Irishman was not asleep either.

"I don't know if it will help," he muttered, "but I was thinking of stepping out for a breath of air and maybe look at the stars. Join me?"

"It wouldn't help me none. Jeremy"—Hadley heaved up on an elbow, his face furrowed with anger—"this world, Lodor is it? It's in a hell of a mess. All the time the old woman was telling us, it seemed like just talk. My mind wouldn't take hold of it at all. But that bit of a girl down there, that Molleen—she was scared stiff of me! Of all of us. Just because we're men! Sure and that's a terrible thing to happen to anybody. It didn't come to me properly until I touched her hand. Like a rabbit, she was."

"You managed to charm her, all right!"

"I've a knack for it right enough. I was brought up on a farm, and I was always good with wild things. But I've never seen that look in a human face before."

"It is pretty hard to grasp," Thorpe nodded. "Seventy

years is a hell of a long time. Three or four generations. Incidentally, that brings up the point you made when we were being hauled out of the pit. Remember? About parthenogenesis. I wonder how they keep going, how they breed?"

"However it is, I'll bet it's something to scare the daylights out of them all. You see, that's what I was thinking. That child was afraid of me. Now you'd expect her to be nervous, or curious. An animal is like that, too. But when you see an animal that is shaking with fright at the sight of you, then you can bet it has learned to be afraid. It's been hurt, or it has good reason for its fear. I'm thinking the old woman was right when she talked about Satan."

"I wish I could think that Earth is safe from this, Paddy, but common sense tells me it could happen there, too, unless something miraculous happens."

"Ah, they would not be let to land so easily on Earth. They'd have a hell of a fight of it first!"

"You're right, there. Ah well, I think I will take a turn in the air. Tell Skoda where I am, if he comes back before I do." Thorpe raised the bolt, and found himself in a short corridor that was no more than a recess.

Three steps took him to a broad gallery with a stout wooden guard-rail on its outer edge. It apparently ran completely round the superstructure of the building. He saw down into a series of dark gardens, caught the glint of light on the pool where they had bathed earlier, and his nostrils filled with the rich scent of night-flowering blooms. Horrors were remote and unreal here. This was sanctuary, surely? It was a clear night and the stars were glorious. He had a basic knowledge of star-fields and astrogation, enough to pick out one or two familiar lights and to guess when he was staring in the direction of Sol. But fifteen or more light-years is a long way, and Sol is not a large star. He had to be content with believing that he was looking in the right region.

A ghost of motion caught the corner of his eye, high up over his head. Keeping quite still, he waited for it to come again. There—a flutter of white. A garment, and a face dimly seen in the starlight. He moved to the guard-rail, set his back against it and looked up intently. The flutter of white came again, closer now, almost overhead. He saw that there must be a flat roof above, and someone moving on it, circling it. He peered, and smiled as he recognized the face.

"Shanne? Can't you sleep either?"

The apparition vanished as if it had been snatched back. Then, very cautiously, she peered over and down. He kept quite still, sensing that he had startled her. He saw now a wooden ladder braced against the wall.

"Earthman Thorpe?" Her voice was no more than a whisper.

"Right. May I join you?"

"If it is your wish." Her face backed away. He went up the ladder to a flat circular surface some twelve yards across. In the center was a low seat, mushrooming from a thick support. Shanne sat there, staring at him. He took a step towards her, and she stood up so abruptly that he had the conviction she was poised for flight. He halted. He saw now that she, too, wore a dangling strip of gauze, exactly like Molleen, with the same embroidered symbol. Was there some ritual significance about it? He moved again, very steadily, and saw the sleek muscles of her leg leap and tense, saw her bare foot clench on the rooftop. Her arms drew back behind her, as the panic flared within her, and he halted again.

"Please don't be afraid of me," he said, trying to be gentle over the anger that filled him. "I'm not going to hurt you!" Her eyes were glassy. Her lips moved but no sound came. She panted, her breast heaving and swelling until he felt an ache just watching her. And he could no longer fight off his rage that this thing should be. He turned on his heel abruptly and went back to the edge where the ladder was, intending to return to where he had come from. Hadley was right. These women had learned, somehow, to fear men the way an animal fears the hunter. He had to go. It was that, or frighten her still more by showing the anger he could hardly control. His foot was on the first rung when she cried out—

"No! Come back. I will try not to be afraid!" He went

slowly back to her. She shifted her feet, stood sideways to him. He saw the shivers run over her curves, her gauzy apron quivering like an aspen leaf.

"Why are you afraid of me?" he asked, making his voice gentle.

"Because I am defenseless. For this period of vigil I wear the seal of hathar. It is a ritual."

"You mean you haven't got your daggers, it that it?"

"Yes. At all other times we always wear the twin blades, one in each pocket, the right one for the man who touches me, the other for my own life."

He strangled on bitter words, made himself be patient. "And you're on some sort of sacred duty now?"

"A vigil. To keep watch, and meditate, trusting to hathari."

"I'm sorry. I've interrupted." He turned away again, but she spoke to halt him, turned to face him bravely.

"No. You are not as other men." The way she said it, she was trying to convince herself. She put up a slim arm to point to the sky. "You do not come from Satan's nest, as they do!"

"Hold it!" He moved close enough to be able to follow her pointing arm. "That one? Below and to the right of the three in a line? How do you know they come from that star?"

"It is said that some of the first men spoke and said so."

"Well now, that's Alpha Lyrae right enough. The constellation of the Harp. Or, as we know it, Vega."

"Can you point to Earth's star, that I may know it?"

"I'll try. It's pretty small, from here." He swung round, raised his arm, and the bare flesh of his wrist grazed her shoulder. She shivered away instantly, but he affected not to notice. "You need a glass, a telescope."

"We have those."

"Look"—he tried again—"I can understand why you hate the Shining Ones, but not why you transfer that feeling to me!"

She moved one step away, then came back. Deliberately she put one foot up on the low seat, crossed her hands on that knee, and stared into the dark.

"I will tell you." Her voice became singsong, like a recitation. "Then the men came forth from the ships looking neither to left nor right but sought out other men, those who had not yet been perverted. These men went into the ships and were perverted. By the third day the ships were full, and departed, other ships coming in their stead. Many men tried to flee, but were caught. Many women, wives and mothers, tried to detain their men. These were slain with the fire-weapons. By the fourth of a year all men had been perverted and there were none left pure. All were taken away in the shining ships, save five hundred, one hundred in each of the five cities of Lodor."

"So there are only five hundred men on the whole planet! And every one of them a Vegan puppet, bossing you about?"

Her eyes came round to him, wide with surprise. "No. I have explained badly. They do not rule. They treat us like cattle. They collect women to breed and build ships, and that only. For the rest, we do as we please. They are not interested in us at all."

"Wait a bit now." He sat by her foot and looked up at her. "I'm confused. They don't rule?" She abandoned her sinsong tone now.

"No. They capture women and train them into a work force, make them build ships. One hundred for each city. Then, once every year, five more ships come, and five hundred go away, with men to crew them."

"They certainly have this thing organized. Did you ever work on ships?"

She stiffened as if he had whipped her across the face. "I am Hathari! Know this. When the Shining Ones first came, many of them sought out the holy shrines of Hathar, all they could find, and destroyed them. And slew those who served there. The Shining Ones hate and fear hathari!"

"So Nick *was* right. The Vegans don't have radio. Sorry!" Without thinking he put out his hand to pat hers. She whipped them away in a flash, so that his open palm slapped softly on her knee. He felt the rigidity of her muscles

73

under his touch, and his pent-up anger burst out. Still gripping her knee he stood and glared at her.

"This is ridiculous! All right, maybe I shouldn't have touched you, but I have. I'm touching you now. Does it burn? I seem to remember only a few hours ago several of you laid hands on me and my friends and stripped us of our clothes. Were you so frightened then? Did you fall down dead?"

"It was I who investigated the wound on your forehead." Her words came stiffly through clenched teeth. "Had it been deeper and central, you would have died instantly, and I with you."

"Don't be a fool! You satisfied yourself that I was an ordinary man, and that hasn't changed. I'm still ordinary. You have nothing to fear from me, surely you must see that?"

"You are a man! In Heklon, as in the other cities, there are a hundred men. They live in great domed dwelling. By day they stand over the women who work. By night, each one takes to himself a woman, into the dwelling-dome, and there tries to impregnant her with the seed of another life, whether she wishes this or not. Some resist, and die. Most go without complaining, and submit themselves."

"And then?" He hardly recognized his own voice.

"All are marked for identification. Only young and healthy women are chosen. Those who become with child are set aside and watched. When the child comes—if it be male—she and the child are put in another place to be cared for until the child is three, then she is set free. Should the child be female, she and the child are dismissed to do as they please. But should the child be in any way sickly or defective, then mother and child are killed!"

Thorpe let out a shaky breath with great care. His mind reeled before the sadistic and inhuman implications. Brood cattle and ruthless eugenics.

"I'm sorry," he breathed. "I didn't know that. I don't blame you one little bit for loathing men."

"You are hurting me."

He snatched away his grip on her knee, and groaned

as he saw the red weals where his fingers had gripped. "I'm sorry about that, too. I didn't mean—Shanne, you'll just have to make allowances, and believe that neither myself nor my friends mean any harm to you or any of the people here. All we want to do is somehow to take a crack at the Shining Ones, to strike at them in some way."

"What can you do? You are three, they are many hundreds!"

"Sounds hopeless, yes. But we have a saying, while there's life there is still a chance—" A faint silver chime interrupted him.

"That is the end of my vigil," she said. "In a moment Varis will come. You had better go, lest she see you."

"And that would get you int trouble, more trouble. All right, thanks for everything you've told me, and my apologies for breaking your meditation."

"You have given me much to think on," she whispered as he went quickly down the ladder and back to the room. As he went in, Skoda was just entering by the opposite door.

VIII

"WHAT'S UP WITH you fellers?" Skoda said. "Can't you sleep? Me, I'm just about on my last spark!" He settled wearily on the bed nearest him and sighed, rubbing a hand through his spiky black hair. Then he grinned all at once. "I'm so knotted in the head that I went strolling into the wrong door." He halted himself and squinted at the doorway to the left of where he sat, then at the door where Thorpe stood. He pointed a finger.

"What's on the other side of there?"

"Fresh air and the night, why?"

"Then that door must lead into the room—it was full of girls, all fast asleep! D'you suppose there's more, on that side?"

"What did you expect, men?" Thorpe muttered. "I thought you said you were tired?"

"That's right, I am. Man, have they got the craziest radio setup I ever saw! If I hadn't seen it with my own eyes . . . they use practically all biological materials, for a start."

"What's that mean?" Hadley growled. He had rolled up his spacesuit into a bundle to prop his head and was sitting up watching his companions. "Leaves and plants and such?"

"No! Not that way. They use juices for acids, and metal plates, and silver wiring, stuff like that. No trouble there. We started off on current electricity that way, too. But their detectors . . . no wonder they're delicate enough to pick up Earth signals! And selective? I've never seen anything to touch it. And they use the nerve fibers of insects and beetles! Fact! I didn't believe it myself until that Molleen got me a magnifier and let me see for myself. Talk about hearing a gnat cough at a hundred yards!"

"They actually dissect the nerve fibers out of insects?" Thorpe moved to his own bed and sat on it. "No wonder their receivers are sensitive, if they are using the sensory equipment of insects."

"It's a funny thing, but logical in a way"—Skoda rolled over and lay flat out in sighing ease—"because they have practically no power at all on the transmission side. I suppose they never bothered much. Never had to. And they have no theory at all on high-tension stuff. No vacuum technique, either. Everything is done with vegetable acids and chemical batteries. Clever . . . it works fine . . . but it seems so cockeyed, when you think that this little unit here, out of my suit, is about ten times as powerful as anything they can do with their biggest transmitter."

"Eh? You're sure of that?"

"Positive. I've just been playing with it, haven't I? It's right down below us, the Supreme Shrine of Hathar. And the master transmitter. If it puts out a quarter of the power of our units I'll be surprised. It's hard to take, isn't it? But, like I said, they have the receivers to handle it, and their ionosphere is as steady as a millpond. So they manage. Manage! Hell, they do very well, all things considered!"

"Had you baffled, did they?" Hadley chuckled, and Skoda sat up at once, his expression very serious.

"You were joking, and I know it. But get this. I may be a dub at most things but I've played around with coils and capacitors since I was a kid. I was a ham, and a good one. I know radio, even if I know nothing else. And those girls are smart. Their theory leaks a bit in places, but they manage. Given just a bit of a hint or two and any one of them would make a first class radio-mechanic. On their terms they are first class, if that kid of a Molleen is anything to go by."

"I'll take your word for it." Hadley murmured. "Sure and with a name like that it would be inevitable. Tell us, did you get to listen to Earth?"

"I did," Skoda's voice sounded oddly, and Thorpe sharpened his ears. "I can tell you this. We are closer than we figured. No more than ten lights, at the most." Thorpe leaned forward intently.

"You mean by the material you heard?"

"Right. Not to put too precise a date on it—after all, I don't know what today's date is, or if they have any such thing here—but the bits I heard were right out of the early stages of the war. I remember that much. When we were still reckoning we were going to clobber them good and proper any minute. And news about the big Procyon carve-up was still fresh. You can date it from that, just as I can."

"You've got it, near enough," Thorpe nodded. "About ten years is right. Not that it makes a lot of difference. One light-year is as good as a hundred, the state we're in."

"That's not what I was thinking of," Skoda muttered. "I remember that period pretty well. I joined up just about then. Soon after, the radio-ban came on, and broadcasting was stopped, except for the minimum longwave stuff. And the news was bad, too, at the last. I'm thinking what it is going to do to these people when they hear that . . . and then lose touch altogether! We represent a kind of forlorn hope to them. The last they have."

"No news is good news," Hadley rumbled. "Better they

should hear nothing at all than have the horrible truth, up to date, from us."

The three men fell silent as they each pondered this thought. Thorpe lay back on his bed, his mind fermenting with frustration, his naturally aggressive violence finding nothing to fasten on.

"You know," Skoda murmured, "that Molleen is a nice kid. Only nineteen. She told me. Bright as a pin, and smart, once she got over being so scared of me. I know you put the charm on her, Paddy, but still it was a long time before she quit shaking enough to be able to talk. And she just would not touch me, nor come close enough for it."

"And she had good sense!" Hadley scoffed. "A nice little girl like that! You should be filled with shame!"

"Hold it!" Thorpe sat up. "This is not funny, but something you both ought to know about. That girl was scared and with good reason. She fact that she was able to talk to you at all shows she has guts." In bitter detail he told them what he had learned from Shanne. "So you see, for her to be alone and defenseless, with a man—is about the way it would be for one of us to go swimming in an ocean full of man-eating sharks!" There was a thick silence for a while, then Skoda snarled.

"What in the name of hell do they do to those men? Treating their own flesh and blood like that! And I walked into a room full of them, all fast asleep! Christ, if I'd disturbed them . . ."

"You'd have been dead, fast. You saw that they even sleep with their knives at the ready?"

"But it's crazy!" Hadley growled. "We wouldn't harm a hair of their heads, the poor things."

"After three generations of this you'll have a hell of a job persuading them of that! Damn it all to hell, if only there was something we could do!"

"I was kidding myself," Skoda whispered, "that I might be able to teach them a few tricks. How to boost up their transmission-power. Maybe even fudge up a condenser or two. Thinking I would be doing some good . . ."

"It would!" Thorpe got to his feet restlessly. "Don't discard that idea yet. Anything we can do to break down this evil will be a good, no matter how small. At least we can be friendly."

"What's the use? What can the three of us do, bare-handed? Sure we have a bit of knowledge to give them, but then what?"

"Perhaps there's more!" Thorpe was snatching at straws now. "You say our units are much more powerful then anything they have?"

"Must have rattled their eardrums when we spoke to them. Must have made them think we were ten feet tall!"

"Maybe we are. Look, I know only a smattering of radio. You say it is a question of power? All right, then why don't they use power? They know how. They build ships for the Vegans, don't they? I know the Vegans don't have radio, but they do have fusion-power for their drive and Pauli, just as we do. And ion-power for their jets. And this is an isotope-battery job, isn't it?" He tapped the unit that he had slung at his belt by its clips, as they all had. "Why don't they use isotope-energy conversion for power? It's right there under their noses, isn't it?"

"Wait—wait!" Skoda begged, sitting up. "You're jumping a bit. It's the same stuff, true. But you don't just move from chemical batteries to radio-active isotope units in one breath. It took us a hundred years to see the connection, remember?"

"All right. You have the chance to catch them up a century. To do some good."

"But why?" Hadley was sitting up now. "You have something else in mind, I reckon. What?"

"It could take a little while, but we might work up to being able to build a transmitter big enough, powerful enough, to send a message to Earth!"

"Huh!" Skoda's face twisted in a sneer. "I figured it was something like that coming. Message to Earth! For what? Pass the time of day, or shout for help? And when they shout back—if they do—to say they're coming, it will be twenty years later. Twenty years! Do you reckon Earth is going to care one distorted damn what happens to us, twenty years from now? Why don't you suggest I go ahead and build a Dirac sub-etheric, and be done with it!"

Thorpe felt foolish, but swallowed it in his eagerness to snatch at the last phrase. "Would you know how to build a Dirac?"

"Of course, given the materials, and the power. Different system altogether from plain wave radio, but not all that more difficult. If I had the gear. But I haven't!"

"The pair of you are forgetting one other thing," Hadley rumbled. He glowered at them as they turned to him. "Suppose you conjure up the stuff, and Nick does his magic, and you Dirac a message to Earth H.Q. eh? Would you be so kind as to tell me what would happen then?"

"What are you getting at, Paddy?"

"Just this, Nick my lad. You're a radio man. You just send and receive messages. But what about the people who get them. H.Q. gets the word, right away, that here is a Vegan base. Just one planet, with only women to defend it, and a handful of Vegans, a few ships half-built. And only ten light-years away, too!"

"Say! That's right. This *is* a Vegan base. Man, would they ever knock the daylights out of it! Fighter screen; move in the heavies; away anti-matter bombs; exit one base complete with facilities! What a strike that would be!"

"And what a bloody mess there would be, afterwards! Is that what you want to do to these women? After what they've been through?"

"That's no way to talk!" Thorpe snapped, fighting back his own instant revulsion at the picture that came to his mind. "I know there's a damn hard choice to make, and we stand the chance of being wiped out along with the rest, but it's something we have to do if we can. We're Earth, remember? And this *is* a Vegan base, the very first one we've ever known about."

"It's all talk," Skoda muttered uncertainly, "and a waste of time. We haven't a hope of building a Dirac. You can talk about these women building ships. All right, maybe they do. But how do we get in there, and get out again with the loot? You can bet the men keep a sharp watch. I'll tell you something else, too. While I was getting Molleen to show me round the stuff, there was a message going out, to all the faithful of the hathari. Earthmen have arrived. They are here, on Shallon, the holy island. Now"—he stretched out on his bed again deliberately,—"there are a few hundreds of the faithful, and I would not care to take bets that there is at least one bad apple among them. So that news is going to leak. And go on leaking. So what would you like to bet that long before we can get organized to start looting the Vegans—they will be here looking for us? With their dinky little flame-throwers. Or worse!"

"That's an evasion," Thorpe snarled "We can talk about our own personal problems later. Right now I want the answer to one question. No, make that two. First, if we can get the materials, will you try to build a Dirac? Second, if it works, will you cooperate with me in sending the message that we *know* has got to be sent?"

"I don't have to answer that, mister. I'll think about it. And, if you don't mind, I'd like to go to sleep now. In peace. While I have the chance!" His tone was too pointed to be missed. Thorpe stared at him for a furious minute then whirled and went to throw himself on his own bed. Two against one, and he was on the unpopular side. *This is war*, he thought. *This is what it does to you.* Minutes ago he had been watching the seductive sway of a beautiful girl's body, and thinking thoughts that any ordinary warm-blooded man might feel. And now he was contemplating ways and means of achieving her almost-certain death and destruction in the merciless holocaust that would accompany an all-out punitive attack by Earth ships on this planet. He felt sick. His mind coiled in on itself in vain search for some way out of the crunch.

If it were possible to give the alarm it had to be done. To fail would be to lend his weight to the process that was daily sapping the manhood of Earth. It was five years since he had last seen Earth, and could not know what it was like now, but he could imagine what it *would* be like, if the Vegans were not stopped. The stark evidence was all around him: A world in which devout maidens were in constant dread of things they called men, in which women were made to slave and sweat—and bred like mares for some invisible stock-master. A world in which men became senseless and inhuman puppets, not even recognizing their own mothers and wives. This could happen to Earth. . . . Nick Skoda would have to be made to see the sense of it, somehow. . . . He finally slept, but his dreams were filled with fiend-faces that were at once beautiful and hideously inhuman.

He woke with a sore head to the lively clanging of a hand-bell, and got his eyes open just in time to see the vanishing of a young girl in the familiar white apron as she rushed through the chamber. Her fleet speed set his memory back in tune with last night.

"One more day I never thought I'd see," Hadley said, as they rose and made shift to tidy their beds. He got no response. The ill-feeling of last night still tainted the air. Thorpe swung round as a girl came cautiously to their doorway to peer, and make signs to others who came at her heels with bowls and large jugs of steaming water. The one in charge looked about twenty-five, about Shanne's age. The four followers were younger, barely out of their teens. They deposited their burdens and departed.

"I am Edda," the older one stayed to tell them, "and it is my pleasure to serve you. In a while food will be brought."

"Wait!" Thorpe raised a hand and she stopped, her face smoothly but guardedly attentive. "Please give my respects to Mother Hathar, and tell her that we don't want to cause any more trouble than need be. What I mean is, we can eat with the rest, unless there's some rule says we mustn't."

It was impossible to tell what Edda thought. There was, to him, an odd quality of arrogant aloofness about her as she bowed her head just a fraction.

"I will tell Mother Hathar your wish, and return." She turned and went in barefoot silence. Hadley scratched his head with comical dismay on his heavy features.

"And to think that she'd run a knife into me if I so much as went to put my arm around her! It's a queer world and all. If they're so spit scared of man you'd think they'd have more sense than to dress the way they do, with that little jacket-thing . . ."

"Probably doesn't mean a thing to them," Skoda retorted as he began washing. "I read a thing once about fashions where it said the function of clothes is to focus attention on whatever image you want other people to have of you. So a normal woman would dress so as to make you look at what she thinks is her best aspect. But you can't judge these women that way. This whole setup is off-beam. It's abnormal!"

"More's the pity, with every one of them as pretty as a statue."

"Pretty?" Thorpe growled. "When you remember why, is it still pretty? These are the cream. The sub-standard ones are destroyed at birth. Pretty?"

"You can grieve about the past, but you have to live in the present, and plan for the future," Hadley retorted. "No matter how it's happened they are a fine body of women, and if things were different I wouldn't mind if I spent the rest of my days right here."

"You're liable to do that in any case," Skoda said, with point. Edda spoke from the door, gently.

"Mother Hathar will be glad if you will join the Superior Sisters at breakfast. This way." Thorpe was too intent on his own savage thoughts to notice their path. He wanted a showdown, to know how he stood with everybody. And he wanted to pick an urgent bone with the old woman, too.

She was at the head of the long narrow table, presiding over a gathering of girls all of this same age, somewhere between twenty-five and thirty. They stood, rustlingly, as the Earthmen entered, and edged along willingly to make room for them at the head end of the table by Mother Hathar. Then they all sat once more and began silently to eat, carefully keeping their eyes on their plates and their tongues still. Edda found herself a seat. Thorpe saw Varis, and Shanne, before he sat himself by the old woman's right hand, with Skoda opposite. Youngsters of no more than ten or eleven came scurrying with plates and goblets and strange cutlery for the guests. Even these little ones, he saw, were double-daggered like their mature sisters. He glanced along the rows of faces. Hadley was right. Every one as pretty as a picture, the picture of generously mature femininity arrogantly displayed. Surgent sex thrust forth like some kind of challenge. Or assurance? His mind snapped back from the speculation as the old woman said—

"I trust you had a restful night. I am told that you," she turned to Skoda, "were good enough to praise our efforts and equipment, that this is your special interest. True?"

"That's right, to both points. Your methods differ from ours, and your theory is a bit shaky in spots, but the equipment is first class. There's not much I can tell you about receivers, anyway."

"Praise indeed from one who understands how to compress the mysteries into such a small space as the boxes you carry. If you could teach us that art, we would be forever grateful."

Skoda grinned. "That's not so easy. You'd need tools to make the tools you'd need to start along that line. But it could be worked out, given time!"

"And time is just what we do not have!" Thorpe dropped the words into the conversation with deliberate intent. The effect was an immediate hush, and then an electric tension all along the table.

IX

"Is there something wrong?" the old woman asked, turning a chill eye on Thorpe. Her tone suited him perfectly.

"You are dead right there is. I understand you have broadcast the information of our presence here, all over the world?"

"That is more scope than I would claim, but substantially

you are right. The hathari have been informed. This displeases you?"

"You might have consulted us first, before throwing the story away. Spreading information is your business. You ought to know how hard it is to set limits on that kind of thing. Who knows where it will end up?"

"Ah!" She nodded and smiled a cold smile. "I understand now. You think I have been indiscreet, that I should have kept your presence a secret, is that it?" He felt the quiet lash of her scorn and seethed inside.

"I think so, yes! Only a fool makes a gift of information to a deadly enemy. How do you know somebody won't pass the story along to the men?"

"Strong words," Mother Hathar purred. "You do ill to offend us, Jeremy Thorpe. You speak of consultation. Did you consult us when you decided to seek refuge on our planet? Should we have consulted you when the Shalla had their points on you and were poised to strike?"

"That was different. We were in no position to choose!"

"Quite so. There was no choice, neither in your case nor ours. Do you think ours were the only eyes to see your ship fall from the sky? Or to hear your voices when you shouted in the instruments? Was there a secret to be kept? Do you think the Shining Ones are stupid?"

For one hideous moment he was too stunned to think at all, then the blood burned on his face as he realized the extent of his inanity. The cold impact of two dozen pair of scornful eyes stung him.

"I'm sorry. I hadn't thought . . ."

"There is much you do not know. For instance, in all the honored history of the hathari only once have we given false information to the people. Only once, and that was because we ourselves were deceived. That was when the Shining Ones came and we proclaimed them as Earthmen. We spoke in good faith, but in error, and we have paid dearly for it ever since. Our order was reviled, our instruments seized and destroyed, many of our order were killed. That was seventy years ago. Now, by degrees, we are winning back something of our former respect among those who matter, but we still have enemies and the past is not yet buried. We exist on sufferance and on our reputation for integrity. We still give out information. This is the field in which we are without peer. We spread the news, and even our enemies are forced to admit that we are honorable, that we speak true, always."

"You must be very proud of that reputation," he muttered, "and I am sorry I spoke in haste against it."

"But I have not done yet." The old voice was clear and relentless. "Our reputation for integrity is almost all we have, that and a few skills. Know then that yesterday I sent forth the instruction that the hathari were to spread a lie! It was deliberately done. To the members of our order the truth is known—that you are indeed from Earth, that you are well and unhurt, and that you sympathize and are on our side." She let that hang in the air long enough to make him burn again, then went on. "They know this, but by my order they are even now causing it to be believed that the ship which fell yesterday was destroyed and that there were no survivors. That is for the common ear, and for the evil ones, to protect you!"

"And yourselves!" he retorted, his anger flaring up again. "Let's be honest both ways, shall we? All right, you've made a sacrifice on our behalf, and been cunning about it. I'm grateful for that. And I was wrong. I'll admit it. But let's have your side clear, too. You know that if the men suspected we were alive and here, they'd be here too. And that wouldn't be so good for you, would it?" An angry buzz along the table greeted his words, but he turned to face the glare of their eyes and raised his voice to ride over their protest.

"Mother Hathar herself used the word integrity. I don't blame her, or you, for wanting to save yourselves from what the Shining Ones would do if they came here. I'll go along with that—but let's not throw all the responsibility on us! You're protecting yourselves too! If your integrity is worth a damn you have to admit it!" The words had hardly died away before a lithe shape left her seat, quick as a cat, and was by his side. He turned to stare and froze as a razor-

edged blade kissed his throat. He kept as still as the death
that was so close. He saw her wrist and there was not a
quiver in it. . . .

"You think we value our lives, man? You think we value
yours, either?" Her voice was wire-taut. "We have nothing
to lose but honor, and I for one regret that we risk ours for
your sake. Say but the word and we die together and settle
the question for all time!"

Now he heard a chorus of ready voices, all in agreement.
"Speak—Earthman! Speak!" and there would be no doubt
what they wanted him to say.

Then the old woman snapped a dozen lashing syllables at
them and they were silent. She drew breath and spoke a-
gain. "Speth! Put up that blade and return to your seat.
Now! Truly I cannot blame the Earth people for thinking we
are fools, on this showing. For hathari, go!" Her arm slackened
and the deadly blade went away, so that Thorpe could
draw a shaky breath and look up into her face. Hadley had
said they were all pretty, and this one, Speth, was no
exception. Somehow her clear young loveliness lent added
force to the intensity of her hate. Soft lips writhed on her
gleaming teeth as she muttered:

"I withdraw—man!"

"Now listen to me," Mother Hathari ordered, as soon as
Speth had regained her seat. "You are all young, even these
men, and youth speaks in haste and with hot blood. But
there is a time for haste and anger, and a time for wit and
wisdom. To say we have nothing to lose is to say that we
have already lost. To take an enemy with you into death
is one thing; to plunge each other into death is something
different, and futile. But above all try to grasp this thing;
that these are men—not Shining Ones—that there is a difference! You will find this hard. You have never known men.
But you must try not to confuse one with the other!"

"It may be even so," Speth spoke up and her tone betrayed
the hatred that she could not let go yet, "but whatever strange
breed of creature they may be, that one talks like a fool!"

"Ah now!" Hadley cleared his throat and spoke, his massive
voice rolling in the sudden surprised silence. "Might I just

say a word here? We all talk the same lingo, which is something to be thankful for, because I can put this to you to think over. If I have the wrong of something, and I talk like a fool, which I have done many's the time, you'd have the right to tell me so to my face. And I would argue with you. I might even lose my temper and shout. But if I've any sense at all, and you can show me I'm wrong, then I'll have to admit it. And I would do the same for you, if I had the chance. Isn't that how we all learn things? By finding out what fools we are? But what good does it do to stick a knife in a man? Does it make him any the less a fool? Would you rather have me dead wrong, or alive and a bit wiser maybe?"

"You speak well," the old woman declared. "And with wisdom. Let us dispute, if it be to some purpose, but let us not have any more show of knives and killing. Not here. If I may say this without offense, the very fact that these men say foolish things should prove that they are not like those things we know as men—who say nothing at all!"

"So they are with us"—it was Speth again, still not satisfied—"and on our side. You say it. But what can they do? What can any of us do, but be ready to die when the time comes?"

Thorpe, his anger now confused with reluctant admiration for what he recognized as a kindred spirit, ached to be able to offer some stirring answer, but the cold facts tied his tongue. Even Hadley's ready joviality had no word to offer. The old woman frowned and was about to speak when she was interrupted by a hurrying youngster bringing a message. The chatter between the messenger and the old woman cut off. She turned.

"The Shalla send word that they have secured the small vessel in which you escaped. They wish to know whether it is of value to you or not?"

Skoda stopped eating and his guardedly polite expression gave way to sudden excitement. "That's our pod!" he said. "And I reckon we do want it. We certainly do."

"Drive unit," Thorpe nodded. "Batteries, instruments, all sorts of stuff we might be able to use. That's if it's not ruined."

He turned to Mother Hathar and said, candidly. "We can use some help from you, again, but if we're lucky it shouldn't be too long before we are able to do something for you in return."

"What form of help do you need?"

"Interpreter, I suppose you'd call it, between us and the Shalla. Transport to wherever they have the pod cached, and to carry back whatever we can rescue from it."

"And tools!" Hadley growled. "Or did you think we were going to rip the thing apart with that diddy little tool-kit of yours, Nick?"

"That could be a snag," Thorpe nodded again. "Those things aren't just blown together. But let's worry about that after we've seen the way the thing has survived. It may be a total wreck."

"Very well." The old woman cast her eyes over the attentive sisterhood. "Better that two of you should go. One of you, and a junior? No . . ." she corrected herself, "it had better be two Superiors, in view of the unusual nature of the task. Who is willing?"

"I will accept the duty." The voice was gentle but firm, and Thorpe was not surprised to see that it was Shanne who had spoken. He hid a smile, but stared in amazement as Skoda spoke up.

"I'll take a chance and say that I'd like to pick one—if it's allowed. I'd like to ask the lady who was so fast with her knife just now. Speth, was it? How about it?" That electric silence chilled the table again. Thorpe frowned, wondering what Skoda was up to. A deliberate try to stir up trouble, maybe? The eyes were on Speth. She put her chin up.

"Very well, man. I will talk for you."

"That's fine," said Skoda with a grin. "All right, I'm ready if everybody else is."

Ten minutes later, with the two Superior Sisters silently leading, they emerged from the quiet of the establishment into a chatter of many voices in what served as a forecourt to the Shrine. It took Thorpe a hard stare to recognize the Shalla women who had come with the message as being kin to those hard-eyed wardens who had held longbows on their captives only the day before. The half-dozen who were here now were jovial and at ease, each one in a sarong-type garment of vividly dyed and patterned cloth. Something of the ease went away with the appearance of the Earthmen, but not to the extent of the open hostility that had been their expression before. Perhaps they were reassured by the hathari's acceptance of the strangers. But he noted, nevertheless, that every one of them wore a double-bitted small-ax tucked in a belt, a thick-bladed knife strapped to the right calf, and the neck strap and chest-strings of a sheath down the spine, to hold a two-foot swordblade. Then he looked past them to the vehicle they had brought, and the thing which stood in the traces, and forgot all about belligerent women.

"What in the name of all that's holy is that?" he breathed, hearing a gasp from Skoda by his side at the same sight. It stood no more than four feet high at shoulder level, but there were three shoulders on the side they could see, with an assumed three more on the other side to go with its six legs. These were massive, as thick as a man's thigh, and equipped with short claws. They needed to be powerful, to support a broad body that was ten feet long from neck to stumpy tail tip and armored with overlapping scales. But it was the huge head that caught the eye.

" 'Tis like a crocodile that's had its face bashed in!" Hadley mumbled. "Glory be, are we expected to believe a thing like that is tame?"

"They don't seem to be scared of it," Thorpe pointed out. "I'd hate to meet that on a dark night, but it may be just its looks." The beast swung its great head round to peer at them, opened the expanse of its scoop-shovel mouth and gave out a growl like the distant mutter of thunder. A Shal-la woman standing close by reached her flat hand and slapped it so hard the smack echoed. The thing heaved its head to front again and stood placidly undisturbed. "There's your answer," Thorpe grinned, and went forward, trying hard not to cringe too far away from that fearsome muzzle.

The vehicle was as much like an earthly farmcart as to

be immediately familiar and reassuring. The wheels were large and leather-tired, the front pair mounted on a swivel, and the cart itself was lashed and roped together with leather, rather than nailed, but the general idea was familiar. Until Hadley said—

"How the devil do they steer that beast, then? I can't see anything that looks like reins, at all!" Shanne and Speth had climbed into the cart and stood up to the front end. Thorpe heaved himself up along with the other men and waited, watching. There were three Shalla on either side of the animal. At some snapped word of command they began in concert to thump and beat on the bulky body and to kick the thick legs with their bare feet. It began to move, rolling as its legs moved three one side then three the other, slowly and pondersouly. The women moved with it, persisting in their urging until the beast had worked up a creditable rate of progress, equivalent to a fast walk. Then they left off their urging and dropped back, all except one who took a flying leap square on to the squat muzzle, swaying gracefully with the seasick motion as she worked her way rearwards and wound up standing precariously on a bony ridge where the head rose in a hump to join the neck and body. There she remained, her feet astride, her bottom resting comfortably against the hump, and hands on her hips in full control of the situation.

At least that was what it looked like. "She's the driver, sure enough," Hadley declared, clinging to the side of the cart, "but I still can't see how she controls the beast!" What added to their unease was the discovery that the lumbering animal was still working up speed, and the other women were now being left behind, although they were running fast.

"Down a track like this who needs a guide?" Skoda gasped, as the cart jolted over the narrow tree-lined pathway. Thorpe, peering ahead, saw a fork rapidly coming near.

"Demonstration coming up," he said grimly. "This ought to show." It proved to be elegantly simple. He was just quick enough to see the driver-woman casually shift her foot to place it over the animal's left eye, where it was shrouded in bone. As immediately as its weight would allow, it heaved its head round to the left, and the rest of its gross body followed as a matter of course. Whereupon she removed her foot and reclined in indifference as the great thing thudded on. Thorpe grinned. His eye fell on the two white-jacketed, white-skirted Sisters who stood up front in silent dignity, and the grin faded.

"What was the big idea suggesting Speth?" he demanded of Skoda, keeping his voice low. "You wouldn't be trying to get me put away, would you?"

"If you're thinking of going through with that notion of calling in the Earth ships to blast this place, that wouldn't be a bad idea!" Skoda retorted. "But it wasn't that, at all. Just an idea of mine. I'll tell you later, if it works out. Paddy's not the only one with psychology."

"I called it philosophy," Hadley retorted, "and it's not the same thing at all. I've been thinking about this situation here. And will you look at the hideous beast that's pulling us? A nightmare, but it's tame."

"Leave out the riddles," Thorpe growled.

"Ah, but listen, because there's a point. We look like hideous things to these women, too, remember that. They don't know that we're tame. But I would ask you to think of something else now. Not only are we the only three men on a whole planetful of women, God help us, but these are not really women at all. Be still now, Nick; what I mean is, a woman is only a woman by comparison to, and responding to, a man. How can she be feminine, otherwise?"

"If you have a point I wish you'd get to it, Paddy."

"All right, then. You've seen—you can't help seeing—the way all these lovely creatures emphasize their feminine aspects. Did you ever see a muscle-man showing off? And what's he doing, but trying hard to kid himself he's really a man? He's insecure. A sane and healthy man doesn't need to show off. A sane and healthy woman's the same, she doesn't need to make a thing of it. Bernard Shaw—an Irishman, of course—said something about it that I don't recall exactly, but to the effect that when a woman wears too much paint and not enough clothes, she is getting worried."

"You've got me worried now," Skoda retorted. "I don't know what the hell you're talking about, and I doubt if you do, either."

"I do. I know, you see, that these creatures are female, deep down inside in their biology. They can't alter that, no matter how much they might hate men on the surface, consciously. So each and every one of them is like a bomb, all wound up and ticking, and we are right in the middle of it all. We have only to put a foot wrong and the whole boiling will go up. Or down. Or sideways. Anything can happen."

"It need not," Thorpe spoke with all the confidence he could work up. "Women have been afraid of men before, and got over it."

"Three of us . . . and three million of them, maybe? And after three generations of blind hatred?"

The lumbering beast dragged them bumpily out of the tree-lined path into the sunshine at the head of a beach, and they dropped the uneasy conversation in order to study the scene. They were looking down on a large landlocked cove, the spurs of rock running out almost a mile into the sea on either hand. And the enclosed harbor was rich with small boats, some lying alongside a timbered pier on their left, the others bobbing at anchor in regular rows. They were flat-bottomed sailboats, square-prowed to let them run up on the sand and disgorge their cargo, and with shear-leg masts braced and rigged with an intricacy of cordage. A fishing fleet, every craft neat and trim. Thorpe recalled the way they had dismissed the Shalla as savages at first glance, and smiled wryly. Then his attention moved to the stained and pitted metal hulk that bobbed sluggishly at the far end of the pier.

"That's it," he said, "and still buoyant, by the look. Couldn't have been too badly shook up, after all." The Shalla woman blotted out her beast's vision entirely now, one foot over each eye, and it lumbered to a ponderous halt by the end of the pier. Shanne spoke a brief word to the driver-woman then turned and gestured to the passengers to dismount.

"The calla will wait for us here, if we require it," she said.

"Calla? That's the wagon? And what do you call that six-legged nightmare pulling it?"

"The mok?" she frowned. "It is no nightmare. Ah, you mean it is strange to you. But you have beasts of burden, surely? The mok is a very placid, rather stupid animal, but very hard working and reliable." She led off, with Speth, along the pier-planks.

Thorpe followed and looked at their mutilated craft. "Full of water," he said, "and we can't pump it out, even if we had a pump, because the door is open. And we can't pump air into it for the same reason. Because the door is open. And if we shut the door the damn thing is sealed!"

"Oh great!" Skoda scratched his head. "Now all we want is diving gear, so that we can work under water on it, in the dark with no tools!"

"What about our suits?" Hadley suggested. "We could weight the feet a bit?" Thorpe shook his head.

"We might have to, but I'd rather not if I can help it. Too damn clumsy." He paused, then went on, "I was thinking of tipping it up sideways. We might be able to buoy it so that the door stayed on top, and bail out. But it's too damn heavy. And it would be unstable, anyway."

"What d'you reckon it weighs?" Skoda wondered. "I know it's about five ton, empty, but with all that water in it it must be double, at least."

"Thinking of hoisting it? I doubt they've got tackle that powerful, but we could ask, I suppose. Shanne! You understand what we've been saying, and what we're trying to do?"

"I think so," she nodded her head very slightly, "and I will ask for you. You wish to know whether the Shalla have tackle strong enough to lift the damn thing up and let the water run out, yes?"

"Huh?" Thorpe gaped for a moment, then closed his mouth hurriedly and nodded. Skoda let out a smothered sound and he rounded on him in a flash, putting his hand up. Speth had stationed herself several feet off, aloofly indifferent. "Hold it, Nick. Not a word! I think we are about to prove you wrong, Paddy. My fault for being a bit free with my language in front of an innocent. She obviously doesn't

94

catch the intention of the word, only that I've used it with emphasis. And she is copying me. Which means she is willing to learn, even though she may not know it, from us. How does that square with hatred, Paddy?"

Hadley scowled and fingered his jaw, which made a scraping sound. "I'd say maybe we have instinct working for us, at that!"

Skoda gave them both an odd look, then turned as Shanne came back from a rapid colloquy with one of the Shalla women on a nearby craft. She shook her head regretfully.

"They think, from their experience in towing the damn thing, that it would be too heavy to lift out of the water. Objects gain weight as they leave the support of the water, as you no doubt know.

"Yes . . ." Thorpe sighed, then snapped his fingers suddenly. "Towing! That's it. Why can't we tow—haul—the damn thing up on the beach and just let the water run out?"

"We might get it as far as the beach, sure!" Skoda agreed. "But it is going to be one hell of a job from there. Same problem, isn't it?"

"Not a bit of it! From dry land we can get power. What about the mok? And we can surely find the equivalent of rollers with all these seafaring people about. Are you still understanding me, Shanne? We mean to haul it along this pier as far as the beach, and then heave it up on to the sand and roll it over to let the water drain out. We could do with the help and cooperation of a few of the Shalla. And the mok. And all the heavy cable we can beg or borrow." The infection of his insistence reached as far as Speth, who drew near to listen. She was sent promptly to explain to the mok-driver. Shanne passed urgent advice and instruction to the Shalla boat-women and within moments the pier was a froth of action and bustle.

Boats were hastily shoved off to give clearance. The three men laid on the lifeboat's mooring-cables with a will, hauling and struggling to get it moving and keep it moving sluggishly along the pier towards the beach. After the first five minutes on their own they found the women joining them, setting their feet and heaving lustily so that the water-logged cylinder bobbed and bumped rapidly into the shallows and leaned over, coming up heavily on the ropes. By this time the mok had been beaten and harried into position, its head aimed up the sandy slope and heavy ropes trailing back from it, ready to bend on to the mooring lines. Thorpe flipped the sweat from his face and studied the line.

"We'll try a dead haul first," he decided. "See how far we get that way. Then, if we have to, we can run a rolling-line round her and roll her up the beach." In a rapid interchange with Shanne and several of the Shalla, he had been made to see that rollers would not serve on sand. "Quite right," he had admitted, with an apologetic grin to the women. "I should have seen that myself. Too soft, damn it!" So they tried brute force, and the mok responded gallantly, lumbering into the drag of the harness until the massive cylinder had ploughed a wet furrow for three quarters of its length. Then it could do no more, but floundered helplessly in the holes dug by its own straining feet. Thorpe called a halt, running up the lines to slap the great beast's heaving side in reward.

"Easy, boy!" he panted. "Save it for later!" He pantomimed to the driver to stop, then explained with gestures just how the ropes should be recast, wading waist-deep into the water to throw the first one. Several of the Shalla had by now discarded their gaudy sarongs and were stripped for business, down to the hip-strap harness they had worn on their first encounter. But there was no hostility now, only eager interest in their mutual task. Thorpe was surprised to find Shanne up to her knees in the slight surf to meet him as he walked out with the rope over his shoulder.

"It's too damn heavy to haul direct, see?" Thorpe explained. "But this rope goes round and under and over, and if a few of us haul on this end it will roll. Nick, better have another line ready to loop the top end when we get her swung round. Paddy, you throw your weight on this, with me. You too, Shanne, if you want to. It all helps!" She seized the rope willingly. And the pod rolled, heavily at first then more easily, until it had twisted on its upper extremity and lay parallel to the slope of the beach. Halfway in the rolling the hatch door swung in to show a dark interior, and a fair amount of water dribbled out, but the capsule leveled with the all-important door on the upper side of the curvature.

By this time, at the risk of getting himself crushed once or twice, Skoda had managed to get a second long line looped about the cylinder at the top end, and he and Hadley, along with several Shalla, were holding on to it. Thorpe spoke over his shoulder to Shanne.

"See they hold this thing safe for a while. Nick! Hold on. I'm going up there and secure that door open somehow." With the ropes to help, he managed to get on top of the pod, and then down through the hatch into the capsule itself, down into five feet of surging water. He groped for the ruins of the shock-harness and managed to get enough of it to lash the heavy door so that it would not swing shut again. Then he was up, out, and leaping down to the sand, waving to the crowd to haul away. By now several of the Shalla had realized what he was up to, and as the pod rolled, and the dark orifice came over and down, gushing water, they crept cautiously round to the lower side with lengths of lumber. He saw them, and grinned approvingly. At the right moment he gave them the signal and the chocks were driven deep into the sand, hard up against the curved metal.

"That's it!" he cried in relief. "She's safe now. We can relax. Shanne, would you express my thanks and gratitude to the Shalla for their help? They did a damn good job!"

Again there was that familiar look of wonderment, almost of struggle, then she nodded, raised her voice and spoke to the little crowd of fisher-women. He was astounded at the way the friendly spirit of cooperation suddenly fled. In an uneasy silence the crowd looked at each other, then, one by one, they drifted away about their own business, leaving only the two Sisters to stay with the three men.

X

"What was all that about?" He threw the question a
Shanne, but it was Speth who answered him.

"The words reminded them that you were men and tha
they had helped you. Just as we are helping you and won
dering why."

"I am not wondering why!" Shanne contradicted, more
sharply than she usually spoke. "These men are not like
the other kind."

"Never mind that," Skoda broke in. "We have other things
to do. I would like you," and he indicated Speth, who lifted
her chin instantly, "to come along with me—in there!" He
nodded to the dark entrance of the pod, now at ground
level. Without thought her hands crossed and reached for
the twin dagger hilts by her breasts.

"Do you take me for a fool?"

"You'll be a coward, and a fool, if you don't. I want to
show you something. And I may need your help, too." Thorpe
saw her hesitate, and then set her jaw. Moments later she
was crouching in the sand watching the radio-man squirm
in at the awkward angle dictated by the lie of the pod. A
second or so later the interior lit up with a blue glare. Speth
knelt, peered in, then went all the way. After a moment
Thorpe nodded to himself.

"You too, Shanne. There's room enough, and things you'd
want to see. Go on, there's no danger." She too hesitated but
soon had disappeared into the pod with Skoda.

"What's the game? What's he up to?" Hadley seemed
worried.

"Professional enthusiasm. Skoda's using his head. Those
girls are radio-experts, remember? It's their religion. And he's

showing them a marvel or two. There's enough life left in the batteries to energize the instruments, if nothing else. And they've never seen televisual stuff before. I'll bet their eyes are bugging." He had guessed right. The two Sisters emerged in a stunned glow.

"These are the inner secrets of hathari such as we have dreamed of but never been able to unravel. Truly you are not like other men if you understand these things. Now we have no more doubts," Shanne said. Speth put it even more pointedly. She came to stand before Thorpe, and with a swift gesture plucked out her daggers and offered them to him hilt-first.

"Never again will these be used against you, oh man. All I ask is how best I may serve the masters of this mystery."

"Keep your blades," he told her. "We are only three. There are still the other men to think of. As for help"—he turned as Skoda came dusting sand from his knees—"you're the expert here, Nick. What's the shape in there?"

"It's not all my stuff. Instruments, sure, but there's a lot more. The batteries can be recharged if we can lay hands on some hydrocarbon fuel liquid. And the drive-converter looks O.K. What we need most is tools."

After some effort and pantomime, with plenty of description in the nearest words available, it seemed there was a fair amount of tool skill among the Shalla. They worked mostly in wood and stone, of course, but they did handle a small amount of metal-craft, mostly copper and the various bronzes. They could and did make very fine quality copper and silver wire in many gauges. "And," Shanne said, "many of them, of course, have worked for the Shining Ones, on their spaceships."

"They have?" Thorpe was stunned. "These women here?"

"Some of them, yes. Does this surprise you?"

"Never mind the surprise," Skoda said; "just get us some of those ladies, if you can. Experienced spaceship builders are just what we need."

"I'll say we do!" Thorpe had a sudden flash of larger ideas. "Not just for tools, either." Speth went away at a trot to seek information and came back excitedly to tell them there was an establishment only a short walk back from the beach where several of the experienced women had set up a kind of advanced workshop for the benefit of the harbor fleet.

"That figures," Thorpe grinned. "Come on, gang, this is just what we need. Now we're getting the breaks. Nick!" He drew his companions aside as they set off. "You and Hadley can concentrate on the breakdown angle and getting out everything that could possibly be any good. Speth can talk for you. I want to take Shanne and sort out whichever of these women knows most about those ships. If I can get anything that will do as paper and pencil or pen, I aim to find out everything I can about those shining ships. We know their main power-source and drive are the same as ours in principle, but there must be a hell of a lot more we don't know. How they compensate for high-gee, for one. And their intercom technique, for another."

They had reached the tree-line by now, and came to a wide road that was deeply rutted with the passage of many heavy-laden carts. That sight lifted his hopes still more. It indicated that whoever was at the far end of that track was accustomed to big stuff. "I wonder if they reckon their output in mok-power?" he mused, and chuckled at the thought. Shanne came to his elbow, and gave him a side-glance as they strode along.

"You are pleased, Jeremy Thorpe? Is that why you smile?"

"I like to be getting on with something, to have something to aim for," he explained. "Hope. Prospects. A chance. Does that make sense?"

"Oh yes, I understand that. And when you smile I feel I want to smile too, and be happy with you. What is damn?"

"Ah now," he shook his head in thought hard, "it's not easy to explain. It's not really a word at all, but a sound to indicate a feeling that is too strong to put in a word. Look, when you saw what there was to see in that capsule you were impressed, yes? Now, suppose I tell you that the instruments you saw are only small things, crude emergency instruments, and that the ship itself had the same things, only one hundred times as good. What then? And before you can speak, suppose I add this, that on Earth in time of peace we have instruments which bring huge pictures in color, and full sound, from one side of the Earth to the other, and so common that all people have these instruments in their homes. Now—have you words to express how you feel about that?"

She shook her head and sighed. "Truly yours must be a wonderful world, with such marvels, and for everyone, even the common people. It is as you say. There are no words to tell how I feel."

"That's it. We haven't got the words, either, for the times when we get excited. So we use meaningless sounds to let off some of the effect. You mustn't pay too much attention to it. But tell me, how come some of the Shalla women have been spaceship workers? Do the Shining Ones actually come here, to this island, and take them?"

"They would not dare!" she snapped. "We would die, all of us, before that should happen, hathari and Shalla alike!" Then, with a rueful smile, she relaxed her belligerence and said, "Damn!" Then in a gentler tone she explained. "The Shalla are a proud and pure people. Their elders in council made the choice long ago, the choice between suicide or honorable survival. Now, once a year they have the great games, to decide who shall be the most fit. The winners, about fifty or so, then take ship and sail to Heklon, and allow themselves to be taken by the Shining Ones."

A chill ran along his spine at the implication of her simple words. She went on in steady calm. "Those who bear males are never heard of again. They lose the gamble. But those who bear females return here. And so the Shalla people survive." He wanted to ask how the hathari managed their own survival problems, but they had now reached a clearing among the trees, and there was the workshop establishment. Four large wooden buildings lay two by two on either side of the rutted track. Chimneys gushed smoke. They heard the clank and ring of hammers on metal and buzz of machinery. The air was rich with the scent of newly cut wood and scorched metal.

The workers not only had paper and drawing instru-

DANGER FROM VEGA

ments, they had offices where nothing was done but drawing and designing. They met the "factory-manager," an older Shalla woman with authority in every line of her face and stance. She deferred to the Sisters, but kept a sharply hostile eye on the men until both Shanne and Speth had spent some time in convincing her that it was all right. Eventually Speth and the other two went off to the shed where all the hammering sounds were coming from, and Thorpe was left with Shanne and the still-suspicious manager. Shanne called her Marcath, and Thorpe saw that she must be in her fifties. But there were lines on her face, not wrinkles, and there was no sign of stiffness or withering about her shape. The only marks of authority he could see were the silver armlets she wore and the decorated inserts in the leather of her equipment. For the rest she wore as gaudy a sarong as any, and had all the uncompromising hostility that was so common to all these women. At last, however, it seemed to dawn on her that Thorpe only wanted to know what she knew about the Shining Ships, that she had secrets to reveal to someone who might be able to use them to strike at the Shining Ones. Then she moved.

In a matter of minutes the three of them were heads-close over a drawing board in one small office, and joined presently by two more, who were dexterous with charred stick and straight-edge. Marcath began with the crude outline of the ship itself, making it clear through Shanne that all the ships were exactly the same. Thorpe watched as she sketched in the various compartments, rubbing and altering until she had the general proportions right. Then she instructed her help to prepare enlargements of each space, with much to-and-fro discussion and argument. The pattern unfolded into familiarity for him. Control-space, main-drive stem and fuel storage, power-room and controls for local handling, places to eat and sleep, blisters for the weaponry. And then items not so easy to grasp, not so familiar. He put his finger on one, conveyed his question via Shanne, and the to-and-fro jabber became complex. At last Shanne said—

"This is the device, so Marcath explains it, which makes things heavy toward it? Does that mean anything?"

"Ah!" he nodded in understanding. "The pseudo-gravity unit. Yes, we have those, but not nearly as big as that. It's a damn big unit, by that drawing, but maybe their design is different from ours." He intended to pass on to something else, but a younger assistant had already begun a detailed sketch of the unit in question, viewed from the outside, and he was caught, suddenly, by one or two odd features of it. There was what looked like a sheaf of output leads, for one thing. He had never heard of output, certainly not along wires, from a grav-unit! Where would be the point? The unit generated a field analogous to a magnetic stress, not a current flow.

"Check up on those will you, Shanne? Ask what they are for." The chattering and gesturing went on for some time, and she said, at last—

"They say that these are wires, thick ones, which run throughout the ship structure and are terminated in the outside shell. Marcath says that it is very important that the ends be melted into one piece with the shining outer surface in all cases, that the Shining Ones are very particular that this be done properly."

"So it must be important. I'll remember that, though I can't see the point of it, at the moment." They went on to other matters, to detail on the heat-beamers and the fragmentation-bomb throwers, the mechanism of opening and closing the ports for these. He had no idea, at this stage, what might be most important. The only thing was to grab everything he could get. It took the raucous scream of a hooter to remind him that time was still passing at the standard rate and that he was acutely hungry.

"It's about time we packed it in," he said. "For the day, anyway. I'd like to take away the best of these sketches, and I'd be obliged if our good friends here could turn out a few more sometime. Anything in detail that we haven't covered so far." When Shanne had relayed that, he added: "And please tell Marcath, and her assistants, that I'm very grateful for all the help, that I hope to be able to repay this somehow!"

He remembered what Speth had said, the last time gratitude had been expressed, so he was not too surprised to see a similar reaction here. But it was less marked. The three Shalla stood back, stiffening in hostility, putting on the look they had lost in the absorption of their work, but after just time for one deep breath, Marcath stood forward again, and raised her right hand to lay it across her body to her left breast. She bowed stiffly and said something that made Shanne stare and think before answering. As soon as they were outside again, and the Shalla had gone to tend to their neglected business, Thorpe demanded an explanation. Shanne was pink with confusion and distress.

"Without thinking," she muttered, "I have done you a disservice. In speaking to the Shalla I have used their word for 'men'. There is no other word, you see? But of course, men—they have the same feeling as we, or anyone, about men. The men we know of. So when I say—'These men are grateful to you'—it is the wrong thing! I should have had more wit than that. I am ashamed! Damn!"

"That's all right!" he laughed. "You couldn't help it. We shall have to work up some different kind of image, that's all. But what about the old woman, Marcath, and that little ritual she performed?"

"She is older, and perhaps more sensible than most. She spoke the general words which are used in saying greetings and good-byes—but the gesture of hand-on-breast is one I do not know. I will ask Mother Hathar."

"Meantime, we'd better get back down to the beach and see how the work is going. I hope Nick and Paddy got the tools they wanted, or all our dreams are shot!"

The mok had been hustled back into harness again and the cart was loaded with precious fragments. Hadley came toiling up the sand with the medicine chest in one hand and a battery-module in the other, to lay them in the cart.

"There's a few more battery-clusters left," he puffed, "and the main body of the drive-unit. We can't get that out without cutting-torches, and it would be no good if we had it.

But the rest came apart fairly easy once we got started. Bailing out the last of the water was the bad bit. Here comes Nick and the girleen now. She's a worker, that one!" Speth was pink-flushed with effort and her hair had come down to stream about her face, but she strode steadily with a battery-module in each fist. On her heels came Skoda, weary but looking pleased with himself.

"Enough stuff here to keep me busy for weeks," he panted, laying his burden on top of the rest. "That's the lot. So far as I can tell, it all works, and there's plenty of power available now, for just about anything we are going to need, short of blasting off. What a day! I could do with something to eat—and a shave!"

"That gives me a notion," Thorpe muttered as they scrambled into the cart and the starting-up performance began. "Shanne—to your knowledge, do the Shining Ones have hair on their faces?"

Both she and Septh were baffled by the question. Weary as she was, Speth leaped down from the cart and went off to inquire among the Shalla, to come running back just as the mok began to get lumberingly under way. She sprang for the tail-board, accepted Skoda's outstretched hand as help, clambered aboard, and then shook her head.

"None of them have ever seen a Shining One so afflicted," she told them. "How would such a thing happen?"

"You are about to learn. Gents, fellow-sufferers in the fight for glory, we are about to become the Bearded Ones!" While Skoda and Hadley stared he explained the matter of image. "We're men, but different, get it? If we look different, it will make things easier all round."

"Me with fur!" Skoda scraped his bristling chin and groaned. "And just when I was breaking down a few barriers, too. Do we have to?"

"Don't be too quick to write it off as a loss, Nick. Not only will it make us different from men—their version of men—but we'll be very different from them, the women, too. And that's a help. Right, Paddy?"

"I'll go along with that. They can't grow whiskers, begod!"

"And you're not doing so bad anyway," Thorpe added meaningfully. "You gave Speth a hand just now and she never turned a hair. When I was talking with Shanne last night she nearly died because I accidentally touched her. We are getting on."

"You still think it's a noble idea to tip off Earth that this is a Vegan base, then?" Skoda jerked the question, and Thorpe frowned.

"Maybe not. There might be a better way, it all depends. Does that mean you will be able to make a Dirac?"

"I can't guarantee it will work, and I haven't a hope of making a receiver to check. I told you, the detection technique here is completely out of step with anything we know. But I ought to be able to do a lot on the transmission side. Apart from raw power, theirs is pretty much the same as ours. It'll take three or four days before I can tell for sure, but right now the prospects look all right."

Hadley braced his back against the side of the cart and put his foot on a shaking stack of battery-units. "You're all confused," he said to Skoda. "First you say you're against bringing violent warfare to this nice quiet planet, and I'm with you. Then you say you think you can build a Dirac transmitter. Why bother? Why say it? You could have told us it was impossible and never a bit of difference would we have known."

"Because I have another idea, that's all. A message to Earth will get there in about ten days. And sure they could send a heavy fleet and blast the place. But they could also send, maybe, a couple of shipsful of experts, sneak them in quietly, and we'd have an underground movement, see what I mean. These shrines might have been made for the job—with exclusive radio, and the girls will cooperate given the chance. We've proved that, and we're just third-rate crew. Think what experts might do, in our place!"

It was good thinking, and Thorpe was slightly disgusted with himself for not having had the idea earlier. But there were snags.

"You were the one who talked about leaks, I recall," he said. "We know a bit more now. It's not likely that these women will betray us to the Vegans, agreed. But they could be made to talk. Or rooted out and put to whatever is Vegan for torture—if they get any sort of hint as to what is going on. We're only three, and we've been lucky so far. But a gang—is a different matter."

"It's worth a try. It's a damn sight better than your notion, of advertising the place as a base and getting it pulverized!"

"All right, Nick! Don't fly off the handle. I'm just trying to suggest this: Whatever we try to do, we owe it to these women to let them know, to pass their opinion for or against —first. When we get back, you and Paddy can handle this stuff, tell them what you've got, what you can do with it. But I'm going to see the old woman and warn her what's likely to happen, see what she says."

Mother Hathar was almost affable as she greeted him in her chamber. "I hope you have managed to gather much valuable equipment, enough to show us some of your advanced secrets. We are keen to be taught."

XI

"WE MAY BE ABOUT to teach you something disastrous. With the parts we've secured, and a lot of work, and some luck, we may be able to send a message to Earth."

"That would be a wonderful achievement." Her voice was neutral.

"A different kind of radio. The message would get there in ten days or so. It could bring an Earth fleet here within thirty days."

"A fleet of Earth ships? And their purpose?"

"That's the point, isn't it?" He explained the alternatives. An all-out devastating attack on a Vegan base, with all the slaughter and pollution that would ensue; or a sneak infiltration of skilled and expert fifth-column agents, and the inevitable reprisals. Her small, sterile bosom heaved just once.

"Why do you tell me these things?"

"Because you deserve the chance to choose. We know where our duty lies. Our job is to hit the Vegans, if we can. But this is your planet. You people are human, like us. We've come to like the place, and the people. We don't want to bring you misery, although it seems our fate to do just that."

"Life seldom offers us choices," she said, "and when it does, they are difficult ones. You have already brought unrest. My sources of information are many and detailed. You disturb my Sisters. You upset the Shalla. Chief-constructor Marcath is almost as old as I am, and remembers the old gestures between man and woman. Real man, that is. Such delicate matters would be best left forgotten."

"I'm sorry about that, but I'm talking about real trouble now, not trivial matters."

"Trivial?" Her old eyes flashed for a moment. "You think it a trivial matter to agitate my little flock and make them think and feel futile and impossible things? However, I have an answer of a kind to your big problem. Is it not true that you would risk much, even your own survival, if you could strike a blow at the Shining Ones?"

"That's part of the hazard of war."

"Of course. Credit us, then, with the same high purpose. But, because we lack any resource, any positive weapon, we have had to consider other means. More subtle ones. Do you know anything of medicine?"

"Not much, why?"

"We could do with help in our research. We seek a way of determining the sex of the unborn. We have been working on this problem for many years. A way to make sure that only female children are produced in the nests of the Shining Ones."

It took him several stunned seconds to grasp the full import of her quiet words. Then, "But wouldn't they suspect—suppose you made it possible? Wouldn't they—?"

"Exact vengeance? Perhaps. We think not, but does it matter? In fact, they would probably just go away. They do not think as we do. They stay, they use us, only so long as we are useful. If we ceased to provide male children, they would leave."

"And then you'd be faced with planetary suicide!"

"We would have a few peaceful years, before the end. You see, your talk of bringing disaster is not so frightening, not to us."

"How many people know about this sex-control thing?"

"Not just the fanatical few," she answered his unspoken question. "For instance, that message I was attending was to say that on the day after tomorrow the Queen-Mother of Heklon is visiting us."

"For what?"

"Not because of you." She cracked a sneering smile. "We hathari preserve an uneasy alliance with the civil power against the common foe, even though we disagree on everything else. Ruthel of Hecklon, with her gaudy retinue, will come to make pilgrimage to Hathar. That is for show. In fact she will want to know how our researches are proceeding, and whether or not we yet have a weapon of some other kind." She put her dry old hands on the table and studied them. "We have tried in many ways to strike down the evil ones, but without success. They go armed, always. They strip those women they use, and search them. And they move always in numbers. Two or more. Never alone."

"But surely," he growled, "a dozen husky women could lay for a couple and smash them? There's only a hundred all told!"

"It has been tried. Strike two, and in two breaths there are two score coming to aid. With no cry or sound. As if they share a common mind. Such is the myth, indeed, that they all think as one."

"Telepathy?" He chewed his lip at the notion. "That's not a myth, necessarily. Our science was investigating that kind of thing, before the war stopped it. We never got any answers that I know of, but we did have some funny results. It would explain a lot if they do have mental links of some kind. However, it won't help us right now. About this royal visit. You want us to keep out of the way?"

"You are men!" The simple phrase was sufficient.

Thorpe made his way back down to the laboratory room slowly and in sober thought, elusive problems itching his mind. He found Skoda in the heart of a cluster of bright and engrossed faces. From somewhere the radio-man had acquired some sheets of a clear flexible stuff on which he had made ripple designs in an attempt to clarify wave-theory and modulation. He was now showing them the elegantly simple proof of the Dirac ultra-wave method.

"This wave," he said, "travels at the ultimate speed, which we call 'e.' So does any other wave. No wave can travel faster. But an impressed modulation can. Let me show you just how. I put this wave on top of that one, see?" and he laid two transparencies one over the other against a white paper background. "Now, if I move one of them just a little—the interaction between the two moves quite a lot. See that? What moves is the relationship between the two, not the waves themselves. It's that idea that we use in making a transmitter that will send messages—modulations—relationships—at many times the speed of the carrier waves."

Thorpe worked his way round the group to where Hadley leaned against a wall watching and looking bored. "The girleens are lapping it up," he whispered, "but it's all Greek to me. I feel useless!"

"Not much call for a beamer-mechanic here. What they really need is a fertility-clinician." Hadley furled his brows in bafflement but Thorpe was too desperately depressed to care to explain. An isolated word came out of Skoda's talk, and rang a bell in his mind, one that he listened to with avidity. Power! Batteries using vegetable acids and plates was all the hathari had. Skoda had said so. But they knew about copper wire, and the old woman had said they knew how to make falling water work for them. Water-mill

—copper wire—now if only they had magnets. He gave Hadley a wink, and a nod.

"Come on," he invited, "with me. I've just thought of a way we can help. I need you to put the charm on the duty-announcer!"

There was a different startled-faced teen-ager in the transmitter-room this time. Hadley had her gentled and co-operative in less than five minutes of talk. Her name was Lyree, and she was only too willing to serve the Earth master. Yes, they knew of the steel so treated that it clung to other steel or iron. Yes, it was common and the Shalla metal-workers would surely know of it. Was that all the Earth men wanted? Lyree seemed just a trifle disappointed at the briefness of her danger. Thorpe was growing sensitive to nuances by now, and he appreciated Mother Hathar's comments about her flock beginning to forget their vows. It is one thing to swear off men when the only samples available are viciously inhuman, but quite another when that situation is drastically changed. Thorpe pulled his mind away from dizzy speculations in that line.

To Hadley he said, "We have a job on, you and I. Skoda can teach them all he wants about powered transmitters, but so long as he has the only available source, those batteries, it is not going to help the other shrines all over this world much. We are going to show them how to make power without batteries. Where there are water-mills, or windmills, and copper wire, and magnets—and a bit of know-how—"

"Got you!" Hadley said. "It should be a pushover. When do we start, first thing in the morning?"

"You bet. And that means an early night. Which is right now, for me. I could do with just one night's sleep!"

It seemed that he had no sooner stretched out on his bed and shut his eyes than he was opening them again, muzzily, to the sound of Skoda coming to bed. The radio-man was draggingly weary but jubilant.

"Wake you up? Sorry. You must be as bushed as me. But those girls are dead keen and they catch on fast. They'd have me talking yet if it hadn't been for some duty roster or something. Vigil, they call it."

"Ah yes." Thorpe smiled to himself and turned over to sleep again, wondering who would be keeping watch on the roof tonight. Again it seemed he had scarcely dropped off before a hand shook him, very gently. His irritated growl was smothered as he sat up to see a familiar figure dart back from his side and stand trembling.

"Shanne!" he whispered. "What's wrong? Trouble?"

"Of a kind. Are you very tired?"

"Not all that much. Can I help at all?"

"It is my vigil time in a moment. Would you—come and talk?"

"If that's what you want, sure. Shall I wait for the bell and then come up there?" She nodded and went silently away. The vision of her seductive curves retiring from sight gave him a momentary alarm as he remembered what Hadley had said about explosive repressions. And the old woman's veiled hints about disturbing her flock with "futile" longings. The chime stirred him. He buckled on his skirt and went out. As he gained the roof she was sitting as before. She rose to meet him, shaking visibly with nerves.

"I am torn," she said abruptly, "between loyalties. I will tell you and let you judge. I believe you will speak true."

"I'll try. But what loyalties?"

"I am a priestess of hathari. Mother Hathar is Supreme. But you have inner secrets of hathari such as we have only dreamed of, so you must be far above her. Is that true?"

"That's not a fair question, Shanne. I know some things she doesn't, yes, but if it comes to a conflict between who you should obey, I can't say one way or the other until I know what the point is. I'm no high priest."

She turned away, moved a step, then swung back to him. "Last night I spent a vigil here, with you. As you know. I was defenseless, yet you did not harm me. You touched me and I was afraid, yet you were kind. You were moved by my story of the evil that has come to our land." She made a gesture of groping. "It was all so confusing that,

112

in the morning, I went to Mother Hathar and confessed all, every word."

He stood very still, keeping his face straight. So this was what the old woman had been hinting at!

"What did she say?"

"She was angry. She said that although you were a man of Earth, and to be respected, yet you were still a man, and thus to be feared and suspected.

"She could be right, at that. But go on, what made you doubt?"

"Today you and the other men showed us that not only were you great masters of hathari and other mysteries, but that you work as we do, sweat as we do, and even the Shalla were impressed. So I think that perhaps Mother Hathar is wrong, or that perhaps she is envious of your great powers." Her green-silver eyes were wide on his, seeking his opinion. He would have laughed had the situation been less fraught with peril. Hadley was right about the instincts, after all. Was there some way he could turn a fact of nature to good account? Putting the question that way reminded him of another fact of nature and suggested a daring scheme.

"Come and sit down," he invited. "This wants some explaining. Let me ask you one thing first. Are you aware of the idea Mother Hathar is working on, about predetermining the sex of the unborn child?"

"Oh yes," she nodded. "All the Superior Sisters have studied it."

"So you know all about sex. And you yourself told me that the Shining Ones impregnate women, so you know all about that, too!" He watched her keenly from the corner of his eye as he spoke, saw her stiffen and shudder, and then he knew what he was up against.

"You don't have much happiness here, do you? Shanne, one of the the greatest of all joys is the deep affection between a man and a woman. That is something Mother Hathar knows nothing of, because she was still a baby when the last real men vanished from your lives. We three are ordinary men. If I speak for myself I speak for all when I say that you are a lovely girl, very attractive. Any man would feel as I do. Any real man, that is. The last thing I want is to do you any harm."

"Are Earth women like me?"

"Not very many of them are quite so lovely. But I can show you." He dug out the 3-D photographs and she produced a night-light from beneath the round seat. She was fascinated both by the texture of the pictures and the subjects. And delighted when he told her one was his sister, and the other his mother. Her shivering had disappeared by the time he put the pictures away again.

"More great wonders," she sighed. "Is there no end to them?"

"Let me show you a greater one still," he said, and put his arm round her waist as she sat by him. For a moment she was as tense as a guitar string, sitting quite still. Then, insensibly, she began to relax, to lean against him.

"It is a strange and disturbing feeling," she whispered. "An uneasiness, but pleasant, like nothing I have ever known before." She turned her face to his, very close and wide-eyed in the starlight.

"Now try this," he breathed, and kissed her very tenderly. Breathless moments later she snuggled close to him and heaved a deep sigh of pleasure.

"This is the way it's supposed to be between real men and women," he told her. "Something Mother Hathar has never known and cannot possibly understand, so there's no point in telling her, because she would forbid it. She would rather defeat the Shining Ones by making the whole of Lodor a place of women. We three hope to do it differently. If we can get an Earth fleet here and destroy the Shining Ones, this planet can breed men again, real men."

"And then all women will be able to feel as I feel now?"

"That's it. Now, who's side are you on?"

She sighed again, turned her face up to his and answered him in the simplest and most convincing way possible. When the silver chime sounded she was shocked into exclaiming—

"It cannot be! So soon? Never has a vigil passed so

swiftly, or so joyously for me. Will there be other times like this?"

"Why not?" he said, with a touch of grimness. "We could be stuck here for a lifetime if things don't work out."

"Not I. My time is short. The Sisters of Hathar do not live long."

"Eh! What's that mean?"

"I told you the shrines had been destroyed by the Shining Ones. Some escaped, some were rebuilt, all are secret, but regularly the Shining Ones seek out our shrines and try to wipe them out. Here on Shallon is the Supreme Shrine, and from here the Sisters go out, as needed, to keep the holy skills alive. Soon it will be my turn to go."

He chilled despite himself, because this was something he could do nothing about. It made sense. At all costs the line of communication had to be kept open. But what a way to do it! Persecution and martyrdom! He was more than ever glad that he had brought a little happiness into her life before it was too late.

It took him long to fall asleep, and he woke early.

"Nick! Paddy!" he stirred out his companions. "I want a word, while we have the chance. Listen. Our coming and being here is beginning to upset the old woman. She's on our side up to a point, but you have to remember that she is the supreme boss, the high priestess—and now that we've come along, we are making her look second best, and she is liable to get nasty."

"What d'you want us to do" Nick grumbled. "Overthrow her regime?"

"Nothing like that. Look, I've managed to break down a lot of the fear between me and Shanne. The instincts you were talking about, Paddy. I think I have her on my side. How are you doing with Varis? And how's your influence with Speth, Nick? What I'm getting at, can we count on some support if it comes to a clash? We may need all the help we can get, any time."

"I think Varis is getting a bit fond of me," Hadley admitted awkwardly. "I didn't want to push it. She's a fine girl."

"I know you," Thorpe snapped. "I know you won't do her any harm. I know Nick, too. It sounds like taking advantage, but if we can keep those girls on our side, we'll be six instead of three, and it might make all the difference." They argued awhile but he had his way in the end. He pursued the other leg of his plan as soon as they were seated and he could get Mother Hathar's ear.

"A waterwheel?" she echoed. "Yes, we have such things. There is one very near here. In season it is used for grinding grain. It will be deserted at this time."

"Good. Then I won't be disturbing anybody." He laid out his ideas for her approval. He and Shanne would find this wheel. Nick had promised to supply a generator. It was nothing more than one of the pod's servo-motors slightly modified. And Hadley, with Varis, would lay a twin wire all the way from the shrine to the wheel. "Then," he explained, "we will be able to provide you with power for hathari such as you have never had before."

Her old eyes glittered, but her face gave nothing away. She said only, "If it is for hathari then I will not speak against it. You may do as you wish."

That was a day that the three were to look back on as an interlude in the urgency of war. Rigging and securing the generator took very little time. Shanne was awed and impressed by the violence of the spark he showed her, once the motor was spinning, but her greatest delight came when, after they had shared their picnic meal, she asked him to show her more of the magic feeling between a man and a woman. He discovered, to their mutual rapture, that her instincts were as true and deep as any normal, healthy woman's. It bothered the happy pair not at all that Hadley and Varis took a long, long time to appear with the double wire, but it was obvious to Thorpe that Varis glowed more beautifully than ever when he saw her, and that Hadley had not wasted any time winning her over.

Once the connections were made, sparks must have been flying at Skoda's end, for it was less than an hour later that he and Speth came excitedly to report that all was well. And there were other sparks, for those with eyes. Speth clung to Skoda's hand unashamedly, and no one would have believed that this laughing girl was the same who had been so swift with her knife only a little while earlier. They were becoming human and normal, Thorpe mused, and they looked glorious in it, but how much longer could it go on? And when, when would they be able to do something positive to strike at the Vegans? Dynamo-power was fine. Skoda would describe how to make it, over the air, and in short order every shrine in Lodor would have a boost. But that didn't hit the Vegans, at all! And tomorrow was the state visit of Ruthel of Heklon. Thorpe wondered. Perhaps he might get more sense from the civil power!

XII

NICK SKODA WAS BUSY in the laboratory next to the radio-room, trying to devise a workable twelve-volt lamp with limited materials, and happy with his struggle. Thorpe had asked permission from old Hathar for himself and Hadley to be somewhere where they could watch the ceremonials. Now it was close on noon and the two men, together with Edda, who had gone along to show them the way, were secreted in a small niche high above the Chapel. It was a place to remember. This was where they had stood, naked and defenseless, while the old woman deliberated whether to spare them or not. Now they were respected guests. Or were they? Thorpe had his own opinions on that. From where he stood he could see the hathari assembled in rows on either side the throne where the old woman sat. Now, for this occasion, they all wore a long cowled robe of white, even Hathar herself. Thorpe was reminded, grimly, that this was in fact a quasi-religious order.

The chatter of voices and the rustle of feet brought all

heads round to gaze at the entrance as the Royal party made its appearance. Thorpe looked, and could hardly believe what he saw. This was culture confused and run riot, insanity openly declared. This was what happened when the balance of nature was violently upset. He could pick out Queen-Mother Ruthel only because of her place. It would have been an impossibility for any one person, however unusual, to stand out plainly in this peacock motley. She was regally tall, arrogant, and spectacularly lovely, but so were they all. Her hair was elaborately coiffed, laced with gold wires and brooches, alive with jewels, and it was as vividly blue as any sapphire. But there were hair-styles all about her in every hue from the glint of silver to the purple-black of iodine. Around her slim neck lay bands of pearls and flaming gems. A gown bellowed from shoulders to feet in flame and green. Her skirt was of the same clashing color scheme. Her fingers were thick with jewels, and bands circled her wrists and ankles, and from the fair smoothness of her brow to the tips of her sandaled toes she was as pure a yellow as a primrose.

The eye-catching beauty on her right was blush-rose pink. On her left swayed a Venus with a rich mauve complexion. Complexions came like an insane spectrum, matching and clashing with gowns in garish hues. They smiled and chattered, those bright-eyed beauties, in skins of emerald green, in wine-red, in sinuous indigo, or the purest flame-orange, and they were gowned, jeweled and trinketed until Thorpe's eyes reeled from the sight. Hadley, just that little bit harder-headed, noticed a common factor in all the extravaganza.

"Will you look, now?" he muttered. "Just like the others. They all manage somehow to keep their breasts bare. And their stomachs too! D'ye see that?"

Thorpe looked again, and had to agree. However outré the gown, the plaster of jewelry, or the billow of skirt, each one took care to be revealed down to the navel in front. Thirty or more dazzling figures now rustled towards old Hathar's throne, and there was no exception to the rule among them all. Edda anticipated their question.

"It is the only way to make light of an evil," she said.

"The Shining Ones will not allow any woman who is with child to venture far from their reach, not even Queen Ruthel herself. So it is the fashion to let the stomach be freely shown. It is almost a pride!"

"I suppose they'd never have been allowed to take a boat-ride otherwise?" Thorpe growled, his anger flaming at this further evidence of the inhuman qualities of the Vegans, and his admiration immediate for the courage of these women in so boldly accepting the affront and turning it to a kind of mockery. "But those colors of skin—are they artificial, a dye?"

"No one knows." Edda gave him a twisted smile. "The women of Lodor began to change color long ago. Some say it was because of accidents before they knew the proper ways of handling the strange machinery of the shining ships. . . ."

"Stray radiation, you mean?"

"It is believed so. In the first days many children were born puny, or deformed, or dead. And some were—colored. Others say that the new colors were because of whatever it is that is done to the males, or because some of the males came here from other worlds, where things are not the same as here. Whatever the true answer may be, it has become the custom for all women so to stain and dye themselves that no one knows what is their true tint, and thus the shame of impurity is hidden."

Camouflage, he thought, and again he admired the courage that had prompted them to act to hide their scars.

Edda went on, "Some of us are born pure, by great good fortune. Of these are the hathari chosen. The white ones. That is why we wear all things white. With the Shalla also, only white ones are accepted. They are a very proud people. There are a few other such groups, not many."

The accoustics of the chapel were such that the three could hear all that passed between the two so-dissimilar rulers, but neither man could understand a word. Formalities, Thorpe supposed, until he saw a tense smile on Edda's face, saw her bob her head as at some satisfaction. Then she turned to him, very close in the small space of the niche, and the smile on her lovely face was such as to make him feel a chill.

"Hathar has just requested Ruthel of Heklon to give passage for three of us when her ship returns to the city this evening. Three of us for whom the time has come to leave the Mother Shrine, to go into the world and become Superiors of other shrines far away."

Shanne had warned him of this. His tongue felt dry as he asked, "Which three?"

Edda smiled again, evilly. "Shanne, Varis, and Speth!"

"Eh?" Hadley grunted. "What was all that?"

"The old woman has just shown her hand. She has arranged to get rid of three Sisters. And you need no help to guess why those three. Shanne and me. You and Varis. And Speth practically hangs on Nick's every word. So she has decided to break it up, the old bitch!"

Edda gasped and made double snatching movements, but Thorpe was seething with rage, and faster than she at grabbing. She hissed as he caught each of her wrists in a savage grip. Her bosom heaved mightily as she strove to break his hold, but in vain.

"Pig-stick me, would you? I ought to take these toys away from you and tickle you with them. Hold still, damn it, or I'll snap both your wrists. I mean just that!"

She groaned as he applied pressure. Her teeth showed as she said, "I do not fear you, or death!"

"Maybe you don't, but there's something you might think worse, and I am a man, remember?" For a moment he thought she was going to faint. She went limp in his grip.

"What do you want of me?"

"Nothing from you, particularly, just that you'd better not try to do that again. You can do something *for* me, though. You go see Hathar, urgently, and fix it so that we can have a heart-to-heart talk with her. Right? And tell her it *is* urgent, that if she doesn't play ball we have a trick or two up our sleeves that will scare the daylights out of her, and the rest of you. Now get!" and he released her arms so that she could stalk away.

Hadley sighed. "Now what?"

"I'm not sure, but whatever happens, we three have got to stick together on it. Come on, let's find Nick and tell him what goes on."

Skoda had his arm up to the elbow in a tangle of gleaming wires, with Speth craning over and peering to guide him. The glow left her cheeks as she saw their grim faces. It took the radio-man a long and scowling moment to grasp the point of their news, but Speth understood it instantly.

"It is my duty," she whispered. "And my honor, but I wish it were otherwise." Thorpe choked back the scorching words that came to his lips.

"Duty? I'm not buying that kind of coincidence. This is a deliberate move by old Hathar to break up our relationships. I *thought* she was hatching something!"

"But what can we do?" Skoda demanded. "There's only three of us up against a couple hundred females armed to the teeth."

"They don't mind getting killed, either," Hadley reminded. "I'd like to have a crack at some of them, but where would it get us, apart from sudden and uncomfortable death?"

"There are ways." As always, Thorpe's wits functioned better under pressure. To Skoda he said, "Didn't you say our suit-units were a lot more powerful than the best they can do here? Can they be boosted more?"

"Nothing to it. Bypass a capacitor or two and they'd output up to ten times as much. Wouldn't do the batteries any good, mind, but it would work for a short while. But it would play hell with their delicate receivers . . . hey!"

"You've got it. That's one surefire way we can twist their arms. Hathar won't risk having her holy hathari shattered."

"But what good will it do to challenge Hathar?" Speth demanded. "Even if she has chosen us three deliberately, it is still our duty to go, or if not ours then someone else's. The holy places must be kept!"

Before he could answer there came the scurry of soft feet, and they were joined by Shanne and Varis who came throwing back their cowls and openly revealing their distress.

"You've heard," Thorpe eyed them. "No need to dwell on

it. I think Hathar has done this on purpose. I also think I can call her play on it. But let's settle one issue first. Which would you rather do, abide by the rules, obey, do your duty, and hope some day either to die the death along with a Shining One, or find some way to promote the mass suicide of the whole of Lodor—that? Or take one hell of a gamble with me, now, and possibly find some way of taking a crack at the enemy and doing him some damage? You pick it."

"Ah now, hold on, Jeremy," Hadley objected. "That sounds fine and grand, but what the devil can we hope to do?"

"A lot. Listen. We have—or will have, soon—a Dirac. Right, Nick?" He threw the question to Skoda, who nodded.

"Twenty-four hours and she should be ready."

"That's one strike. We have, also, a lot of stuff about Vegan ships. Not everything, but a lot. It may not make much sense to us, but it will to the double-domes back on Earth."

The two men shrugged in concert. "That's a gamble, all right." Hadley growled, "I've had a look at those drawings. The only thing new to me that I can make anything of is that pseudo-grav unit. . . ."

"You mean, with all those leads to the hull?" Skoda queried. "I saw that. You know what I thought. I did a bit of pseudo-grav theory one time. Inertial-field stuff. If those leads actually flow the field out to the hull then the whole of the ship's interior will be inertialess."

"Strike!" Thorpe cried. "Nick, you know what you've just said? You have put your finger right on the reason why the Vegan ships can fly rings round ours in combat. Got to be. And dead obvious, too. *Now* do you see what I'm getting at? We have a stack of stuff that must be equally valuable, that we have got to get out. And there's a lot more we can get, by the simplest method of all. We can get it, if we take a chance!"

He had his next words all ready, but a chill voice from the laboratory doorway chopped him off short.

"You challenge my authority, Earthman Thorpe?"

Hathar stood there, bleak and calm, with a dozen of the Superior Sisters ranged on either side of her, all with daggers drawn ready. Thorpe edged aside just enough to be able to whisper to Skoda:

"Pretend to be fixing your suit-unit, Nick. I'll tell you when to put on the act." Then he moved away and stood clear, looking the old woman full in the eye, just as bleak and determined as she was.

"Call it a challenge if you like. Let's say I question your motives, your personal and private motives in deciding to send away these particular three at this particular time."

"You have neither authority nor power to question anything I do."

"It's not my power, or authority, but your boast. You claim the hathari always speaks true. And you are Hathar, more true than any. So I challenge you to speak true, by your boast, your faith, and tell us all exactly why you choose to send out these three at this time. The truth!"

The words cut deep. Not all her age and skill could hide the fact that she was inwardly torn. And doubt grew the longer he hesitated. At last, in a voice thick with fury, she cried—"Seize them! Kill them, and those other three faithless ones!"

"Wait!" Thorpe snapped, as the white-robed figures surged forward. "Hathar fears the truth and dare not say it. Therefore hathari is false, you are all deluded, and I do not hesitate to destroy your instruments!"

The surge halted, the lovely faces uncertain and confused. Only the old woman stood firm.

"He cannot destroy hathari. Pay no heed to his nonsense!"

"Nonsense? Think again, old woman." He snatched his suit-unit from its place on his hip and raised it close to his mouth. "Have you forgotten that I once spoke to you through this, in a voice like thunder. Hear now your own transmission." He pressed the receive switch and they all heard the steady voice of the vigil-operator on duty in the nearby room relayed by the thing in his hand. As he released the switch again the laboratory was as still as death, so still that tiny rustlings from the agitated robes were plainly audible.

"Think of this," he told them. "This unit is set for low power, low by our standards. Nick has just reset that one he's holding so that it is a hundred times more powerful. You saw him do it. Do I speak true?"

"That's right," Skoda nodded, holding the unit up.

"And now," Thorpe said, "listen, foolish old woman, to what *this* one can do!" He thumbed the talk switch, held the unit close and called, loud and long, "Hathareeee!" The howling roar of the speaker in the next chamber was instant, and terrifying. The white-robed sisterhood wilted. Hathar herself ducked and raised a hand to her face in fear. The giant sound echoed and died, and they heard a scream and crash as the unfortunate operator recoiled from her instrument. Thorpe glared at the assembly.

"Now let's have the knives," he challenged. "Take us. Come on! No matter how quick you are, Nick has only to scream once into his unit and your sacred hathari will burst into fragments—and you know it!"

The deadlock held in silent fury for three long breaths, then broke in the only way it could. Hathar dredged up what was left of her dignity.

"What do you want of us?"

"Two things, for now. First, nobody gets sent anywhere just yet. We need all the brains and skill we can get, right here. Second, I want audience and cooperation from you on a plan I have in mind, just as soon as I can work out a few final details. Before that ship departs. Right?"

Hathar bowed stiffly, whirled round and stalked away, taking the Sisters with her.

XIII

"MAN!" HADLEY SIGHED. "That was a hell of a bluff you put up. My hair was turning whiter every minute."

"A bluff?" Varis slid out of her cloak and stared at him. "What is a bluff?" Hadley took her cloak and folded it to lay on a bench.

"You didn't think we would really bust your precious hathari, did you, me darlin'? We were only pretending!"

"It's a thought, though," Skoda said. "I reckon it might be a good idea to change the wave-lengths on our units, switch over to a higher frequency altogether. Then we'd have private air and no eavesdroppers. I'll do that right now, while I think of it."

"What's this plan?" Hadley demanded, passing over his unit, and letting his arm find its own way about Varis, without any objection from her.

"The robes gave me the hint," Thorpe replied. "You can't tell who, or what, is under those things. So if we could borrow a couple, me and Paddy, and hitch a ride on that ship . . .?"

"To do what?"

"To see if we can't knock off a Vegan!" Thorpe waited until the storm of protest had died a little, then, "I'm not out of my mind, at all. Look, we can do it this way." He spelled out his tentative scheme for them, and they argued. They tried to prove it was suicide, but he matched them point for point with ready suggestions. The exercise had its reward in that he was able to use the experience to match the same objections all over again from Hathar as he laid out the plan for her ears.

"It is sheer madness," she declared. "It is well known that when one is struck, many others come at once and all are armed."

"Do they move at night?"

"In the evening, when the workday is over, yes. There are those who prowl for any unfortunate women who may be so unwise as to be about."

"Those are the ones I'm after. We will hit 'em so fast and hard they won't know what's happened. And we'll blind 'em so they can't tell tales. And then we'll make 'em talk, some-how."

He won his point. Skoda was furious because it was insisted that he stay and carry on with the Dirac, with Speth. Thorpe wanted either Shanne or Varis to drop out, to keep the number right, but in this one case he was met by opposition that would not yield. Varis offered to cut his throat there and then at thought of letting Hadley go without her, and Shanne said nothing, but held his hand and shook her head. So it was that when Ruthel of Hecklon set sail with her peacock court and her gaudily decked craft there were four silent and aloof white-robed figures in the prow, and only those four knew that a little Shalla ship set off to follow at a horizon's distance, as part of the mad scheme.

The red flush of sunset stained the sky as the ship came to its first sight of Heklon. Thorpe was more and more impressed as the outline of the city grew into view. To Shanne, by his side, he murmured, "I didn't expect anything half as big as this. It's huge. Those buildings must be tremendous!"

"I have been this way once before, on a duty visit to the shrine which lies beyond the city. It looks imposing, but you will find that a lot of it is decaying and neglected. Especially about the center, where the Shining Ones build their ships. Do you see the dome, now?"

"Just noticed it. What is it?"

"That is where the Shining Ones live. It is like nothing we have built, being made of many hundreds of lesser bowl shapes joined by edges to make one huge hemisphere. All the Shining Ones build thus, even for the smaller places where the parts are made for the new ships. Soon it will be time for the ships to go. Already the Shalla are starting the games to decide who will be fit to go. Then the whole thing will start all over again."

"Perhaps it won't, this next time. There's got to be some way to stop them."

They hushed as the ship slowed and the agile crew began reefing sail to bring her alongside one of the many piers which lined the harbor. At this close range he saw that many of the tall buildings wore the marks of desolation, windows shattered, paint long since flaked away, banners tattered and grimy from neglect. The four watched as the fine ladies of the party scurried ashore in threes and fours, to be scooped up and driven off in ornate carriages drawn by beasts very like Earth deer, but smaller and one-horned. Thorpe smiled a wry smile in the privacy of his cowl. "Unicorns, rainbow women, mermaids, and a devil's brood nesting under a geodesic dome," he said, under his breath. "Bows and arrows and spaceships, and nuns with daggers. Who's to say anything is crazy, in a setup like this?"

"Mark the pier," he advised as they gathered for a last minute talk. "We have to be able to find our way back here. Now, you know the drill. Me and Shanne go ahead. You keep us just in sight. And if there's any more than three, we all fade until they've gone by." He led off into the dingy deserted streets with Shanne pacing by his side and all his senses alert. There was no time to dwell on architecture, or to speculate on what this city had been like in the past. This was enemy territory. The minutes went by. They worked further away from the dock area. There was not a sign of life anywhere. He began to question the feasibility of the hunt. A whole city, one third of it in ruins, was just too big to hunt through. In any case, all sensible women would be snug indoors and abed by this hour, and the Vegans would know that.

"I'm afraid we're wasting time," he mumbled as they turned a corner and started down yet another dark canyon of silence. No sooner had he spoken than Shanne seized his arm and hissed, "Listen!"

Holding his breath, he caught the faint and distant click and slap of booted feet—and the sounds were coming nearer. He touched her and they hurried forward to meet the oncomers, eyes straining into the gloom. He saw starlight on a distant glint of metal, and gripped her hand, dragging her aside into the first doorway handy. In black shadow they pressed well back and waited. Fifteen seconds and the footsteps were loud, then going by. Only two of them, two big and brawny fellows, bare-headed and blank-faced, each with a silver disc glittering on his forehead, each dressed from neck to knee in rustling metallic fabric.

Vegans! Thorpe clenched one hand on the short length of lead rod he had brought just for this moment, raised his other hand to hold the radio-unit ready to his mouth, and nudged Shanne to move out. From here the plan was utter simplicity. Hadley and Varis would move straight at the Vegans, to focus their attention, while he and Shanne drifted up behind them as silent as ghosts—and strike! He thumbed the talk switch as he moved.

"Paddy? Here they . . ." the words dried in his mouth, for at the first whisper both Vegans halted as if they had slammed into a brick wall, hung there for a breath, and then slumped and fell like dead men. Utterly baffled, he could think of only one thing.

"Come on!" he cried. "They're down. Let's grab 'em and get!" As he ran he saw the other two sprinting to meet him. Skidding to a halt he said, "You take that one, Paddy, I'll bring the other. Away you go, girls, ahead. We'll follow!" It was heart-cracking effort. The sack-limp Vegans were monstrously heavy after the first few yards, and the streets were long and turnings few. Ten minutes of shambling brought Thorpe to the point where he had to stop, or fall down. Hadley collapsed beside him, whooping for breath. The two girls needed no telling, but spread out to either side, watching and listening for pursuit.

"What'd you hit 'em with?" Hadley puffed.

"Never laid a finger!" Thorpe gasped. "They just dropped!" Varis came back, then Shanne, to report not a sign of chase. They set off again, making an awkward shift to share one body between two. They stumbled down alleyways. They gambled on guesswork short-cuts. They shambled on until legs were like string and breath was agony. They found the pier and the Shalla boat. They dragged and dumped their captives down into it, then fell in themselves and slumped in the bottom, utterly exhausted, while the three-woman crew shoved off in stealthy silence and the boat went drifting out to sea.

After a while Thorpe levered himself up enough to throw off his heavy robe and let the cool air suck the sweat from his body.

"That was a damn fool, gamble," Thorpe muttered. "We never deserved to get away with it. And we forgot the damn hoods, at that." He dragged out a thick cloth bag he had carried ready and clumsily fitted it over a Vegan head, while Hadley did the same for the other one. The Irishman put his head close, then felt for a pulse.

"If this one isn't dead he's putting up a fine imitation. How's that one?"

Shanne leaned over. Thorpe reached for a wrist. Varis heaved herself up in agitation. "If they are dead," she cried, "we have failed!"

"Hush!" Shanne lifted a slim hand. "This one lives, barely."

"Now how the devil could they just drop?" Thorpe muttered, casting his mind back. "It was exactly as I spoke to you, Paddy, over this." And he lifted the little suit-unit and stared at it. "Could it be this? Just a radio-wave? I know high-frequency stuff can affect tissue, but surely not a midget like this!"

"Listen!" Shanne whispered. "He weeps!" They hushed, and against the click and squeak of canvas and the lap of water they heard the quietly feeble sobbing of their captive. And then a broken hardly-audible voice. "He says," Shanne reported, white-faced, "that he remembers, now. That he is himself again. That the great and wonderful Queen has departed from him. All have departed from him. He is alone, and afraid. Where are they all gone? There were many with him, in his mind. Now he is alone, and he is afraid!" The feeble babble rose to a sudden eerie cry. The Vegan gave a convulsive start, and then was quite still. Shanne put a fluttering hand to still the turmoil of her breast and stared in fear at Thorpe.

"What does it mean, Jeremy?"

"I'm not sure, but I have a feeling this is wilder than we thought. I doubt if he was speaking of any Queen we know, but something that was going on in his mind. His mind!"

"Anyhow," Hadley muttered, "he's dead. That's the both of them. I doubt we'll get any secrets from them now."

"Don't be too sure, Paddy." Thorpe lifted the radio-unit to his mouth and spoke. "Nick? Nick Skoda, do you read?" On the second try he got a response, very faintly.

"Read you, Jeremy. What's new?"

"We are on our way back. No sign of pursuit. We have two dead ones. I want you to contact old Hathar and ask her to have ready her best in the surgical line. I want these two opened up. I want to know just what it is they have planted in their skulls!" Skoda made him repeat it, then cut off. Hadley stirred uneasily.

"Do you thik they can do a brain operation, then?"

"Ask them, not me. How about it, Shanne?"

"We can do it," she nodded, looking sick. "I think Mother Hathar herself will want to take charge of this."

They reached the island shortly before dawn, and then there was the dismally grisly business of carrying the bodies to the shrine, made more gruesome by the need to fend off those who were savagely eager to mutilate the remains of their enemies. Hadley secured and carried off the two hand-weapons he had taken from the bodies. Thorpe took his problems to Skoda, who was relentlessly plugging away at the construction of the Dirac.

"Micro-waves certainly do affect tissues, in all sorts of ways, but I can't see the feeble output from these things doing any harm. Not to knock over a full grown healthy man. If that's what knocked them down then they're not as human as we thought."

"But they must be human," Thorpe argued, "or they wouldn't be able to breed with these women!" At which Skoda elevated his shoulders and said, "You pick it. You can't have it both ways."

Thorpe chewed his lip savagely. "What sticks me is the obvious. If they *are* vulnerable to radio-waves, why haven't we hit 'em before?"

"Because it's a fleet order that we keep radio-silence except for short-range internal use. That's common sense. You never know what you might give away."

"That's it, then. They have some sort of communicator surgically implanted in their skulls. And we shattered it. And the voices in his mind went away. That's it!"

"Not for my money," Skoda shook his head. "Not radio. What you're talking about is a thought-wave amplifier. Mechanized telepathy. Our lot have tried it, years ago. Never came to anything, though."

Telepathy! Thorpe mulled the notion in his mind. Hathar had said something of the kind, too. It would explain a lot, if it were true.

Hadley had his problems, too. He and Varis had stripped one of the little heat-guns. "I can take a laser-beamer apart with my eyes shut," he claimed, "but I'm no good with the theoretical stuff. Power-pack and leads, and switches, those I can find, but for the rest it looks like long-wave stuff all jumbled up with infra-red output."

"Never mind. Just so long as you can describe it, for transmission, somebody else will unravel it. I wish that surgery would hurry up!"

It was halfway to noon before Hathar sent for him. She was alone in her private chamber, looking older and worn. Her hand shook as she uncovered a flat tray on the table for him to see.

"These are what I took from the brains of those unfortunate men," she said. He looked. His stomach heaved, but he clamped down on his jaw and swallowed, then looked again. The two were identical. From a fish-belly white three-lobed body no bigger than his little fingernail there spread eight hair-fine tendrils, each about nine inches long. The pulpy body was black and yellow-spotted, the tendrils coppery, with a mass of delicate extensions almost too fine to be seen.

"I would call these antennae," she said, "and they are extremely tough. I found them intricately woven into and spread through the brain-tissue. Judging by the physical damage, they must have contracted very suddenly and strongly, to cause fatal lacerations. Is this what you hoped to find? If so, what do they mean?"

"I expected something, but not this," he mastered his voice with an effort. "They resemble—spiders."

"That is true. I would assume that these are female, if they follow the same pattern as other insects. It would be logical."

"Spawn of the devil," he muttered. "In this case the devil is a female. A Queen. These are some of her brood, parasites on human males. A lot of things make sense now. Men are needed as hosts, workers, servants, for the Queen-mother of this lot. Through these she controls them, like puppets. They all think in tune, in mental rapport. They probably steal the skills and knowledge of the man they inhabit and add it to the common pool. By her instructions they work, and fight, and breed, to make more hosts for more daughters."

"Can it be true?" Hathar went as white as ashes. "All this, from a super-insect mind?"

"It's true, all right. You've seen the dome they've built. What is it but an oversized hive? I'm willing to bet there's a sub-queen on every ship, and a senior queen in each dome —and the grand queen of all squatting in her nest back on their home planet."

"It is supposition. You have very little evidence."

"You think so?" He was savage now. "You add it up. They take only males, ignoring females except for breeding. They don't talk to each other, nor do their ships communicate— and where's the need, when they are all of one mind? And they seek out and destroy hathari, your radio. You know why? Because it irritates them, gives them a headache or an itch. Your very weak stuff does that. Ours knocks them dead! It killed them so fast they never knew what hit them, so they couldn't report, so there was no pursuit, this time! Don't you see it? These things died, instantly, but the men lived on for a short while. What more evidence do you need?"

She nodded slowly, and then her old eyes took on a hard glitter. She sat up, stiffening her spine in determination. "You are right, it is enough. Earthman Thorpe, you have a weapon with which to strike the evil ones, the shining Satans!"

"*We* have." He corrected her instantly. "We're all in on this. We can forget private quarrels for the moment. Now we can hit them, the next question is how? What's the best way? It's a gamble in any case, but we have to try, all of us!" She drew a deep breath, lifting her withered old breasts defiantly and touching her daggers.

"For the chance, however dangerous, to strike at the evil

ones, I pledge you our absolute support. All hathari is at your service. You have only to command us!"

But it wasn't as easy as that. There were a dozen difficult decisions to make, and hazards to be considered. Skoda stressed one.

"We have got to keep radio-silence on this shortwave stuff until we're ready to lash out close. If we mess about at long range we might tickle them and tip our hand." Then there were simple mechanics to think of. They had enough battery-packs from the lifeboat to power up some thirty possible units, and without any kind of mass-production facilities, every one had to be handmade. If the entire complement of the Shrine worked day and night they might just do it in forty-eight hours. And that became their deadline for several other reasons. The Shalla games gave the strongest hint.

A spokeswoman said, "As it nears the noon hour of the day after tomorrow there will come a new Shining Ship from the void to descend on Heklon. On the day after that all the new-built ships will fly away, and the work will begin all over again. On that day our winning maidens go to Heklon."

Thorpe hammered the point home. "It's the key day. A new ship and a hand-over. They'll be all gathered and busy swapping jobs and information. That's when we have to strike. Too early and they'll be dispersed, or alert. Too late—and we lose a hundred ships from Heklon alone!"

So everybody labored, even old Hathar herself. Skoda was the key man. He and Speth worked delicately and ceaselessly on the Dirac, yet kept a constant and ready eye on the many crude micro-wave emitters that grew under determined fingers. And two devout juniors kept weary watch and constant reports to other shrines throughout the time, and spelled each other in compiling exhaustive notes about the Shining Ones, their ships, their ways and their still-to-be-proven vulnerability to micro-waves, for transmission via Dirac just as soon as the apparatus was ready.

"That," Thorpe insisted, "is vital. We may flop. We may pull the most disastrous bust. But so long as we can get the data out to Earth, we won't be a total loss."

And so it was that just before dawn of the crucial day, half a dozen little ships of the Shalla stole silently over the heaving sea to come quietly alongside the decaying piers of Heklon and disgorge thirty white-robed figures into the shabby dockside area of that once-great city.

Thorpe and Shanne made their way, like the others, in wards to the most convenient deserted building within a certain distance of that vital center area. The great dome was their target point and they were to ring it and wait. He found one derelict structure to suit him, parted from her, and began making his way to the rooftop. Fifteen minutes later he stood out in the first sunlight and saw her distant figure appear, away to his right. He waved. After a minute or two he saw another white robe appear, away to his right. He waved. After a minute or two he saw another white robe appear, far away to his left, and waved again. Edda, contritely apologetic to him but bloodthirstily eager to see the Shining Ones die, had taken her station. And so, one by one, the thin ring of retribution formed itself around the Vegan space-field.

Thorpe had set up a short stick to cast a shadow by which he could gauge the time. Ahead of him he could just see the humping top of the big dome. From his hip-strap hung a battery which trailed wires to the crude instrument in his hand. The shadow shortened and his skyward glances grew more frequent.

There! Very high up in the blue he saw just a glint of silver, of polished metal. This was it! He threw his arm up, saw his signal answered on either side, closed the rough switch on his weapon, and heard it fizz and then settle down to a shrill whine. He went down from the roof swiftly, fanning the air with sweeping waves from side to side. On the street again he paused one moment to orient himself, then began to march, steadily and silently in towards the city-center, always as he went being careful to sweep a wide arc before him.

He felt foolish, futile and ineffective. He had no way of knowing whether he was discharging death or just making motions. He hoped fervently that the others would be able to overcome the same feeling, that they would have faith. He came upon a chattering crowd of gaudy women, and they hushed to give him reverent room. He crossed a street and plunged into another. A fast-moving carriage turned a corner and made him dart aside. He kept on. He began to sweat under the heavy robe. He sprayed the air like a priest bestowing benediction. And now he was moving into dereliction again, but of a different kind. Here the houses and stores were ruinous, with gaping walls, gashed and distorted pavings, gangling beams, roofs leaning at perilous tilts, and piles of rubble on all sides. He moved more slowly now, sweeping wider, taking no chances. Through gaps in the shattered ruins the dome loomed huge, its very size a threat.

Then all at once he stepped out of devastation into order, across a perimeter line as precise as if drawn with a giant compass. The hard-packed ground had a very shallow depression, yielding a scene that was geometric in its arrangement. The massively gleaming ovoids of ships stretched away on either side in the arc of a grand circle, and nestling round each one were little domes. Factory-buildings, he guessed, each to its own ship. And in the center, dominating all, the great bulk of the main dome, its shell dully gleaming like a many-faceted insect's eye. And all was still. Nothing moved. He halted where he was. That was the order. He glanced to right and left, and waited. In a moment or two he saw Edda. And then Shanne. He waved greeting but stayed where he was, steadily but ceaselessly fanning the area. Orders again. He glanced up into the sky, and the new-arriving ship was growing rapidly as it fell. In another two breaths he could hear the first shrill scream of its dive through atmosphere. He shut off his weapon, and waited, remembering his own hard words.

"The new ship *must* land. We have to let it. If we don't, it may get just a fringe dose, take alarm, and go back up again. And we're all dead!" So he waited. This was the testing time. The scream grew to a howl and then a gargantuan bellow, and the air about him thrashed with shock-waves. The glittering ovoid fell, sat down on spouting ion-fire, settled, and the jets winked out. The sudden silence was shattering. He counted fifteen seconds, and there came the buzz of hatches and the ringing clatter of a telescopic ladder thrusting itself out from a dark orifice down to the ground. Still he waited, a nerve twitching in his face. It had been easy to plan, but it was nerve-wracking to do.

Now they came out, two by two, stalwart and handsome men from space, striding and marching easily, each in glittering metallic uniform. "And each one with a spider in his brain!" he muttered, his thumb on the switch. The double line wheeled, headed for the dome, had almost reached it, when the whole picture shattered and broke apart. As if on some hideous cue, many-colored women broke from the work-domes, running and screaming. Staggering figures reeled from the many entrances of the main dome. And the double-line of new men broke into milling disorder. Thorpe switched on, began fanning and running. Skoda had guessed right. The metal of domes and ships had partly shielded the people inside from the radio-waves. Hit—fatally perhaps—but not dead, not yet. The men in the open had gone down instantly, but his mouth went dry at the thought of those others who might still have enough life left to bite back, those inside the ships, the work-domes, the big dome. And they all had heat-beam weapons! Switch to stage two, already planned.

He ran towards the nearest work-dome and straight into its semi-circle entrance, dodging the screaming women who ran out. He had no time for more than a snatched glance at the interior, at long rows of weirdly intricate machines and the stink of scorched flesh. He waved his weapon generously around, ducked out again and ran on to the next. He had no time to think, to observe the shape of the battle, to bother about anything or anyone else. He was counting domes. He backed out of the eighth and last, and a searing breath burned the air by his ear. He fell, rolled, rayed the area, all in one frantic movement, and saw two Vegans fall where they had been sheltered by the curve of the dome.

Up again, he ran on and in, to the inviting gangway of a

new-built ship, straight up and into the hatch, the beam-emitter whining in his hand. A writhing man screamed and fell the last ten steps of the inner ladder. Thorpe stood, gasping for breath, to count a grim five as he sprayed the interior liberally. Then it was out, down the ladder, run again for the next ship, and repeat the performance. Part of his mind was dividing by thirty into a hundred and being prepared to do his three and a third and then more. But he had underestimated the unleashed savagery of the Sisters, once they saw how effective the whining weapons were. He knew it was all over when he found himself almost having to use force to hold back one vengeful girl from going back over his tracks, just to make sure.

They were a breathless, much-scorched, yet jubilant group as they gathered by the latest-arrived ship and surveyed the fallen. Thorpe made a rapid nose-count. All present and accounted for.

"We busted them good!" Hadley growled, throwing back his cowl to show a grin made ferocious by a four-day black stubble. "But it's going to be a grim job picking up the bits and pieces."

XIV

"WE'LL HAVE TO leave that for somebody else," Thorpe declared. "We aren't out of the wood yet, by a long way. We've got to assume that some of these creatures lived long enough to scream a warning, even to shout for help. And there are four more bases like this."

"You reckon the others will come here?"

"I don't know, Nick. They don't think the way we do. But we have to assume they will, and be ready."

"With what? We're sitting ducks here. We'll never knock 'em down out of the sky with these midgets!"

"And we'd not stand a chance trying to hit them with their own stuff, even if we knew how," Hadley added. Thorpe cast a hard glance at his little band. It was a time for desperate measures, for a scheme he had been nursing and trying to firm up. A gamble to go far beyond anything they had so far endured.

"Suppose we don't wait here?" he demanded. "Suppose we take a ship, this new one—we know it's fly-ready—and go to meet them? I reckon I can learn to fly the thing without too much trouble. After all, they are built to be flown by men like us!"

Hadley sucked in a long shaking breath. "Begod, even if you could get us off the ground, what would we fight them with? We've no crew, and they will be bound to know their own weapons better than we do. There's only the three of us, Jeremy!"

"Three? I can count thirty!" He looked round at the scorched and disheveled Sisterhood. "You want to bet they're willing? As for weapons, we have workshops all around us. You said, Paddy, that the heat-beamers are electrical—long-wave and infra-red stuff. It shouldn't be too hard to convert them, Nick. You have skilled work staff here, by the hundred, once it gets across to them that they have a chance to hit back for real. What more do you want?"

Skoda scratched his jaw, eyed the ship close by, then turned a grin on Speth by his side. "Come on, green-eyes, we have more work to do."

"That's the stuff!" Thorpe snapped. "Paddy, you and Varis can get the work-detail organized. Pacify the women. Put them in the picture. Stop them from wrecking everything. And collar some of those who know how to tackle heat-beam units and how to run the machines. Shanne, you come with me. We are going to learn that ship, so far as controls go, from top to bottom—and sideways!"

It was not as difficult as he had feared. He had done this once before, in training, and although this was an alien ship, it had to fly in the same environment and by the same forces as any other ship. When you had a shrewd idea what a thing was for, you knew near enough where it had to be, what it ought to look like, and, eventually, how to work it. He ran into one grisly surprise. Sealed away in the ship's heart was a tank-room, a space filled with an ammoniacal liquid. In the thin broth floated the grossly enlarged body of a thing exactly like that pair he had seen on old Hathar's table-top—and clustered round the big body were thousands of pinpoint-sized little ones, her spawn. He radioed the gruesome brood thoroughly, just to make sure, then sealed off the tank again.

He and Shanne settled at last in the control-space. Many things were readily familiar here. He explained to her the handling and function of various levers and grips, and why it was so helpful to have all these things arranged in twin form to provide dual control. Most of the indicators and instruments were comprehensible, if different in design. But he was bothered more than anything by the total absence of anything even like a viewscreen. As she sat by him in the copilot seat and listened and nodded, he took her over everything he was sure of, but he had at last to confess that this one thing had him stopped.

"And it is vital," he muttered. "Unless I can see what goes on outside, somehow—I daren't leave the ground. There has to be some way of knowing where we are. Unless they do that by telepathy too, and if that is the case, then we're sunk!" It had not occurred to him in just that form before, but the more he thought of it, the more it appeared obvious. You couldn't have external views without something like radio, so far as he could conceive. And the Vegans were antipathetic to radio, for obvious reasons. Thus —no viewers! Then Shanne, peering about as keenly as he, happened to look straight up over her head. She said "Oh!" and reached up. Before he could do more than begin to mutter a warning about mucking about with strange gadgets, she had hauled down a hollow bowl-shaped thing and drew it completely down over her head. He held her wrist anxiously.

"It is all right!" her voice came hollowly from inside the hood. "I can see out. It is wonderful. You try!" Looking up, he saw that the twin of the thing hung over his own seat. A moment later he was pulling it down over his own head. There was ample room to turn his head and stare. And stare. Because it was almost as good as being outdoors. On the curved interior before him he saw the airfield. If he turned his head to the right he was looking at the big dome. On the left were the other ships. He could even see the near-ground below, down by his chin. He marveled, shoved the cover up and stared at it in wonder. There were wrist-thick loops of cables coming away from the outside, dozens of them. He snapped his fingers in sudden understanding.

"Optical fibres! Of course! Masses of them from all over the skin of the ship. So simple, but how effective! Shanne," he turned to her in delight, "you're a wonderful person. What would I ever have done without you?" There was fire in her green-silver eyes and an eager understanding on her lovely face as she moved towards him. His breathing was fast and unsteady by the time they sundered contact.

"Damn!" she sighed, and he chuckled.

"As you say, damn! But this won't do. We have work to get on with. I wonder how the others are doing?" He managed to raise both Skoda and Hadley on the little radio-unit.

"Nothing to it!" the radio-technician gloated. "Man, those machine-shops are really something. Fully computerized. You just specify what you want, hit the right buttons, and out she comes. Our total armament is eight heat-beams. Give us another half hour and they'll all be mega-watt micro-wave emitters. How's your end? Think you'll be able to fly?"

"No sweat. Some of the stuff is strange, but no trouble so long as we don't have to do a warp-jump. Which we won't. How's the mopping-up chore coming, Paddy?"

"Just fine. The women are keen. A bit too keen, with the beamers. Better keep your robe on."

"I'm not going anywhere. I'm sending Shanne down to check round all the Sisters and make sure all the weapons are manned, that they know what to do. I'd just as soon not have any lay-women aboard for the trip. It might be risky—know what I mean?" So Shanne went away down the ladder and left him to that tedious but essential practice—

140

practice—practice, that is so vitally necessary if a man is going to be able to grab and hit the right lever and button at the right time without having to stop and think. By stages he fed power to the various relays until he had everything alive but the main drive and jets and could go through the most complex shift with smooth familiarity. Then Skoda beeped him on radio.

"Everything converted and ready to blow, skipper. Shanne wants a word with you first." Skoda's voice sounded hag-ridden weary. So did Shanne's. As she spoke, Thorpe realized that he was ache-tired too.

"Jeremy," she said, "all is ready. Some junior sisters from Heklon Shrine have come, offering help. But our sisters are so tired!"

"Yes, I know," he sighed. "Me too. I can barely keep my eyes open."

"What do we do, sir?" That was Skoda again, and Thorpe felt a stir of irritation at the title, but recognized how inevitable it was. He saw by the view-hood that sunset was racing on them.

"We'd be crazy to take off half-doped with fatigue. It's nearly dark. Look, have the weapon-crews camp right there by their posts, as best they can, and bed down. Post the Heklon juniors to keep a watch, a vigil. They are to scream a warning if anything shows during the night, and roust us out about half an hour before dawn. Right? And I want Shanne up here with me, as copilot."

The control seat was very comfortable. He was practically asleep in it before she arrived to settle down by his side.

Hadley's voice and none-too-gentle shake roused him. "Sunup in half an hour, sir," he growled. "The rest are stirring. Ready to lift as soon as you like." Thorpe knuckled the grit from his eyes, stretched, and took hold of the controls, tugging the view-hood down over his head. The ship went up as effortlessly as a dream. He had painstakingly traced out the pseudo-grav leads and controls, and he had known it was alive by the shiver of a red column in a sealed transparent tube, yet for all that he was astonished by the utter absence of any sensation of lift. It was as if the external scene just fell away below.

"Ready to lift any time you like, sir!" Skoda's voice came edgily.

"Take it easy, Nick. We've been airborne for five minutes, must be close on a mile up by now."

"Begod!" Hadley growled, "It's just struck me. We can't see what we're doing, and all these gadgets are just Chinese to me!"

"Look for an inverted goldfish bowl kind of thing, probably up over your head somewhere. Put it over your head. Right? Pass it on to the rest—" The ship fell upwards swiftly. Heklon was now no more than a smudge of grey with a hundred-point star in its center. He reached to put his hand on Shanne's wrist. "Up to you now, girl. You point me the way to the next city." With a little trail juggling and a few errors he was able to level off and set course by her directions. Below them the continent unreeled steadily. He jockeyed their speed until they were skimming just ahead of the first flush of dawn.

"Arreck soon," she warned, and then, suddenly, "There, ahead!"

He caught up the suit-unit to his mouth. "Nick, Paddy, pass it on to the rest. I'm going to try a fast low-level pass, then turn and come back for another. All weapons fire at will, at anything, and full-bore!"

He was getting the different, gossamer "feel" of this ship now, the barely audible whisper-sound of power, the superbly effortless response to his controls. And now he could see the dark cluster of buildings that was Arreck—and the plain target of the space-field with its ring of ships and center dome. He put his own ship into a steeply dipping approach, leaned on the power, and heard the shrill screech of tortured air whipping past the hull. The space-field sprang up at him, swelling into hugeness, slipping past below and behind in a flash. Cringing instinctively for the drag that did not come, he spun into a tight bank and aimed back and down, over the target again. There was a sense of anti-climax. Nothing. Not a sign that anything had been achieved.

One sure way to find out, he thought, and jockeying the ship round he brought it to hover-halt about a thousand feet directly above that central dome. And waited for a grim count of thirty. Still no sign. Arreck space-port was dead.

"All right," he growled to Shanne, "let's try the next one."

Again she pointed the way and he set the ship skimming, racing on the verge of dawn's grey light, slanting southward now to Panator. And in due course the pattern was silently and efficiently repeated. It gave him no satisfaction.

This is more like butchering cattle, he thought, too easy by far. But then he thought of seventy years of ruthlessly inhuman exploitation, degradation and killing, and the distaste seemed less important. Now, for long steady hours, they sped over the rolling ocean, the sunlight at their heels and lagging behind. Then they raised land and Shanne gave her words of guidance. Once more he passed the word to "Stand by to hit 'em!" and they stormed in over the sea to Rotalan, to crisscross the now familiar geometric target. But this time his hard eye noticed something different about that pattern on the first pass, and confirmed it on the second. The hundred in a ring were there, and the big dome, but there was no sign of the new arrival, the odd one.

"Either it didn't arrive yet, or it's spaceborne already," he reported, "and waiting for us somewhere. Maintain a-lert!"

The thirty-second count dragged to its sterile end and they sped away again for their last target. Shanne briefed him on it.

"Merdan is a large island. The city of Merdan is on the far shore. Very soon now, but we have time to eat and drink something. I will see to it." She came back very quickly with curiously shaped jars, one each, brimming with wine, and an armful of orange-like fruit.

"Have yours," he suggested. "And then you can watch out while I take five." It was one of those moments to treasure, sitting there by her side, surrounded by the quiet hum of unfamiliar power, the surge and dance of outlandish instruments, yet nothing more outlandish than she herself, in that setting. The view-cowl covered her down to her chin. She had her slim hands on the steering levers between her knees and was utterly engrossed in what she was doing.

She snatched a sudden breath, in quick apprehension. "We approach Merdan," she cried, "but the Shining Ones come to meet us!" He had his viewer down in a flash, crackling the warning to the others by radio. And Shanne had spoken no more than the cold facts. There ahead was the dark smudge of an island just cresting the far edge of the sea, but between that and him came a ring of gleaming ships, a formation showing instantly that they meant business. He hit his retard-jets hard and fast and then went down, in his mind a picture of his own armament, that ring of eight beamers around the belly of the ship. Strategy, now, was to somehow jockey the enemy into such an approach that he could use his weapons to best advantage, while minimizing theirs.

It boiled through his mind ten times faster than he could have spoken it, a hundred times faster than he could have begun to explain. He snatched a glance down, to see the waves virtually lapping his bottom, slammed the up-drive on, snatched a second glance up and saw the ring-formation turn over and drop on him. There were fast and deadly, their intention obvious. They had him boxed.

"That's what you think!" he grunted, and bore down on the lift-throttles hard, sending the ship arrowing straight up through that ring of death. He caught a blurred glimpse of open weapon-ports spitting their venom, and then the outside scene went crazy, jerking, looping, tumbling in a mad whirl. He knew why, instantly, a hit. A frag-bomb hit. Because the ship was inertialess, there could be no sensation of impact, but the shock had sent them bouncing and spinning like a soap-bubble. The drill to stabilize was automatic and unthinking, and then he could look down. It was a sight to gloat on. The ships in a ring plunged straight down, smacked into the sea and disappeared for a moment in a circle of spray. Then they surfaced, to lie there and roll. *Dead hands at the controls,* he thought. Then, *God, if their weapon-ports are still open—!* He stared, and winced as one leaped into a searing fireball of destruction. Then two more.

And he missed the rest as his own ship reared and plunged in the shock wave from the explosions. His shiver gave way to renewed caution.

"That was only ten," he muttered to Shanne. "They might have a lot more yet. Keep your eyes peeled!" He picked up Merdan again and headed for it, swooping down low and close to the sea. He watched the coastline leap close. He wondered how badly his ship was hit, but he did not dare take his hands off the controls. He hoped they would try that ring-formation again. Not their usual form. In the past he had seen them pop out of Pauli-drive in a tight cluster, and spit their death outwards on a large and dispersed force around them. This was different, and if it had been devised on the spur of the moment, then he was up against brains, and in for trouble. They would try something new next time. If there was to be a next time.

Mountains loomed and he lifted the ship up to skim over them. A red blossom on his control-panel went purple and then blue. Altitude? Couldn't be. Air-pressure, then. The ship was holed somewhere. He went down the far side of the mountain ridge and he didn't need to be told he had found Merdan. There ahead were shining ships lifting off in all directions. *Here we go!* he thought, and put into effect the craziest strategy anyone could imagine, just as it seethed into his mind. Devoting a grudged second or two to getting aimed straight for that last base, he threw the attitude-drive hard over and then caressed the tangential correctors just enough to set the ship spinning on its axis like a lazy top. Then he snatched for his radio.

"All weapons full-bore and hold them down. Never mind whether you can see anything or not." The scene in his viewer was enough to bring nausea as they howled and spun simultaneously straight for the air space above the space-port. So far as his bemused senses could tell, they got through and out the other side without damage. He checked the spin, braked the drive and swept the ship round and up, squeezing his eyes tight before trying to see what the results were. It was a sight that was to stay in his memory a long time. One ship went screaming up in a crazy broken-winged spiral, spitting ion-fire, and then to vanish in a coruscating flare of destruction. Another shot after it, faltered in mid-flight, and fell like a stone square on the roof of the great dome, smashing a mighty dent in the many-eyed surface. Two more spun in blind flight and ran headlong into each other, to perish in a flare that blinded him for several seconds. One squatted where it was and melted itself into a puddle of fused earth with its spouting jets. Two more had just begun to lift and were now scuttling crabwise over the field, wreaking havoc and destruction before they shuddered into stillness. High above he saw a familiar sight, and hit the throttles again.

He slid the ship steadily along, close to the ground. The vengeful ring stormed down on him. He waited, feeling cold, judged the moment, then bore down on the lift-drive. Again they dived straight up through that ring of death. Again they leaped and spun in a crazy pattern from impact. And again, stabilized, he looked down to see the circle of ships scream down and plunge straight into the ground.

And it was all over. He felt drained, weary, an old man, as he touched Shanne and said, "Better go and see what the damage is, honey. We're on our way home now. I can manage this on my own."

Her report was nothing as serious as he had dreaded. The first hit had been somewhere in what was the crew's living space, the second had come close to Hadley's weapon-blister, and there was a hole through which the air whistled. The Irishman was down, a blow on the head, but Varis was caring for him. Edda and the two others with her had been scorched, but not seriously. And that was all.

"We're very lucky," he sighed. "Very lucky." There didn't seem to be anything else to say, certainly no feeling of triumph. It was a sadly silent and chastened party that climbed down from the ship as soon as he had grounded it again in Heklon. Varis lent her shoulder to Hadley to lean on. Edda's weapon-crew were a sight, their faces and hair singed and their garments in tatters. But they were whole, and uncomplaining.

Shalla boats took them back to the island, and the Shalla

women seemed to have caught the gloom too. As Shanne said, "Truly, all the Shining Ones are destroyed. The hathari has reported it. We should be glad. But what is to become of us, now that there are no men left at all?"

Thorpe had no answer. Yet another sadness awaited them as they reached the shrine. Hathar was stricken, had taken to her bed, and had not long to live. The three men were shocked to see the plain truth of it as they stood by her bedside.

"My time is come." she whispered. "I am not sorry to go, not now. I have lived to see the end of the Shining Ones, destroyed by Earthmen, those people we have long admired and reverenced. And I am proud to know that the hathari had a great hand in it. All this is more than I had a right to hope for."

"You have a good life to look back on, Mother Hathar."

"We all make errors. I have made my share. You will make yours, Jeremy Thorpe. But I ask you to take my place."

"Me? How can I?"

"You can. The women of Hathar need men. All Lodor needs men." Those were the last words they heard. They left her to the Sisters. In the hathari-room again, Thorpe sighed his regret. "It's up to me. I wish it wasn't, but I've stuck my neck out, and I've got it." He gathered his wits, forced himself to be practical.

"First thing," he decided, "is to get the word out to all shrines and then to all Lodor. The shining ships are to be preserved, repaired where it is possible, made ready to fly and fight!" The junior sister on duty stared her incomprehension and he realized he had to explain, for her and all those who would be listening. "The ships are valuable. They can be used to strike back at the Shining Ones on other worlds. You will also ask, by hathari, for any and all women who want to avenge themselves, who want to save another world from the evil they have suffered here, to make it known that they will serve. That they will be ready to fly in those ships."

"Women in fighting ships?" Hadley growled, and then blinked as Varis gripped his arm, her eyes flashing.

"We can fight, as you have seen!"

"There you are!" Thorpe nodded. "We can use them, all of them. Except those who are with child. They must be cared for." He speared the junior with a stern eye. "You will also broadcast that. Tell them that all women who are with child are to take care. They are to know—for it is true —that their children will be normal and human, even the male children. Particularly the male children. There will be real men on Lodor again, soon. Tell them that!"

"It sounds fine," Skoda came close to confide, "but who's going to skipper those ships? The women can build them, know how they work, but flying them is something else again."

"Nothing to it, Nick. I learned, didn't I?"

"But you're a trained pilot. I couldn't have done it, nor Paddy, so how can you expect a bunch of women to learn?"

"We'll set up a school. Better still, we'll ask for some! You have the Dirac going?"

"So far as I can tell, sure. Three girls in rotation sending data as hard as they can." They stepped across to where one girl was reciting from a screen while another scribbled hastily and a third monitored the instrument.

"All right." Thorpe put up a finger to halt the operation. "Send this: 'For attention Vice-Admiral Corde personal. Lieutenant Jeremy Thorpe reporting. Lodor origin. We have four hundred Vegan ships fully operational, also many thousands capable maintainance and operational personnel. Need competent executives. Personnel here all female, repeat female. Executives will be welcome only if bearded, repeat bearded.' Send that, then carry on with the data for today. Repeat it again tomorrow, and daily for a while."

He had guessed accurately. The unusual nature of the signal was enough to bring investigations from Earth as fast as they could jump the distance. Five weeks only from the time the signal went out, Skoda's jury-rigged alarms rang and buzzed, bringing him speedily to slide into place before the panel he had built up from salvaged parts. He rattled a key.

"This is Lodor," he said. "Identify!" and he switched on a spotlight.

"Hermes, flagship 15th Battle Squadron, Solarian Fleet, Vice-Admiral Corde in command and speaking. Are you reading me, Lodor?"

"I see you, sir. This is radio-technician Skoda, ex S.S. *Quest.*"

"Let me talk to this Lieutenant Thorpe, would you?" Skoda opened his eyes wide, slid aside to let Thorpe get in view and face the screen. "You young rip, Gerald! By God, those whiskers don't fool me one bit. I ought to have you court-martialed for this. All this time I've believed you safely tucked away on Venus!"

"Just as well I wasn't, isn't it?" Thorpe said boldly, and the old face in the visor went red under its straggle of white whiskers.

"What's all this nonsense about ships, Vegan ships?"

"Why don't you come down and see, Dad? You'll be very welcome, you and your crew. Four hundred ships, and all the personnel you'll ever want."

When the invitation was grumpily accepted and the communication link closed, he turned to smile at Shanne by his side.

"You'll like him. That bark is only on the surface. Along with him will come many men. In a way, this is very like the Shining Ones. They came with men from many other planets. The women of Lodor worked for them, built ships for them, produced children by them. This could be very much the same. Can you believe me when I say that it will really be very different?"

"I believe you, Jeremy. If these men from the stars are all like you, it will be very different. There will be joy on Lodor again when all women can be as happy as you have made me."

Here's a quick checklist of recent releases of

ACE SCIENCE-FICTION BOOKS

F-titles 40¢   M-titles 45¢

F-350 **STAR OF DANGER** by Marion Zimmer Bradley
F-353 **ROGUE DRAGON** by Avram Davidson
F-354 **THE HUNTER OUT OF TIME** by Gardner Fox
M-127 **WE, THE VENUSIANS** by John Rackham
       and **THE WATER OF THOUGHT** by Fred Saberhager.
M-129 **EMPRESS OF OUTER SPACE**
       by A. Bertram Chandler
       and **THE ALTERNATE MARTIANS**
       by A. Bertram Chandler
F-355 **THE DEVOLUTIONIST** by Homer Eon Flint
F-356 **THE TIME AXIS** by Henry Kuttner
F-357 **YEAR OF THE UNICORN** by Andre Norton
F-361 **THE DAY OF THE STAR CITIES** by John Brunner
F-364 **THE MIGHTIEST MACHINE** by John W. Campbell
M-131 **BEHOLD THE STARS** by Kenneth Bulmer
       and **PLANETARY AGENT X** by Mack Reynolds
F-365 **NIGHT OF MASKS** by Andre Norton
F-367 **THE MAKER OF UNIVERSES** by Philip Jose Farmer
M-133 **THE CAVES OF MARS** by Emil Petaja
       and **SPACE MERCENARIES** by A. Bertram Chandler
M-135 **SPACE CAPTAIN** by Murray Leinster
       and **THE MAD METROPOLIS** by Philip E. High
M-137 **BEST FROM FANTASY & SCIENCE FICTION:**
       11th Series
F-372 **SPACEHOUNDS OF IPC** by Edward E. Smith
F-373 **THE SWORD OF LANKOR** by Howard L. Cory
F-375 **THE WORLDS OF ROBERT A. HEINLEIN**

If you are missing any of these, they can be obtained directly from the publisher by sending the indicated sum, plus 5¢ handling fee, to Ace Books, Inc. (Dept. MM), 1120 Avenue of the Americas, New York, N.Y. 10036

ARMAGEDDON IS TONIGHT AT TWELVE!

You might have thought that the Fiesta of the Holy Hermit in the Mexican town of Los Remedios was just another of those quaint colorful ceremonies that the Indian natives put on each year for the mystification of tourists. And perhaps for the past few hundred years it had been nothing more than that—but this year was to be different.

For Jacob Clay, the American expatriate, had been poking into the buried secrets of that mountain community which dated back before the Aztec Empire, and he had begun to entertain a shocking suspicion. Before that fiesta was over he was due to learn the volcanic reality behind:

The Holy Hermit—a mummy that was not a mummy...

Tlaloc—a statue that was not just a thing of stone ...

Huitzilopochtli—a legend that was stark realism ...

And what started as a holiday turned into a nightmare on which pivoted the fates of the very stars themselves!

Turn this book over for
second complete novel

AVRAM DAVIDSON has been a respected figure in both science-fiction and mystery circles for a decade or more. He has won both the Hugo award for the best science-fiction short story of the year, and the Edgar award for the best mystery story, and was editor of *The Magazine of Fantasy and Science Fiction* until turning to full-time writing.

Ace Books has previously published a collection of his best short stories under the title of *What Strange Stars and Skies* (F-330), and two novels:

ROGUE DRAGON (F-353)

THE KAR-CHEE REIGN (G-574)

CLASH OF
STAR-KINGS

by

AVRAM DAVIDSON

ACE BOOKS, INC.
1120 Avenue of the Americas
New York, N.Y. 10036

I

THE INCREASE of population and prosperity in and around that great and ancient habitation, the City of Mexico, has brought with it a great many innovations, ranging from the brilliant new Museum of National Antiquities and Patrimonial Treasures to very unbrilliant smog. The visitor who has enjoyed the riches of the former and finds, if he is fortunate, his view of the outside world unimpeded by the latter, can look up and away—very far, indeed, away—and observe the snowcapped outlines of two great and sacred mountains: the splendid shining cone of Popocatapetl and the magnificent snowy sierra of Ixtaccihuatl. The latter, the "white woman" (thus, the meaning in the Nahua language of these syllables, so all but insurmountable to the Anglo-Saxon tongue), was believed by the Aztecs to be the bride of the sun; and, indeed, bears an uncanny resemblance to the figure of a reclining woman: head, bosom, body, hands and feet, all covered in white. Her companion, "smoking mountain," was set there to guard her.

5

Little guard was needed to keep away the Indians, whose religious awe alone restrained them—as it did, until too late, from resisting the Spaniards. Cortez, thinking in terms of a different universe, knew a volcano when and where he saw one, sent his lieutenant, Diego de Ordaz, with nine men, to make the ascent. They ravaged the sacred and burning mountain and descended with enough sulfur to make gunpowder. The snows of Ixtaccihuatl remained unsullied. The record does not say if the sulfur was wrapped in fennel stalks like the stolen fire of Prometheus, or if eagles tore at the liver of the audacious Iberian. Probably not.

In the confrontation of the conquistadores with the civilizations of Mexico and Peru we have a situation almost Science Fictional: the potent monarchs submitting in scarcely comprehending resignation, and all their millions of subjects, to the handfuls of men who might well have come from another planet—so alien were their weapons, their manners, and their minds. It is ironical that the Dukes of Montezuma, descendants of the Aztec Blood Royal, became and are, still, grandees of Spain. There are moments, and not a few of them, when the Conquest seems never to have taken place; when one sees the Indians emerging from their brushwood huts, huaraches on their feet, sarapes of ancient pattern wrapped about their bodies, drinking the immemorial *chocolatl* from tiny earthern pots. . . .

But then the antique and pre-Columbian silence is broken by the roar of the jet plane, and the elder design reveals, once again, that it has cracked into fragments of an almost infinite number. Standing on the threshold of space and all which that implies, it is well to be reflective.

The town of Los Remedios does not attract tourists in any great numbers; indeed, it has few amenities to tempt them. Sitting as it does so high up on the slopes of *los volcanes* and surrounded by forests, it has very pure air—and very thin, too, a heart unaccustomed to altitude tends to pump hard and tire easily. There are few famous antiquities, no night clubs, no swimming pools, and its tiny hotel, though clean, has not even running water.

6

A second-class bus service runs several times a day, requiring several transfers between the town and "Mexico" ("City" being understood), and a cheerful Toonerville trolley of a narrow-gage railroad known as the *mas o menos* because it comes chugging and smoking and whistling to and from the junction at Amecameca twice a day—*"more or less,"* The roads are never in good shape and the weather is usually cold, with frequent rain and often mist.

Now and then a party of alpinists comes through en route to assay the heights of Popo and Ixta, as the mountains are familiarly known locally; or an archaelogist appears to examine the mysterious Tlaloc in the cave; and of course a considerable number of outsiders appear for the fiera of El Heremito del Monte Sagrado. There is one Lebanese merchant, called *el Turco*, one Syrian corn-buyer, called *el Arabe*, a refugee Austrian misanthrope, *el Alemán*, and three citizens of the U.S.A., called—with a shade more geographical accuracy than the inhabitants are accustomed to—*los norteamericanos*. These constitute the only inhabitants of the district who are not in whole or in part of Indian blood.

They also constituted the only inhabitants of the district not, at the moment, seemingly totally preoccupied with the approaching fiesta. Not only had extra and ramshackle buses been laid on to transport the visiting pilgrims, but retired engineer Juanantonio Calderon Cruz—whose boast was that he had once transported Zapata—had come out of retirement to navigate a special train—by the appearance of locomotive and rolling-stock, the same one. There were a great many cars and trucks (though few new ones), a great many horses and mules and burros and crude wagons—and a great many dusty feet. There was even a platoon of cavalry from the Federal District. The marketplace was like an anthill and the top of Monte Sagrado (where now stood the 17th century stone church which replaced the 16th century adobe one, which had replaced the original Aztec pyramid) was like another, with the roads and paths in between like ant-trails.

Every hour or so another procession started up the winding trail with its banner, usually of either the Virgin of Guad-

alupe or the Virgin of Los Remedios (slightly less popular, she was suspected of anti-Republic sentiments), pausing meticulously to make pagan offerings to the sacred *ahuehuete* trees which lined the way. But all these were but opening acts before the day's main event: the procession down from Monte Sagrado and all through the town and then back of the figure of the sainted Heremito. Everyone was anticipating this with great pleasure—with the probable exception of Sarah Clay, the pleasantly plump and sometimes charming wife of Jacob Clay, one of the two male Northamericans of the town.

Sarah, at the moment, had fixed her soft pink mouth into a discontented line and was breathing noisily through her small and freckled nose. The source of her annoyance, Lupita, the Clay's maid, stood before her in the patio making dramatic faces and gestures. She was small and scrawny and squinting and walked with a curious shuffle and was not a very efficient maid, but maids in Los Remedios—good or bad—were hard to get. "Infirm," she was repeating now for the twentieth time, speaking rapidly and mixing in many words of Nahuatl. "Infirm—in bed—mother—alone—mañana—infirm—"

The mere sight of the beautiful Douanier Rosseau patio denuded of almost all its flowers and branches by the landlady, Señora Mariana, to make decorations for the fiesta, had put Sarah in a bad mood. Plus the fact that Evans, the tootsie cat, for whom Sarah had saved a dinner tidbit, was nowhere to be seen. And now this. *This*, being Lupita's intention of absquatulating and the need for Sarah to speak Spanish. "He did not will know why your (plural) mother so often was also infirm," Sarah said. "Why not used to could procure a doctor to was meeting her, and return?"

"Infirm!" cried Lupita, seizing the word, triumphantly. "Malady very malign! Immediate attendance!" She rolled her eyes up, hideously, arched her back, and twitched vigorously to indicate the malignant nature of her mother's malady—adding, encouragingly, "But mañana will be better!"

"Oh, all *right!*" cried Sarah, who didn't believe a word of

it, Lupita bugging out so often on account of maladies unknown to science and holy days of obligation unknown to the church. Adding, too late, "But by favor to wash the utensils since?"

Lupita, already halfway to the gate, half-turned her head. "Mañana, Señora! Mañana!"

Sarah thrust out her lower lip. Unless the dishes were washed for supper the Clays would have to sup off market-boughten prepared foods, and their budget showed a cash-on-hand status of only five pesos. She recollected the tidbit in her hand for the tootsie cat, so cunning with his markings like a black and white bunny. "Evans!" she called. "Evans. . . ." Her voice became disconsolate, her lips more prominent. "Oh, well," she said, after a moment, "maybe he's only gone off to shack up with the convent cat." She smiled a trifle. Then she saw the pile of dirty dishes, the scuttle-butt of icy cold water, and the fibre scouring-pad; and her lip went all the way out and she began to snuffle.

Lupita went shuffling along at a rapid pace down the rain-rutted street. The plaza of Los Remedios had once been paved in preparation for the expected visit of Maximilian, but nothing else had ever been paved before or since. Avoiding the principal avenues and streets, aflutter with women and children and even a number of men preparing the decorations and altars for the forthcoming procession, she made her way by a series of knight's moves to the outskirts of town —very abruptly demarcated here on this side by a deep arroyo. Into this she slid rather than climbed, and passed beneath the shadow of her own house, from which the sounds of groaning and grinding indicated that her mother —an aged blind crone—was preparing tortillas. Lupita did not look up, but she did look back. So. Bautist was there coming along behind. Good. And there, up ahead—Solita. The others were probably already there.

And there, after a long uphill trudge which took her and her two companions alongside ruined walls and across little rivers and through groves of trees and around cornfields— but always away from houses and always uphill—there at

9

last she found them: Ruiz and Dolores and Gustavo. Gustavo had hold of a rope on the other end of which frisked a very young black goat-kid. Lupita broke off a pine branch and swept the ground, Dolores sprinkled it with water from a gourd, Gustavo and Ruiz began the saying of that which needed to be said. Solita built a tiny fire on which they all sprinkled copal-gum and, while one of them waved a turkey wing to spread the fragrant smoke, the others thrust scraps of cloth and hair-combings and bits of colored corn-dough into the crevices of the ancient tree. Then Ruiz took a sharp pair of scissors and cut the kid's throat and, while the others sipped the blood collected in the calabash and sprinkled it around and on each other, Ruiz took up the razor-sharp piece of black volcano-glass and cut out the animal's heart and they offered this at the base of the tree and they all bowed down.

Then Gustavo hid the carcass where it would be safe and on top of it they hid their clothes and they dressed in the coyote-skins which had been there and they smoked themselves in the odorous embers of the fire and then urinated on it and painted designs on each others' faces with the paste of ashes. Then they started off—up, up, always up—twitching their rumps from time to time so that their tails wagged and now and then they went a short way on all fours and now and then they chanted and now and then they howled.

"Josefa, the Widow of Gomez," as she signed her name on the very few occasions which ever arose for signing it, had gone out to gather herbs in the woods and uplands which stretched away so endlessly and sloping until they came to the dead region of black volcanic sand which surrounded Popo or the gaunt escarpments of the base of Ixta. Señora Josefa had a great devotion to the Blessed Crown, to which she had commended herself before starting out on her little expedition, and it was beyond doubt this which had preserved her from death or even worse. The late Señor Gomez had been of a mature age at the time of his marriage, and his death had left the widow with no more than a good name, a small *granja* in the country and a small *quinta* in the

town: plus two children. So Señora Josefa had gotten out the black garments which she had worn after the death of her first husband, rented both properties as best she might, reserving the greater part of the income for the education of her son in "Mexico," and moved with her daughter into the house of her sister, Mariana, the Widow of Matteos. The possibility that she might offer, or her sister accept, money for room or board had never occurred to either of them. By her needle, which was skilled, she was able to supply young Marinita with clothes; and as for other expenses—gifts, for example, or masses—these she supplied by gathering and preparing and selling herbs.

On this occasion she had in mind particularly to gather a great basketful of the tender leaves of the *cedron* tree, which, decocted into a tea, are excellent not only for the kidneys of older men but also for various feminine periodic infirmities which are not the affair of men of any age. She also wanted to find, if possible, some poppies and yellow daisies and violets, all of which make good preparations to wash the bodies of those afflicted with weaknesses and fears. These were her specific needs for the moment. Naturally she kept her keen eyes open for anything else which Providence might place in her path, such as roots and buds and barks useful in cases of irritations of the body, or mushrooms . . . half of which might be exchanged for butter enough to fry the other half.

Although she felt the trip to be necessary—otherwise she would not now be engaged upon it when she had much rather be back preparing decorations for the procession—and although she had made it hundreds of times before, Señora Josefa felt a measure of nonspecific uneasiness. For one thing, there were soldiers in town, and although the manners of soldiery had improved since the troubled days of the Revolution, still, well, soldiers . . . Then there was talk about the Tlaloc; Señora Josefa was not worried about the Tlaloc, not in the least, she was a good Christian and her opinion about the Tlaloc was that he should be left totally undisturbed where and as he was. As for the mysterious lights said to have been seen on and around Popo,

11

she did not doubt but that they were made by sulfur poachers, that was all, there was nothing more to it, and she wished they would go away. As for other things, there were no other things which could justify her feelings. Nothing major. But many things minor. And yet—

What difference did it make if some woman whose figure she had seen for years without noticing, or noticed for years without seeing, should suddenly lift her head and look Señora Josefa in the face boldly and almost threateningly?—she realizing, with a sort of shock, that she had never seen the woman's face even once turned to her before. It meant nothing. Still . . . still, there was a certain change of atmosphere, subtle and intermittent, and it had bothered her. Well. Of nothing. To the work, without dawdling or dallying, then back in time to make the Stations of the Cross on Monte Sagrado and visit the Holy Hermit before he was carried through the town on his annual peregrination. She fell to, her strong fingers nimbly stripping the twigs of the desired leaves.

If one had asked her the meaning of the offerings hung upon the *ahuehuete* trees between the Stations, she would have answered, mildly and gravely amused: "Things of the Indians, Señor—of nothing." And if one had asked her what or whom she meant by Indians, her answer would have been, "Poor people, Señor, who cannot afford proper clothing." And, consequently, when she saw what she saw, and her fingers grew frozen and still, she was neither perplexed nor confused: merely horrified.

Señora Mariana de Matteos was as short and round as her sister Josefa was tall and slender, but her thicker fingers moved, nonetheless, deftly now as they had been moving all day long . . . not alone in the usual tasks of the house, but in preparing for the fiera or fiesta. Let no one be able to say that the Quinta de Matteos did not prepare itself properly for the passage of the procession of the Holy Hermit! Nimbly and skillfully those fingers had prepared chains and garlands of cunningly twisted colored "china" paper, had prepared and set up archways and banners and legends,

12

had stripped the garden of both the front patio where she and her sister lived and the back patio where the Señores Clay lived, of almost all flowers and greenery. The petals had been plucked and dropped into baskets according to color and Señora Josefa had just finished sifting the last of them into a series of flower-petal-pictures and patterns in the road in front of her house. She always did so. But none of them, she considered, as she regretfully turned her eyes away—equally ready to scowl if any passerby showed signs of walking in the road or to beam at any praise—none of them had ever done better than this. It was when she saw that the feet heedlessly trampling the floral designs belonged to her sister Josefa, that she realized something must be dreadfully wrong. She seized her arm and hurried her into the patio.

"Sister, what passes?"

"Oh, woe of me! Sister, what have I seen!"

"My God, Sister, what *passes?* What *have* you seen?"

Josefa dropped her basket, and fled into the tiny room which housed the family altar, pausing only to utter the single and scarifying word, *"Naguales!"* before falling on her knees before the huge framed picture of the two Virgins and the flickering votive lamps, and, crossing herself with her beads, began to pray aloud with sobs and tears and shuddering breaths. Mariana lifted her trembling hand to her gaping mouth, swayed, then, with heavy steps, followed her sister and knelt beside her. It was a while before she had recovered enough to think of anything beside prayers.

Finally the two of them went in the kitchen and, at the table, Josefa sipped a drop of ancient Spanish brandy bought during Señor Gomez's last illness, and then sipped a cup of very potent black coffee. Mariana asked the inevitable question: "How do you know that they were Naguales?" Josefa threw up her hands and rolled her eyes. "How do I know? First, I heard them. I said, "Coyotes here and in the daytime?" Then I saw them, loping along, and I felt my heart grow weak, for whoever saw six coyotes one behind the other in a straight line? And then,—*Cristo Milagroso!*—they

13

rose to their feet and went upright and beneath the skins of the coyotes they had the arms and legs of men!"

Mariana crossed herself. *"Jesus-Maria! Jesus-Maria!"*

"So I knew that they were neither coyotes nor men, but Naguales. Sister—woe of me! Sorcerers and were-coyotes! *Brujos* and *brujas,* witches and warlocks! God alone knows what troubles and evils will come upon us now that they dare to show themselves again in the open!"

The sisters each took hold of one of the other's hands and, as with their free hands they crossed themselves repeatedly, they chanted:

"May we not die of fright,
"May we not die without confession,
"May that fright fall into the ocean,
"May those that cause that fright fall into the mountains,
"May it seize only the wicked and the infidel and the malevolent!"

They gazed at one another in silence a moment. Already they were beginning to feel somewhat better, and a righteous and determined anger was beginning to replace the fear in their faces. "So," said Señora Mariana, grimly, "they are up to their old tricks once more, are they? Worshippers of evil demons! And to pick this day! Oh, the malevolent ones! Oh, how the Naguales hate the Holy Hermit and his blessed catafalque! Oh, how they hate the priests! Aren't the witches always trying to destroy the good Hermit?—and who knows that they might not have harmed him more than once if he did not trick them by slipping away in the night and vanish off to Rome to serve mass there before daybreak! Well!" She rose to her feet and seized her scissors. "I'm not going to rest a minute, I'm cutting rue and rosemary, both so good against witches—and *cordones de San Francisco*: may it bind them hand and foot! And even the little rosebuds, like drops of blood from the Sacred Heart— we will dip them all in holy water and place them all around. . . ." She paused a second at the doorway and looked back at her sister. "For Heaven's sake, Josefa," she cried, "don't just sit there doing nothing: *Pray!*"

14

It was quite different keeping house in the United States, Sarah thought, for the manyeth time. There it was all so simple. There was hot and cold running water, O-cella sponge mops, detergents, Comet Cleanser, Campbell Soup . . . all the conveniences of modern science. *Here* there was nothing but a barrel of water so cold that it burned like fire and a sort of concrete sink without a pipe (there *was* a pipe, elsewhere in the patio, but it lacked a sink) and a fibre pad. You had to dip the dirty dish all cold-greasy into the ice-cold water and scrub it with the pad and your fingers froze and then you put the dish, which looked no cleaner at all, in the sink and dipped some more melted snow out of the barrel and poured it out and it ran and splashed all over your legs—"*Ow!*" screamed Sarah. "OW—OW!" The dish slipped and shattered.

Sarah swore. If it weren't for the few bits of flowers and herbiage still left in the patio she would have wept. . . .

No use telling Jacob. Not him. That stinker. That bastard. Would he offer to light a fire and try to make hot water, let alone for once *help* her? No. He wouldn't. Not him. She knew his rotten, selfish moods . . . just let her put her head in the door of his workroom and *tell* him about mean, selfish, ungrateful Lupita and he would, without doubt, *yell* at her! As though it were *her* fault they had only five pesos left and he had to meet a deadline with the damned story he was working on. *He* wouldn't care that tootsie little Evans had run away or been catnapped or something! And here she had thought Mexico was going to be such a *fun* thing, all loyal smiling hardworking native servant-girls and lovely tropical beaches like Puerto Vallarte in that picture with Liz Taylor. Tropical! Here she stood, risking frostbite and only a few sprigs of herbs and a few stalks of little purple flowers and one bush with tiny-tiny rosebuds on it—

At which, in stomped Señora Mariana and, without so much as *looking* at Sarah, began to cut all the rest of the green stuff and the flowers! The grease congealed, Sarah's fingers got stiffer and redder and colder. "All right for *you*, Richard Burton!" she wept. . . .

II

Luis Lorenzo Santangel knew well the networks of little paths which led through the woods and rocks above even the highest pastures, led eventually to the small *milpas* where grew the life-sustaining corn of the Moxtomí Indians, who raised no cattle, not even so much as a goat. Milk, they held—and it seemed logical—was for infants; and if it came ever to pass that the small brown *tetas* of a Moxtomí mother had no milk for her infant, why, there was always the milky pulque, good for young and old alike. And, if despite this benevolent liquor made from the fermented nectar of the manguey cactus the infant died, why, how sad—only not very sad—it was *destinado* that the tiny soul become a tiny angel in Heaven.

The townspeople were, as a matter of course, scornful towards the Moxtomí, calling them *cerrados*—closed ones— because their minds were closed to all things modern and innovating. They laughed at the Moxtomí, so meek and so mild, at their bare feet and naked legs and blue-black serapes, their ignorance of proper Castillian speech and at their poverty and pagan ways. Townspeople had, over the course of centuries, alienated the greater part of the Moxtomí *ejido*, the communal-tribal lands: no wonder the Moxtomí were so poor! Had the church done anything to prevent this? No. Small wonder, then, that these poor, good Indios were more than half pagan.

Most of all, perhaps, the townspeople scorned the Moxtomí because of their dark Indian skins, unlightened by a single drop of Spanish blood.

This was not the least of the reasons why Luis felt himself to be so close to these Indians and considered them his

16

friends. Why—it was not a week ago that Don Eliseo, the unlicensed veterinarian, come to inject the cows of Luis's father, had asked, "Is this your oldest son?" And Francisco Santangel had answered, grudgingly, hastily, "Yes . . . But you can tell that he doesn't take after *my* side of the family because he is so dark." He always spoke like that of his son . . . his own son. And it was true that Luis was the darkest child of the family. He was the best behaved child at home, and the least favored. He was the brightest student at school, and the most neglected. Fathers and mothers did not favor him as a suitor for their daughters unless the daughters in question were themselves too dark or too poor or too old or ugly or of too ruinous a reputation to hope for a suitor of lighter complexion. Luis, nevertheless, had finished school and, moreover, had even taught himself English—and what might he hope for in the way of a career?

He might hope for the crumbs of the table, the jobs left over after the fairer applicants had been placed—regardless of their other qualifications in comparison to Luis. This was the ineradicable stain in the Mexican garment, the fatal inheritance of the Conquistadores and their Conquest, and he hated it. He even hated "La Conquistadora", the Virgin de los Remedios, because she had come over with Cortez's men and remained the patroness of the Spaniards. Other "true" Mexicans, dark as or darker than Luis, even though they might be less acutely sensitive, would tend to favor the Virgin of Guadalupe, who had no European origins, who had appeared shortly after the Conquest to the humble Indian convert Juan Diego: others might. Not Luis. He didn't speak of it, but in his heart, deeply, he hated the Roman Catholic Church as much as he hated the Spaniards and his family.

For a while more he would still try to swim upstream and ignore the snubs. There was a faint possibility that he might be able, nonetheless, to make his way successfully in the modern world. And yet—still if he failed—what then? Would he be content to live as a failure in the world which had refused him success? No. No, never. Rather than that, he would defy them all and shame them forever. He would do what no one of Christian education and secular, modern

17

training, of even partly Spanish blood, had ever done: leave this corrupt civilization behind forever. Burn his modern clothes. And put on the homespun and the blue-black serape of the Moxtomí, ask for a dark-skinned daughter of the pueblo and an allotment of the shrunken *ejido* land. Already he knew much of the Moxtomí language; he would perfect his knowledge; they would initiate him into the sacred secrets which the townsmen did not know and, indeed, scarcely knew existed. And he would dance the holy dances and perform the sacred ceremonies and sing the chants to the Great Old Ones. . . .

Only not yet.

His heart had begun to beat faster at the prospect, as it had used to at the prospect of a woman before he had ever really had one. But the joy of making a woman part of himself was a transient joy and this other anticipated pleasure would be a permanent joy. And so he hesitated. For, with every delight there is a sorrow, and the delightsome life of the Moxtomí Indians had a very sorrowful side, indeed. Almost every bit of it had its roots in poverty and this poverty was due entirely to the loss of the greater part of the *ejido* lands. He told himself that he might not do it, after all. . . . But underneath the thin meniscus of confidence in his ability to prosper as a modern man was a deep certainty, part pleasure and part pain, that his future lay not in an office or an apartment but in the small huts of the Indians, warm only in love and history.

There was, of course, never any doubt in his mind that the Indians in question were the Moxtomí. The Tenocha Indians were infinitely the more numerous, incomparably the more powerful, and there was even a vigorous movement among them to give official status to their language, the Nahua dialect, which they called *Meshika*. The fact that Luis knew very well that his maternal grandmother had been a Moxtomí did not blind him to the probable fact that the blood of the Tenocha flowed in his veins as well as an heritage on both familial sides. But who and what, after all, were the Tenocha? Who else but the Aztecs! And were they not themselves the seed of a pre-Spanish Conquest? They

18

were themselves aliens here on the upper slopes of the great valley. The Moxtomí, the last and furthest-flung of the Toltecs—it was to them that this land rightfully belonged.

And all the while Luis's feet led him up through the stone-strewn and balsam-scented paths.

But his mind was elsewhere and on a multitude of things. He wasn't going up to El Pueblo de San Juan Bautisto Moxtomí merely to enjoy the friendly presence of such acquaintances as, say, Tío Santiago Tuc, or Domingo Deuh, who was more of Luis's own age. There were *things* he wanted to discuss with them, a variety of exciting things, and he wanted their opinions. There, up ahead, a huddle of brown brushwood and adobe, he saw the pueblo. It was still a good way off. Luis began to form his thoughts into mental conversation.

"There are soldiers in town, Uncle Santiago; soldiers from 'Mexico' with horses and rifles. Why, do you suppose? I don't really think that this time they've come to expel any Indios from Indio lands; their business seems to lie only in Los Remedios *municipalidad*. But there's a further question, you see—*what* business? It has to do with Monte Sagrado, I'm sure . . . everyone is sure of that. Some say that they're here to keep order at the fiera of the Holy Hermit. Some say there's going to be, I don't know, some kind of trouble with the procession. You know that not everyone in town is the *Heremito's* friend—particularly not in the *Barrio Occidental* —that's a mean, tough neighborhood; you know that. Today I heard a saying I haven't heard in a long time: *Scratch a Nahua and you find a Nagual* . . . What do you think that really means?

"And others are saying, Tío Santi, that the soldiers are here for another reason altogether. They say that the government is going to take away the Tlaloc that's in the cave under the Monte and take it to 'Mexico'—I don't know why. And there's talk that this would be a bad thing, that if they do this the Tlaloc will be angry and that there will never be any rain again in the whole Valley. Some are angry about this and some are just excited and of course some don't care at all."

19

The turn in the path at this point brought Luis face to face with a view which might alone make the fortune of a hotelier. To his left the great Valley of Mexico sloped downward like a precious bowl, and he could see the farms and fields below the rim of forest. Very far below him, and seeming quite small, was his native hateful town of Los Remedios, a huddle of red-tiled roofs at the foot of Monte Sagrado—so high it seemed from down there—yet from here a mere hummock, apparent only because crowned with the church. More fields, more forests, dwindling, dwindling . . . a tiny wisp of smoke: the *mas o menos* steam locomotive panting its way uphill from Amecameca. And, to the left of the misty huddle which was Amecameca, from here the land fell away abruptly into another valley and another state and another and altogether different climate. To Luis's right the land rose unmarked by man except by the meager *milpitas* of the Moxtomí, rivulets and gorges and woods and great riven boulders: the Pass of Cortes like a line of demarcation between the gigantic sleeping woman in her white shroud which was Ixtaccihuatl and the looming cone of glistening ice-clad Popocatapetl.

Luis gazed and sighed and resumed his walk and his cerebral conversation. "Domingo Deuh, my friend, have you and your people seen the lights which are said to have been shining and moving about on *los volcanes*? I myself think that I have, once or twice, but I am not entirely sure—perhaps they were stars peeping out from behind clouds, or *aeroplanes* passing high and silently between the mountains and myself. Still, many others and some of them sober and serious witnesses have claimed to have seen them, and in such a manner that neither stars nor *aeroplanes* could account for them. Do you know anything of this? Have your people formed an opinion?

"And what of the smokes from Popo? Mountain-climbers have come down with reports of such. Did they lie? Were they mistaken? Has the long-slumbering Smoking Mountain begun to stir again? Or have interlopers descended to dynamite the sulfur inside the crater and carry it away to sell without having to pay taxes on it? And are these smokes

"Long walk . . . you," the older old woman said, speaking in a deliberately debased Moxtomí, as though he were incapable of understanding anything better. He said, in his best command of the language, "Has Tata Santiago very far to go before he returns?"

"Yes, very far—you. Tired. Hungry. Eat—eat," she said, as though not understanding, and gave him tortillas with beans and a bit of chili. The other old woman poured him some stale pulque. And the girl began to roast a handful of squash seeds over the tiny charcoal fire. It was not until he had dutifully cracked the last of these that it occurred, belatedly, to Luis, that old Tuc was not coming back at all! And he ceased, suddenly, to be the bewildered friend of the humble and dispossessed autochthones and became, totally, the outraged Mexican male upon whom an insult disparaging his *machismo*—his maleness—has been put.

Bad enough that he, having come with warmth, should be greeted with coldness! Bad enough that his sincere inquiries had been repulsed with assumed ignorance and feigned indifference. Worse, he had been tricked! But worst of all, he had been given over to the custody and the ministrations of women, two old hags and a child, as though he were no more of a man than the infants on the earthern floor! It was not to be tolerated! Rage choked him—they did not think he was a man, then? Not worthy of masculine courtesy? So—he would show them if he were *macho* or *hembra!* He half-rose from where he was sitting . . .

But the sudden ugly flame which sprang more from outrage than from lust, died down quickly. The women were too old, dry and shriveled like mushrooms, and the girl was far too young—it would be like mounting a boy. . . . Besides, this was their village, they would certainly make a commotion, and Luis might indeed cease very suddenly to be very much *macho* at all after the men were finished with him.

He muttered a Moxtomí thanks and farewell which almost choked him, and walked off with stiff and angry strides away from the cold and meager hamlet and its empty streets.

With distance, however, came reflection; with reflection, forgiveness. Why should they have trusted him? What, after

all, did they know of him? His overtures of friendship might, for ought they knew, have been false. Wasn't his father a landowner? If he, Luis, were a Moxtomí, with a memory of loss of tribal-communal lands which had gone on over the course of over four centuries, it might very well seem cause for suspicion . . . Only— Why *now?* Why had suspicion of his intentions (if such it was) never manifested itself before? Or, at least, never in this form? What had suddenly upset them . . . for they had, he now clearly recalled, been upset *before* he arrived. The source of their mistrust of him must therefore lie in something apart from him . . . and, almost certainly, in something apart from *them*. . . .

What could this be?

He had no doubt that it lay, somehow, in the very matters he had desired to question them about; which he, in fact, *had* questioned them about. And since they would, and perhaps really could, tell him nothing, it thus behooved him to find out the answers himself and then *tell them*. His imagination began to soar once again, and, looking down from mental heights upon a landscape only partly imaginary, saw things it had been accustomed to see before. But now it saw clearly in detail as well as in outline things of which it had previously seen as only semi-concealed hints. He saw these so clearly and so richly that it no longer was possible for him to doubt them. In his disappointments with the modern world ruled by *guerros* and *blancos* of "purer" Spanish blood than he, in his sullen retreat from it, he had failed to appreciate that his knowledge of it could make it possible for him to use it for his own (and his friends') ends—and thus totally to defeat it. Would this be *machismo* or not?

Thus and therefore . . .

He would not only find out the answers to the mysterious questions which must be not merely puzzling but vexing the Moxtomí—and thus gain their full friendship and confidence —he would do more than that; he would solve, somehow, (details did not concern him now) *the* basic Moxtomí question of all: how to regain the lost *ejido* lands, and by regaining them transform the Moxtomí from the huddled handful they now were to the prosperous people they had

once been, and—with the help of Luis Lorenzo Santangel—would be once again.

The sun on its way down seemed to turn the edges of the Valley into gold.

III

ROBERT MACAULEY, a stocky, self-contained sort of man with shrewd blue eyes and a large blonde moustache, was the connection which had brought the Clays to Los Remedios . . . via the *Concerning The Author* note attached to a story of Macauley's in a little magazine they happened to come across. Jacob had liked the story well enough, more than he had any of the others, which was less praise than it merited, but it was the words *"now lives in Los Remedios, a small town in the State of Mexico"* which had hooked their attention. They had moved, freshly married, from New York City, a place which Sarah declared contained no oxygen, to the Currier and Ives community of Pickering, Pennsylvania, wherein they had learned, by and by, a number of important things, such as that: it had, and for good reason, a suicide rate higher than Sweden or Japan; two can't live as cheaply as one; their landlady, a virago with a face like a malevolent horse—ah, well . . .

"If we can't make more money, then let's go where the money we can make will go further," they said. And they said, "If we've got to move, let's move far away in one jump." And they said, almost in one breath: " *'Los Remedios, a small town in the State of Mexico'*—hey!" They wrote immediately to Macauley and received a fairly immediate reply containing the magic words, "My own expenses amount to about $50 a month," and beat it the hell out of Pickering, Pa., one step ahead of litigious Mrs. Moomaw's latest writ.

The trip south, via a disintegrating station wagon whose sale to them almost seemed to have been arranged by Mrs. M., standard-gage, auto-bus, and narrow-gage r.r., so exhausted them that they couldn't have moved any further if Los Remedios had looked like the Pit of Purgatory instead of rather like an Andean village shoved north by a glacial drift. Finding Señora Mariana's back patio house had been, they were not long in realizing, a stroke of luck, for Los Remedios was not much designed for accommodating foreigners.

Another thing they soon picked up was that living there was not going to cost them anything as low as $100 a month, either. Curiosity mingling with annoyance, Sarah said, "Mac, how do you manage to live here on only $50 a month?"

"I sleep with my landlady," he said, very simply.

"Oh. You didn't tell us that."

"If I had, you wouldn't have come, and I wanted some people I could speak English with."

Their expenses ran them something close to $200 a month, but this was still about $400 cheaper than life in Mrs. Moomaws' semi-renovated barn, plus the fact that Señora Mariana would as soon have entered a brothel as a court of law. Besides her truly benevolent assistances, they had six rooms for $20, including a large studio with a skylight where Jacob Clay, a thin, frenetic man enraged by the difference between what he was writing and what he knew he was in theory capable of writing, typed and cursed and periodically poked his head out to see if the mail had come with assignments or checks. At least once a day they went over to Macauley's house and at least once a day he came over to theirs. Another approximately $20 went to Lupita, but by now Lupita had managed to extinguish any guilt feelings either of them had had for paying such wages.

So now, at the moment, while Jacob crouched at his typewriter like an outraged toad, and Sarah sulked her way through the dishes—only not very far through them: the water was *cold*—Macauley sat on the coping of a dry fountain in the patio and talked. He talked of his stories, for one thing, and his fears (in which Jacob, who mildly admired

the stories, concurred) that despite their merits they were far too far out of current literary fashion to achieve any notable success. "So I decided to take time off—from the one about the childless aunt who schemes to replace her sister-in-law as Foremost Female Figure in the children's lives . . . by the way, a standard plot-item in Mexican soap opera . . . nobody cares about a philandering husband that much—and repair Lenita's kitchen ceiling. I'd like to put in a fireplace but she wouldn't know what to do with one. The Mexicans have never discovered the chimney, they're moving right from the charcoal brazier to the atomic pile; meanwhile, let the smoke find its own way out—that's their attitude. It took me only about half the time that it would have taken a carpenter, but it would have driven a carpenter crazy to watch me!" he said, with cheerful pride. "Carpenters are always driven mad to see the way that miners work because we always do everything ass-backwards . . . according to them . . . but we get it done better and quicker. Any miner can handle wood, but did you ever see a carpenter could handle explosives?"

"No," said Sarah, rubbing her rapidly-chapping hands. "I didn't know you used to be a miner . . ."

"Once a miner, always a miner . . . Say, don't forget the procession tonight. You won't want to miss that. It's quite a thing."

She felt that she would gladly agree to miss every procession that ever was or would be, even if led by Jesus of Nazereth riding a zebra, in exchange for getting the dishes done. But of course nobody would take her up on it. She noticed that young Mexican who spoke the strained English come into the patio, Mac spoke to him in rapid Spanish, the boy asked something about Jacob, and Mac gestured to the study door. Sarah felt too subdued to warn him off, and besides, if Jacob shouted at the boy he might work off all his hostilities and be in a good and sympathetic mood towards her. She sighed heavily and looked glumly at the dishes.

"Tell me about the procession," she said, dully.

"Jacob, you are busy?" Luis asked, entering the long room with its yellow-washed walls and long trestle-table laden with piles of books and papers.

Luis, entering, had no more substance or reality to Jacob Clay than, say, the Ghost of Purim Yet To Come. He thought of a sentence he wanted for his next paragraph, and smiled, vaguely. Luis, encouraged by the smile, came in and sat down in the cane-bottomed chair with the red, white, blue and green floral designs. Jacob jotted down the sentence in pencil; it was not quite ready to go through the typewriter. He looked up and gazed abstractedly at Luis in the chair, not altogether noticing either of them.

"I can speak to you in confidence and in Español?" asked Luis. "I may to make the light?"

Jacob muttered, "Sí, sí . . ." without more than barely understanding the question. It was getting on towards dusk. He peered up at the light, scowling. The light went on. Good. He began to reflect on the sentence. Absurd, that he should allow one paragraph to hold up this whole damned piece, but . . . mmm . . . how did it go, now? ahhh . . . *He was not merely overwhelmed by this new calamity, he was by it* . . . yeah . . . okay . . . mmm . . . so: *He was?* what? *by it* . . .

"You are very kindly. *Bueno. Entonces, mira, Jacobo—*" Luis began his confidences, haltingly to begin with, but with gradually increasing fluency. He felt no contradiction in explaining his secret problems to a foreigner; indeed, had Jacob *not* been a foreigner, Luis would never have dreamed of making him a confidant. True, Luis distrusted . . . feared . . . hated those of lighter skins—but only those of lighter skins who were *Mexicans.* It was they, after all, who had snubbed him; not the gringos, to whom all Mexicans were alike. Jacobo was as polite to him as he was to Don Umberto, the Municipal President. Let Don Umberto mutter about the loss of Tejas and Alta California by gringo conquest, gringo theft. How many thousands of hectares of *ejido* lands had not Don Umberto's townsmen acquired that had once been conquered and thefted from the Moxtomí! It was not the Moxtomí, after all, who had lost Tejas and

Alta California. Luis was as indifferent to the yanqui conquests there as any African nationalist was to Russian conquests in central or eastern Asia. It was his own losses he resented, not losses in general, and the enemies of his enemies he regarded as his friends.

"Entiende, Jacobo, ayer en las montañas . . ." he said, earnestly.

Jacob regarded him, serenely and unseeingly. *He was not only overwhelmed by this new calamity, he was—he was—he was—* Okay, he was what? washed out? flooded out? No . . . no . . . no . . . But something like it. Luis was talking. Luis was asking something. Who knows what. Jacob Clay made a sympathetic noise, continued to search his mind for the *mot juste.*

Robert Macauley smiled a smile of anticipated pleasure and stroked his golden moustache. A chance had been given him to enlarge on his favorite subject, The Secret History of Mexico. Usually he liked to reveal new entries for The Worst Thing That Happened to Mexico ("The worst thing that happened to Mexico was the expulsion of the Jesuits; literacy dropped seventy percent in a generation." or "The worst thing that happened to Mexico was the publication of the Papal Bull against Freemasonry; liberalism and religion were divorced forever."), but Little-Known Insights he cherished almost as much. Sarah's question was right up his alley.

" 'Who was the Holy Hermit of the Sacred Mountain?' " he repeated. "That's a good question. Let's preceed it with another one. 'Why is the Sacred Mountain sacred?' Hey? I suppose that this town has been rebuilt a dozen times at least, since the Conquest . . . but I bet that if you traced on a map the route this procession will be taking you'd have a pretty good outline of its original boundaries and axis. Now, obviously, the Sacred Mountain was sacred when Huitzilopochtli or Quetzalcoatl used to have the concession. The old Aztec flay-'em-alive boys had one of their cardiectomy clinics on top of it, you can be sure of that. It's got an uninterrupted view of both Popo and Ixta, the Super-Sacred

29

Macro-Mountains. And, naturally, Cortez and Padre Olmedo, his chaplain, didn't waste any time in toppling the idols and setting up a cross in their place.

"The Indians wailed a bit, but they didn't really object *too* much. Know why? Know what their big objection was? That the Spanish cross didn't have equidistant arms! Sure. The natives already *had* the cross as a religious symbol. The old bishops claimed this proved that St. Thomas the Wandering Apostle had stopped off here in Mexico on his way to India. And the Mormons, of course, claim that this proves that Jesus was here, just as Joseph Smith said. But the simple fact of the matter is—and there's other proof connecting this with Monte Sagrado, I'll get to that in a minute—the simple fact of the matter is, that a cross with equidistant arms was the ancient Mexican symbol of the rains which come blowing down bringing blessings from every direction, and all four cardinal points in particular. But still: what made *this* hill with the pyramid holier than any other hill with a pyramid? And particularly after it ceased to have the pyramid?"

"Was there anything else on the hill?" asked Sarah, beginning to get interested despite herself.

Mac smiled an a-hah sort of smile and raised his eyebrows and his index finger. " 'On' it? *'On'* it?"

"Well, what then? *Under* it?" she said, at a venture.

Instantly he leveled the index finger at her face. "Exactly. Exactly. How did you know? Who told you? They don't usually care to discuss it with outsiders."

Sarah beamed and raised her hands, palms out, to the level of her ears, in one of her favorite gestures. "You mean that there *is* something under it? Oh my goodness!" She uttered a squeal of sheer delight. "What? Tell me? Hidden treasure?"

"Tlaloc."

"Who? What—what?"

"There's a Tlaloc under, or perhaps I should say, inside, the Holy Mountain. A statue of the rain god. At least, some say there's a whole statue. But all that's visible is the head. I'm not sure there *is* any more than just a head. It's in a sort

of tunnel or cave, or—if my miner's experience is any judge, a combination tunnel and cave. How they got it in there beats me, because the way is so narrow you more or less almost have to wiggle on your belly like a reptile—and it's not carved out of any kind of stone that was ever found in, under, there, either.

"Never mind how I got permission, I have certain strings I can pull if I need to," he said, winking, "but it took some doing. The good clergy have done about all they could to christianize the surface of that little mountain, but *nothing* could ever de-paganize that head. Try to imagine it—" he said, glee giving way to sober sincerity, "this gigantic head —must be a good six feet up and down and across—eyes half-closed—broad nose—full lips—expression of infinite majesty and calm—"

"Gee—!"

"—nothing Aztec about it in the world, it must be *pre*-Aztec, Toltec, maybe, or even Olmec. And—get *this,* now: it's situated under a sort of seepage spot from a spring . . . and the impression that you get, when you turn your flashlight on it, is that, well, damn it! That it's sitting under a sort of gentle rain!"

"*Gee!*"

"Yes, exactly. Well . . . even though hardly anyone has ever seen it, because you've got to go through the church precincts and the priests have got it closed off and shut up with a good ten stout gates with enormous locks, still, everyone knows it is *there*. All of which is background as to what makes the Holy Mountain holy. Now, as for the Hermit himself, well . . ."

What the Hermit's original name was, Macauley had been unable to learn; he wasn't even sure that it was on record. But it was a matter of history that he had been some sort of pagan priest or attendant at Monte Sagrado when the Spaniards arrived and that he was just about the first to accept baptism. The Spaniards made him a catechist and, Roman Catholic priests being then and for a long while thereafter in short supply, his influence as a catechist was immense. In fact, he might well have become a Roman Catholic priest

himself—except that no natives were ordained at that time at all. Weren't trusted not to be relapsable, in short.

But Juan Fernando, as his baptismal name was, nevertheless, had lived a devout religious life, never marrying, showing an excellent example, quietly exhorting and instructing, chastity, poverty and obedience and all that, respect of Spanish and Mexican alike . . . and, when he finally died, was buried right there.

"Right up there?"

"Right up there . . . Only he didn't stay buried. He's still on view, in that glass-covered catafalque that they'll bring around tonight. A sort of local example of popular canonization. To the Church, of course, he is no saint. But to the people, he's very much a saint. Oh, a few times, some superscrupulous bishop has decided that this is an illicit cultus and has tried to suppress it. But not for long. The most the priests here will commit themselves to, if you ask them if it's true, as the people say, that the Hermit takes off at night for Rome every now and then and serves the Pope at mass—oh, they'll sort of click their tongues and give a quick shake of the head . . .

"But . . . you know . . . I'm not sure that they're totally convinced that he *doesn't!*

"And of course there's a lot more. I could talk all night. For instance—I've never been able to find out, to make sure: is that actually the Hermit in the catafalque? Or a wax effigy? Or a waxen covering *over* a mummy or bones? It's all covered with embroidery, except the head and hands, and you can't get close enough to make *sure.* I'd sure like to know. Oh, well—maybe someday I will!"

He smiled. Sarah said, "Gee . . ." Her sense of wonder was very pleasantly excited. And just then a dish slipped out of her slackened hands and crashed into pieces. "More *cachi-bachis!*" Macauley said, pleasantly undisturbed. "Be sure you stick them up in the fork of a tree."

Sarah said, "Damn! Oh—damn it!" And burst into tears.

He was not merely overwhelmed by this new catastrophe, he was . . .

32

*He was not merely overwhelmed by this new catastrophe,
he was ...*

"So there you are, Jacobo," Luis wound up. "Now, please,
tell me, honestly, your opinion. Please." He looked at the face
of his confidant. And the face lit up with sudden insight.
Luis's heart bounded. He leaned forward.

"*Inundated*'!" Jacob shouted. "*'He was not merely overwhelmed by this new catastrophe, he was inundated by it!'*
Ha! Ha-ha! Good! Great!" He leaped to his typewriter and
began to attack the keys. A minute passed, and another
and another, with Jacob uttering little squeaks and grunts.
Then he ripped the papers and carbons from the typewriter. "There!" he cried. "And stap my vitals if we don't
put it aboard the packet-boat to sail at first tide tomorrow
morning!" Then he blinked, smiled slightly, frowned slightly.
"Hello, Luis," he said, cordially. "Didn't see you come in ...
What's new? Anything on your mind? Eh? *¿Que pasa,
joven?*"

Amidst much, much excitement and after many false
alarms, the inhabitants of, and visitors to, Calle de la In-
dependencia were finally outside and awaiting the approach
of the procession. Archways of wire and flowers and greenery
and electric lights spanned the street at several points and
were boasted by a number of individual houses, as well as
banners reading *Bienvenida Heremito.* Down the street, in
front of the house of the Rosario family who kept the pulque
saloon, an altar had been built, like a small stage, a glorious
gallimaufry of gauze, lights, candles, colored cloth and paper, gilt, silvering, angels, crucifixes, images, and Mexican
flags. Even Coco, the idiot cow-tender, usually in a state of
agricultural grime, was cleanly washed and dressed and
wore a brand-new sombrero in his hands. Fireworks sounded,
grew nearer. So did a curious medley of musics. Sky-rockets
hissed and wooshed and shot sizzling upwards and exploded
with bangs and bursts of stars, and the procession rounded
a corner and came into sight.

All the religious confraternities in town, it seemed, were
there, members and banners and huge burning tapers, as

33

well as many from out of town. The women for the most part dressed in white, those who were not in white were all in black, mantillas or rebozas covering their heads . . . except, curiously enough, the women members of the lay religious orders. Their dress was something in between uniform and habit: all bareheaded, as though to emphasize that they were *lay* people and in no way contravening the secular law against the wearing of clerical costume in public. Men, though outnumbered, were numerous, clutching their sombreros; children were present in profusion, and all walked slowly and gravely with their eyes cast down, voices raised in something half-chant and half-hymn. Group after group, band after band, banner after banner . . . Jacob thought, as he did again and again, how, for an ostentatiously secular republic, Mexico managed to be so very and so constantly and so demonstrably religious.

The marchers proceeded on with measured pace, the voices paused, the music was suddenly heard again . . . and a very odd music it was, too: the repetition of a single bar over and over again, of a kind of music which had certainly never come out of Spain—odd, archaic, impressive, stirring, baffling. The musicians came into sight: three Indian men, one with a flute, one with an odd sort of drum, and one with something vaguely resembling an ocarina—

But before he could fully take this in, from down the street, a rather sad and shabby and tiny "orchestra" in run-down uniforms with run-down instruments of the conventional sort, burst into an off-key version of a tune he recognized (after a moment) from having heard it in the United States, to wit, *Good Night, Sweet Jesus*—and the native players fell silent. And on this note of bathos and anachronism, the spectators fell to their knees and the catafalque, born on the shoulders of a dozen young men, approached and passed by.

It distantly resembled a sort of truncated four-poster bed, with frame and canopy of dark and carven wood, with sides of glass. Jacob strained, Sarah strained, Macauley strained, to see what was inside. Again the resemblance to a bed . . . someone was lying down, covered with a profusion of (so

it seemed) embroidered, richly-embroidered, bedclothes, drawn up to his chin. The face was dark, very dark, scantily-bearded, in total repose, on its head what seemed to be a skullcap or headdress of equally rich fabrication. They thought they could see the hands, too, but the procession did not halt. The catafalque seemed to float by in a sea of sighs and candleflame; the rockets hissed and wooshed; the near-19th century orchestra reached the end of its piece; once again the tootling and the beating of the weird and totally non-European, yet tantalizingly evocative melody motif, over and over again . . .

There was a silence. Those who had knelt now rose to their feet. The beautiful and elaborate designs and patterns of flowers had been churned into chaos by the passing feet. Señora Mariana smiled as she noted this. Sarah asked, somewhat disappointed, "Is it all over?"

"*¿Es terminado?*"—Macauley.

"*Si, ya es terminado, Señores.*"—Señora Mariana.

"Well, it's all over, folks. I'll be getting home. I suppose my *chula* landlady has all kinds of goodies waiting in honor of the fiera. Come around tomorrow for breakfast, okay?"

Already the streets were emptying. The Clays proceeded past the kitchen where they saw the two older women and the girl bustling about laying a table, opened the door into the back patio and proceeded through the gloom to their own apartment. "Well, that was interesting," said Jacob, brightly. "Hey, honey, what's for supper?" Sarah, with a pang of sheer horror, remembered the still-largely-unwashed pile of pots and dishes and cutlery—and the evil barrel of water, icier and freezinger than ever! Fortunately, before she could reply, in bustled young Marinita, prettily aproned, and carrying a neat stack of well-filled dishes. She smiled, she spoke, she lifted a napkin, she withdrew.

Sarah's spirits soared. "Well, isn't *this* nice," she cried. "Our landlady has made holiday goodies, too! Look, look, all kinds of luscious things—two, no, three kinds of tamales! and tacos and tostados and enchiladas, and—look! look! Quesadillas, too! Oh, yummy! See how they're made with

colored cornmeal, red ones and blue ones and even green ones. Oh—"

Jacob said, "Eat, eat. Later, we'll talk . . . Don't bother setting the table, let's eat them with our fingers as the Mexicans do."

Sarah said, serenely, entirely forgiving the landlady for denuding the patio, "Very well, if that's the way you want to do it, that's the way we'll do it. Who needs knives and forks? . . . Yum yum yum yum . . ." So much for washing in ice-water. And tomorrow breakfast at Macauley's. Now— if wicked Lupita would only turn up before lunchtime tomorrow—!

And while most of the people in that part of town through which the procession had already passed were snug and happy in their houses, eating traditional foods and dipping them in special *mole* sauces and washing it all down with lots of pulque, there was still a good stretch of town through which the procession had yet to pass. . . . And this included a rather bad stretch of town, the ward called the *Barrio Occidental,* or Western District. Here were the most tumbledown houses, the filthiest pulquerias, the raggedyest children, the raunchiest whorehouses, the highest proportion of glowering faces and of drunken brawls and slashings. And here a curious sort of ceremony sometimes customarily attended the procession's passage—a dozen or so of the younger men would halt the procession and ask, with truculent politeness, to be allowed the honor of bearing the catafalque through the barrio. The offer was always refused (when it was made, which wasn't always); sometimes there was a bit of shoving and pushing, usually the occidentales were bought off with presents of dulces, cigarettes, fiera-foods. But, if so or not so, the procession after a short while continued on its way past the sullen, scowling faces of the neighborhood Indios.

But not tonight. Not quite.

"With permission, carriers—" Permission was not granted.

Almost immediately the women who carried the gifts or bribes in case they be needed, sensed that something was not

as usual. They hastened forward with their baskets of sweets, tobaccos, snacks . . . only to be knocked down, to see their baskets and contents trampled underfoot in the sudden rush forward upon the catafalque. They screamed, there were shouts and curses, clubs thudded, knives were drawn and flashed, the orderly procession dissolved into a riot. One of the carriers clutched his bloody arm. The catafalque sagged. It was swept to and fro. It dipped and it swayed in the dim light here, where no festive lamps burned and tapers fell or were burned out. Luis, who had followed, rushed first this way and that, not knowing what to do.

"The Hermit! Save the Holy Hermit! Assassinos! Thieves!"

It was very dark now, like a scene from Hell, and then, in a sudden hellish burst of light caused by the untimely explosion of all the rockets at once, Luis saw the catafalque come stumbling, heavily, to the ground. He cried out. He saw the Hermit fall, he saw his splendid coverings in the dust, he saw the Hermit rise and look from side to side—

Total pandemonium now. Glimpses of people fighting, fainting, screaming, struggling. Glimpses, totally inexplicable, of figures half-human and half-coyote—

—darkness again—

—the Hermit, with tottering steps, uncertain at first, then very quickly, vanished into the blackness.

And Luis, seeing the footsteps which glowed briefly and phosphorescently as they appeared and then disappeared, Luis followed after them, after the swiftly retreating figure of the Holy Hermit.

IV

LONG AND LONG he followed these evanescent tracks, like the glistening of snail-trails or the fitfully cold flames of the fire-flies, up through the hills into the cold black night where the cold white stars seemed peering low upon the land of Earth.

Sometimes it seemed to him that he knew the path he followed and sometimes he was sure that he did not. Now and then he heard the howling of coyotes and he shivered less from the cold than from the recollection of every tale he'd ever heard about the *naguales,* the men-who-were-coyotes, the-coyotes-who-were-men, and who as part of wicked sorcery, were infinitely more dangerous to men than any real coyotes would or could ever be.

He pushed these fears aside, not only because fear was not *macho,* but because these legends stemmed from the malevolent Meshika, the Tenocha-Aztec people, whose decadent descendants lived in the *Barrio Occidental;* not from the benevolent Moxtomí, the real heritors of the land. If indeed the Hermit of the Holy Mountain had Power or Powers—and, after seeing him rise from the dead, Luis scarcely felt capable of doubting it, than this power ought certainly to protect Luis, who was literally now following in his footsteps. Following in something akin to numbness, something not far from a kind of terror he had never known before, following with feet which stumbled now and then not only from the darkness but from fatigue . . . for he had not made the long, long walk up these same hills earlier in the day and then down again? . . . But, still:

Following.

Now and then he saw below him the huddled handful of lights which was Los Remedios; sometimes, very infrequently, a moving spark which he knew must be an automobile, or, likelier, a truck on one of the roads down on the lower slopes; and once he saw the tiny spurt of flame in the fire-box of the *mas o menos,* toiling to Amecameca with a line of freight cars. And overhead, the deliquescent stars dripped dew and delicate mist upon him.

But for the most part he saw only the shining, fleeting footprints of the Hermit, and he hesitated to plant his own feet upon them to guide his steps before the pallid light faded away forever.

How far ahead the Hermit now was, Luis did not know. A faint notion that the old stories were true and that the Holy man was on his way to Rome took hold of him—but he cast

it off. The mood of it stayed with him, though, with all its intimations. Whatever the Hermit was, he was not a mere corpse or effigy. Was *not*. Such did not rise and walk off into the darkness and the mountains. But in the name of . . . anything! . . . what *did* rise and walk off—anywhere!— after having supposedly been dead for four hundred years?

He had not, surprisingly, formed any answer to this by the time he reached the pueblo of San Juan Bautista Moxtomí. He was very tired, stumbling with stiff and twitching legs, eyes burning; he needed rest and warmth . . . and answers . . . answers . . . answers. He saw the men posted along the path, answered their hail in The Language, passed by them into the small open area which was the plaza, and there he saw the people of the pueblo sitting in a wide circle with faces of awe and joy and inside the circle burned a fire and the night air was odorous with copal-incense. The Hermit stood beside the fire and spoke in a clear and vigorous voice, but antique language and although he was standing and those whom he addressed were sitting, he and they were on a level of eye to eye. When Luis saw these others, saw their massive bodies and massy limbs, their strong broad noses and strong full lips and their heavy-lidded eyes with pupils of burning gold, he recognized who and what they were. And he fell upon his knees and bowed his brow down into the cool dust of the ground before the Great Old Ones, the demigods of the Toltecs and Moxtomí, who had calmly and benevolently ruled over the land before the coming of the cruelty and incessant bloodletting of the Aztecs.

And who had now returned . . .

The Hermit (or he-who-had-been-known-till-now-as-The-Hermit) paused in his speaking. And another voice broke the sudden silence, a voice like a great and deep-toned bell of gold and bronze, saying, in the Moxtomí language, "One moment, you who have so long and so faithfully been the Guardian of the Entrusted Thing; one moment only . . ." The ground shook slightly with the great and measured tread and huge, beautifully-proportioned hands took hold of Luis and lifted him to his feet. Dazed, delighted, stricken still with awe, he gazed into the great golden glowing eyes

and heard the great golden voice say, "Younger Brother, what is in your heart?"

Luis heard his heart beating, his ears rang, he drew a shuddering breath. "Great Old Ones. Is it you whose lights have been seen on Popo?"

"It is so. And then?"

"I . . . Ah! There are so many things in my heart to tell you, to ask you . . . I . . ."

The lips of the giant figure parted in a faint smile. "Not now, Younger Brother. Not yet. Take this—" Something was pressed into his hand. He felt a cord of maguey fibre and something metallic, with an embossed surface. "—take health, take rest, and at another time, Younger Brother, it may be that we may listen . . . and answer."

The disappointment was like the falling away of ground beneath Luis. All day long he had sped and toiled from place to place, asking only to be listened to. But Santiago Tuc and Domingo Deuh had been too busy to listen to him, Jacobo Clay had been too busy to listen to him, and now the astonishingly returned Great Old Ones were too busy to listen to him! Anguish ate at him like acid—but for a moment only. And then sleep, of the most delectable sort as is usually felt only when one knows that awakening is imminent, sleep now wrapped its arms around him. The circle of serenely joyful Moxtomí about the (he now recognized) sacred fire, the still all-but-totally-mysterious figure of the Hermit/Guardian, the titanic figures of the sapient and potent and benign Great Old Ones, all began with a swift slowness to dissolve into the golden mists; and Luis smiled and Luis slept.

The Clays slept, too, in their Krazy Kat style house in the back patio, with barely a straight line let alone two parallel ones in the whole structure, and each room painted in different bursts-of-color tones: restaurant-pea-green, imitation-soda-pop-orange, do-not-leave-within-the-reach-of-children-shoe-polish-purple, whorehouse-madam-red, and so on . . . all, presumably, the work of a previous tenant defined by Señora Mariana only as *el Español*. Why does the roof leak

so much, Señora? El Español punctured it vigorously, Señor.
Why are the holes in the gas-stove burners mostly plugged
up, Señora? Because of the unwholesome foods cooked
upon it by El Español, Señor. Why does the wall in the third
room not meet the ceiling in the corner, thus letting in the
wind, Señora? Thus did El Español occupy himself, Señor,
—Ai, the malevolent one! But take no concern, Señor, we
will make all these reparations, excellently. Ah, good, Señora—and when? Mañana, Señor! Mañana!

It was Sarah who awakened first . . . from a dream in
which she sat bound hand and foot in a barrel of ice-cold
water while Lupita, laughing fiendishly, broke greasy plates
over her head. She considered telling Jacob of this latest
evidence of ill will on the part of that mean girl, but decided
against it because he might kick her for waking him up. But
by the time she was fully awake she realized that he was,
too, and listening.

"Jacob, are you awake?"

"No."

"Well, what's that kind of, well, *singing*, then?"

"Weird, isn't it?"

"It sounds exciting and interesting."

"That's what I said. Weird."

They sat up and listened. The sound of the song or chant
or whatever it was came to them distantly, rising and falling.
For a while it seemed to be coming near, then it began to
die away as though going in the opposite direction. "Do
you think," Sarah began, "that it sounds like that wonderful
little tootsie music we saw in the parade tonight?"

"No. No, it doesn't. Much more weird. Barbaric. But I
see what you mean. Hmmm . . ."

Sarah's mind had meanwhile started on another track.
Tootsie. Evans. Where was cunning little Evans, the tootsie
little cat? "Evans?" she called, hopefully, hoping to hear his
answering preep and the sudden scamper of paws and then
his leap onto the bed and the thrust of his little head against
her hand, demanding to be petted and stroked and scratched.
"Ev-ans . . . ?"

"What's *hap*-pened to him?" she asked, her voice faltering.

41

"I can see it now. There he is, shacked up with the convent cat. And he says, 'Well, time to split, babe. See you.' And she—the convent cat—she says, 'Just one more time, lover-poo?' And he says, 'Well, now that you come to mention it, why not?' "

Sarah snuffled and laughed, said that, well, she *hoped* so. But she could not be reassured. Jacob had inclined his head and even twisted it about and cupped his ear so as to catch the odd and vanishing strains of curious sound. But Sarah continued to fret about the missing Evans. He had *never* been away *this* long. The Mexicans didn't understand about cats. They thought they were just *an*imals. Suppose he were *sick*. Suppose he was lying, *hurt,* somewhere?

"Where are you going?— You're getting dressed? Why?"

In a choked voice she answered, "Evans!" He understood immediately, and swung his legs over the side. "Oh well . . . One more bunch of nudniks wandering through this town tonight won't hurt it, I guess. And"—the thought occurred to him in mid-shoe—"maybe while we're looking and paging, we might trace down the troubadors."

It was cold outside, and Sarah muffled her head up warm into the reboza which she had bought in the Langunilla market their first day in "Mexico." A sense of hopelessness came over her, not knowing where to look, and so she simply followed behind Jacob, who was trying to track down the sound of the archaic chanting which continued to rise and fall upon the shifting wind . . . or so it seemed. And about two or three times in every block she called out, tentatively, distressfully, *"Evans . . . ? Evans . . . ?"* But no answering "preep" came, anymore than they ever seemed on a definite track for the music. And then—

A number of blocks away, barely visible in the light of the exceedingly rare street-lamps, which was, moreover, a number of blocks *further* away, a figure slipped around a corner and went shuffling rapidly across the road. Sarah clutched Jacob and gestured. He said, "Huh?" She said, "There—there—Lupita—" and then, recollecting herself and her purpose, raised her voice. "Lupita! Lu-*pi*-ta!" She trotted forward, turned her foot, fell heavily against Jacob. By the

time they had recovered their balance, the figure was gone. The street, studded with stones and lined with the usual stone-and-adobe houses with peaked, tiled roofs, some of which (with their massive, though worm-eaten, wooden gates) antedated the original Mexican Revolution, was silent and empty.

"Are you sure it was Lupita? And if so, so what?"

"Yes, yes—Lupita—she knows Evans—find her—find her and ask her!" Ask her precisely what, Sarah was not certain of. Ask her if she'd seen Evans, if she'd heard news of Evans, if she had any idea of where he might have gone. . . .

She and Jacob quickened their pace. They were looking for Lupita; they were looking for Evans; they were looking for the singing and chanting . . . gradually the town fell away behind them . . . and all three quests seemed to be leading them in the same direction.

Wherever that was.

V

THE LAST LANDMARK which they recognized was the tottering archway with its weathered Latin inscription, leaning against the one still-standing and still-sturdy wall of the old ruined convent, and straddling what was once part of the Royal Road . . . and was now no more than one of the back alley-ways of town. The Clays had seen it before, but had never gone under it or passed it. Three hundred years of continual traffic—before the route was shortened and redirected by Santa Anna in a rare act of public benefit—three hundred years of iron-shod mules laden down with silver bars en route from the mines to Madrid—three hundred years of lumbering wagons with iron-rimmed wheels, had worn the road down below the level of the surrounding land until it seemed rather like the dry bed of an abandoned canal.

But it had also beaten the surface so hard that even a hundred-odd years of neglect hadn't destroyed it; so that, while the Clays could not see where they were going they had only to follow their feet in order to go there. And by and by their eyes adjusted to the darkness which, of course, began to appear less dark. When the road eventually "surfaced" it seemed to the two of them that they were moving through a light mist suffusing and diffusing a subdued light the source or nature of which was unknown.

Now and then a line of wall ran parallel to the road or went off at an angle, sometimes a palisade or a grove. The scent of the open night was all about, night-flowering blossoms and the sweet suspiration of the trees, the strong and fresh sweetness of growing corn, and, over everything, the powerful odor of the relaxing soil itself.

From somewhere ahead the sound of chanting began once again, a deeper and faster note. "Where *are* they?" Sarah asked. Turning her head from right to left, she called, "Evans? Ev-ans . . . ?"

"Maybe it's another procession," Jacob suggested. "Or—maybe even the same one. Hey? Maybe that's why we don't catch up with it . . . it's keeping ahead of us. Well . . . they'll have to stop sometime. What—?"

She clutched his arm. "Didn't you *hear* him? *Evans! Evans!*"

After a moment he said, "I think I did hear a cat . . . But I can't say that I'm sure it's *that* cat. . . ."

Sarah, however, had no doubts. Of course it was "*that* cat!" Maybe he was following the procession, too! Thinking that it contained his people—trying to catch up with it/them! She quickened her pace, panting, for they were now going uphill. At just what point they left the old main road behind and branched off onto the increasingly narrower path, Jacob did not notice nor Sarah care. Now and then the luminescent mists seemed to part a moment, they could see fires and other lights up ahead, and even once, bathed in the rays of an invisible moon, they saw the incredible heights of Ixtaccihuatl, the serenely sleeping Woman, shrouded forever in her snowy cowl and mantle.

Sarah stopped, breathing heavily. "I . . . I'm not sure . . . that I can go much further. . . ."

"The air does seem a lot thinner up here. Well . . . You want to turn around and go on back?"

Distress and indecision played upon her face. "Well . . . Oh . . . Just a little bit further. Now, don't say anything. I . . . want to be able to hear . . ." Her sentence faded off into a laboring breath. But he understood: to hear if the cat sounded again. He nodded, they started off again, this time much more slowly. But each wondered, secretly, if the sound of the blood pounding in their ears would not prevent their hearing anything so slight as the plaintive mewing of a distant cat.

Sarah, finally, dragged one foot after another, clutched at Jacob, and leaned against him, her mouth open and her breath now a painful gasping. And with that, the winds drove the mists into their faces, wet and chill and pallid. The winds drove the sound of the strange and eerie singing louder than ever to their ears. The winds parted the mists in front of them: and quite a ways away across the more-or-less level land where they now stood, unable to go on, Jacob and Sarah, saw a circle of fires burning . . . evidently fed with some quickly combustible fuel, the thin dry fallen twigs of the pine or piñole perhaps, for here at one point one would die down to a glow and there at another point one would leap up and flare as some stooping figure replenished it. There were two groups involved, one inside the incomplete circle formed by the individual fires, and one outside. This latter band was nearer to them, more quickly recognizable, but not very much less puzzling for any of that.

The first, hasty, and not a little frightening impression which they had was that those inside were seeking refuge from the coyotes outside the circle. . . . Coyotes circling around and around and back and forth, coyotes suddenly howling . . . coyotes . . . But even before the matter of distance and perspective adjusted itself they both realized that coyotes would not be doing a to-the-rear-*run* maneuver whereby each turned and reversed direction and all did so at once, now loping clockwise and now of a sudden loping

widdershins. And they realized, too, that coyotes do not chant, and certainly do not chant *words,* not even in a totally unfamiliar language. . . .

They were prepared, then, for the moment when the "coyotes" suddenly reared up and revealed themselves to be human figures clad (or partly-clad) in coyote-skins. Still, it was marvelous—and eerie, frightening—the way that in stooping and even erect there still remained something so sinuous and animal-like in all their movements. . . .

That was what was outside the fiery circle.

Inside, was something else altogether.

The darkness of night, the slant and diluted rays of moonlight, the flickering-flaring-spurting-blazing-dazzling-dying of the firelight: none of this was designed to help give any clear picture of what was there . . . and the exertion of climbing in the rarified air now tended to obscure their vision from within their eyes. . . . There was a first impression of flashing colors and of odd, misshapen design—as though great grotesque birds had been dressed up by a gifted, but insane, child and set to hopping about in agony upon a great, hot griddle—but, of course, there was no fire within the circle of fire, as there is said to be no wind within the eye of a hurricane. The things moved and jerked about and flashed with gold and brilliant plumes and irridescent ornaments, great grotesque and asymmetrical bifurcated and trifurcated blunted muzzles out-thrust and huge eyes glaring like gigantic burning coals—

"Oh, I don't like this," Sarah whispered.

He said, "Sh . . ."

The things within the circle took up the chant in deep and discordant voices distorted by their masks and danced and jerked and moved about. The coyote-skins flapped, naked human flesh gleaming as though oiled. Only the smoke of the wood fires, mixing in with the mist, seemed normal or natural. And then smoke and mist closed in once more and the sound fell low once more.

Jacob muttered, "Let's go—"

"Evans—"

"Let's *go!*"

She obeyed, yielded to his commanding arm. He could hear her subdued weeping.

Afterwards, he said, "Look, I know that you're worried about the kittykat, but that was no time and no place to break in and say, *Dispenseme, yo busco mi bicho-gato . . .*"

"I know," she said, with a snuffle.

"Boy! Are the natives ever restless tonight!"

They didn't say anything more for a very long time, and by the time they came again to the tottering old archway it was already daylight, though still misty. And here they paused. That is to say, Sarah stopped, and as she had been using Jacob as a sort of staff or crutch, he perforce stopped, too. "Whatsmatter," he grunted.

"So are we going home now?" she asked, in a pity-me-for-surely-you-can-suggest-a-better-notion tone of voice.

"Not necessarily . . . We can go to the Los Remedios-Hilton, if you prefer? What kind of a question is that?—Where else would we go?"

In a teeny-tiny voice she said, "I thought we might go to Mac's house . . ."

"At this hour?" But a look at her woebegone and teary face stopped his sarcasm. "Well . . . He did invite us for breakfast . . . But even for breakfast it's darned early. What say we go home a while and rest up?—*then* we can go to Mac's house. Okay?"

But she, in a voice which was almost inaudible, said that she didn't want to go home . . . because it was full of dirty dishes at home . . . And so he, knowing that her stubbornness was often in inverse proportion to the reasonableness of her request, and that if balked she was perfectly capable of simply sitting down under the archway until she took root, he said, "Let's go to Mac's . . ."

Fortunately, the menage at Mac's also included an aged aunt who retired and rose with the poultry; Tía Epifania had just returned from the *molina de nixtamal* with fresh-ground lime-boiled cornmeal for the breakfast tortillas, and greeted them as though it was the most natural thing in the world for anybody to be up and around at that hour. "Pass, Yourselves!" she cried, cheerily. "This is Your house!"

Some question as to the house's ownership evidently troubled her niece, however, from behind whose bedroom door a sleepy and puzzled "¿ Quien?" proceeded.

"Los paisanos de Roberto," shrilled the ancient, and blew on an ember. The niece-landlady, after an astonished invocation to the Virgin of Guadalupe (whom she addressed, companionably, as "Sweety!"), dug Roberto in the ribs with an audible thud. He broke off in mid-snore, and presently appeared, rather rumpled and sleepy-looking, but as amiable as usual. He looked at Sarah's face and blinked.

"Let me perform some quick hydraulics," he said, "and I'll be at your entire disposal." He did and was. Then, tapped and drained and washed and combed, he sat down and lit a brown-paper cigarette and began to talk of some light and humorous matter until he thought that they were sufficiently relaxed for him to ask if anything was the matter.

Jacob hesitated. "Well . . . We had a rather curious experience last night. Or, early this morning, to be more exact . . . maybe . . . I'm not sure of the exact time." And he proceeded, with help from Sarah, to tell what had happened. The account took a while; Mac nodded and nodded, lighting a second Negrita from the first before they were finished.

Then he laughed. "Well, if there were such a thing as a local chamber of commerce, they'd have printed leaflets which I'm sure would have taken a load off your mind . . . if you'd read them in advance."

"What do you mean?"

He shrugged. "Simply that it's customary to dress up in costume at this time of year. The hills around here have got more old customs and costumes and dances and fiestas and fieras of one sort and another than just about any area of comparable size in the country. You just happened to stumble across one of them without realizing it, that's all."

Jacob, though somewhat relieved, was still somewhat dubious. "Dress up like the old Aztec gods, too, you mean?"

Macauley shrugged again and smiled again. "Well, I hadn't heard of that particular one. Or of the coyote-skin one, either. But, Lord! I don't know all of them, there are so

many. About the only one which is well-publicized is the one that's attached to the Holy Hermit . . . and that one, of course, even though it's technically theologically irregular, well, still, it *is* attached to the church. But most of these others are purely pagan. Which is to say that for the whole length of time of the Spanish rule, they were at least in theory illegal. And hence tended to be clandestine. Then when the Roman Catholic Church was disestablished and some measure, some varying measure of governmental anti-religious pressure came along, varying from disapproval and ridicule down to outright persecution—why, a lot of the pagan cults and ceremonies got it in the neck, too. It didn't make much difference to them if they were suppressed in the name of Catholicism or of Freemasonry—which reminds me"—he chuckled—"no, I'll mention that later. Anyway, so they went right on being underground, so to say.

"Nowadays very few of them have got anything to fear, actually, from the law. But, well, these things are looked upon as silly things which only ignorant Indians engage in. And even ignorant Indians don't want to be laughed at, mocked at. So they go right on going off into the woods, you see. Sometimes whole families sort of split up over it. Say that one family has a son in the secondary school, well, they know he's bound to be too modern to strip down to a loincloth and dance around, say, a post with homemade hootchemacallits pinned onto it. So the afternoon before the thing is due his father may slip him a few pesos and say, 'Why don't you go visit your cousin in Amecameca—tell him we'd like to come, but we can't get away.' Then, with the kid out of the way, they can troop out to the boondocks and carry on the way Grandpa used to do.

"That's all there is to it, really . . ."

Jacob was weakening, but was still not convinced. "This wasn't any mere poor-Injun bare-assing around," he said. "Why, those costumes must have cost a fortune! Besides . . . besides . . . I don't know just how to put it without sounding corny and pulp-fictionary—but—well, damn it! Yes! There was an atmosphere of evil about whatever was going on back up there last night! I had the definite feeling that if I'd let

on that I was there I might have wound up a patient in what you called the Aztec Cardiectomy Clinic! Really, Mac, no kidding around: that was very bad medicine there."

He was about to enlarge on it, seeing that Macauley was at last becoming at least a little bit impressed that this was no mere rustic frolic—but then Lenita appeared. She had so thoroughly repented her of her earlier brusqueness that she clearly neither remembered it nor desired it to be remembered—a plump, dark woman of general good nature and not a single word of English. She bustled Sarah away from the two men with an oh-you-poor-thing manner, reclaiming her for the Improved Benevolent Order of Women—local branch consisting of Lenita, Aunt Epifania, and now, of course, Sarah—and impressed her into service at the business corner of the kitchen. Sarah, as soon as she saw that (a) she was not merely allowed, but encouraged, to take samples of the sundry goodies, and (b) that there were no dirty dishes to be washed, no, not a one, Sarah abandoned the discussion without a pang. She even fell spontaneously into Spanish. "What quality of article will we you were to have making thereunto?" she inquired cheerfully.

Macauley's smile slipped a bit, with her gone. In a lower voice, he said, "Well, there may have been some intended bad medicine brewing around here. Some of the aborigines are really upset, you know."

"Yes, that I gather. But *why?*"

"Government doings."

"Meaning . . . ?"

"Meaning: Tlaloc."

The familiar-unfamiliar word made Jacob frown. Then he remembered. "Tlaloc. Wasn't he the old Mexican rain god?" More than this, the name conveyed nothing to him, because he had been in his studio trying to finish an assignment the while that Rob Macauley had been telling Sarah all about the image in the cave (and/or tunnel) under the Sacred Mountain. But Macauley didn't mind, and he gave his account all over again. Jacob was impressed.

"Sounds as nice as what we saw last night was nasty . . . But how are they connected?"

Over the cheerful clatter of mixing bowls Mac said, "I don't know for sure that they are connected. I just think that they may be. Have you seen the cavalry troop in town? No? Guess you must not have been out of the house yesterday at all, then. Well, it seems to be a fact that the government has decided to remove the Tlaloc to the big new Museum of . . . what's the whole handle? . . . mmm . . . The Museum of National Antiquities and Patrimonial Treasures (how's that for grandiloquence?—not that they haven't got a lot to be grandiloquent about!) . . . yes . . . Down in 'Mexico.' So the cavalry is sort of here as an advance guard to stake out the scene until the moving men arrive.

"The C.O. is a figure in the classical style, tall and leathery and trim moustache, you know. Colonel Benito Alvarez Diaz, and mind your manners, too. I didn't know why they were here, and I said to him, jovially—why not?—'Ah, *coronel*, are you here for the fiera?' Wow! Hey? Guess what hit the fan? I got a fierce little, quick little, stiff little lecture on the fact that the United Mexican States constitute a secular republic. Emphasis: *secular*. And that, in addition, he, *Coronel* Benito Alvarez Diaz, is an educated man and a freemason and—I'm quoting—and that as educated man and a freemason he does not fear and, indeed, defies all superstition, whether Christian or pagan! Hey?"

"Well may you say, 'Hey'."

Macauley said more. He said that he thought that the army unit was there to give notice that the government intended to stand for no nonsense, either from good churchmen lay or religious who might not like any poking around in the Monte Sagrado, or from good (or, as the case might be) bag pagans who might and probably would in one way or another object to the removal of a Tlaloc which had been there, so to speak, forever.

"But it won't do them any good. Lopez Matteos wants it down there in 'Mexico' where the tourists can see it and the antiquarians study it, and you can bet your ass that's where it's going to go. To wit, Mexico. And the poor dumb bastards in the boondocks can dance all they want to and complain that if it's moved there won't be any rain again.

. . . It won't do them a bit of good. I just hope," he added, "that those poor dumbos, some of whom, mind you, are my (ha ha) best friends, don't engage in any transference of hostilities . . ." His manner was thoughtful.

"What do you mean?"

A shrug. "Oh . . . Anybody who isn't from right around here is a foreigner. You're a foreigner, President Lopez Matteos is a foreigner, every savant or non-savant who's ever come here to look at Tlaloc is a foreigner, and, of course, needless to say that Colonel Diaz who's here to start taking away precious potent sacred rainiferous Tlaloc is a foreigner. In other words, to a mind very untutored, which is most minds, all foreigners are linked together in an evil intent—hey?—and design. So—"

"*A la mesa, a las mesa, hombre,*" Lenita directed. "Here are tortillas and refried beans for those who eat the Lord God's food, here is *dulce* of quince and fresh honey, coffee cooked in the aluminum *maquinita,* pure butter of cows, and here is also—look, look—*¡que linda!*—los pancakes norteamericanos which Roberto has so successfully me taught me how to make—"

Sarah, beaming, licking her fingers, said to Jacob, "Isn't it *good?* Doesn't it smell yummy? What is she saying, the tootsie?"

Jacob held out his cup for coffee and his plate for pancakes. "She's quoting from the Popol Vuh. It means, 'Eat, eat; later we'll talk.'"

Later, however, they were too full to talk. And it was even later that they finally and leisurely returned home, full and contented and quite at ease, entering throuh the same back door to the back patio they had left by, and found Evans lying on their doorstep, stiff and bloody and with his heart torn out and missing.

VI

THE FRONT and back patios alike contained a profusion of flowers and fruit and nut trees (there was also an adobe chicken-coop, the inhabitants of which tended to vanish away on the eves of feast-days), but there was also a multitude of such herbs as lent themselves to domestic cultivation; and these Señora Josefa picked and dried and sometimes distilled, as part of her craft and trade. She gave away as much as she sold and had a fair-sized following among the poor, who referred to her as *la doctora;* often as not there were several of them sitting on the bench in the front patio waiting for advice and supply, neither of which would cost them a *centavo.*

This morning, however, the bench was deserted except for a middle-aged and unkempt-looking woman who kept clutching her knee and groaning. As Señora Josefa and Mariana knew very well that she suffered from nothing more than a hangover and a general (and very un-Mexican) disinclination either to work or to wash, and as they were otherwise engaged, she was allowed to go on sitting for the moment. The sisters were in the kitchen going about their work and discussing this and that with their neighbor, Señora Carmela, who was poor but honorable, in low voices.

"And your tenants?" inquired La Carmela.

"They know nothing," said Sra. Mariana.

"She has appeared disturbed, the fat pretty one . . ."

"Yes, because her small cat-beast has not been encountered."

"How sad," said Carmela, adding: "If there were four or five children, there would be no time to be disturbed over cat-beasts."

Sra. Mariana sighed. "They stay up half the night reading books."

"There is still the other half of the night," La Carmela pointed out.

But Sra. Mariana was not to be diverted.

"It would be a disgrace for us all to have this matter exposed before the eyes of foreigners," Sra. Mariana said, heavily. "Woe of me . . . it seems like a bad dream . . ."

"*Life is a dream and the dream is but a dream itself. Everything passes, everything passes, but he who has God lacks nothing,*" quoted Sra. Josefa. Carmela was crossing herself when they heard the screams in the back patio.

The shortest way there, in theory at least, was out of the kitchen by way of the dining room and thence into the sewing-room and then by way of the storeroom onto a small piazza from which two steps descended into the back patio. But their passage, accompanied by cries of dismay and assurance was impeded by the presence in the storeroom of an assortment of items such as sacks of corn kernels for nixtamal and corncobs for fuel, bales of wool and a stack of sheepskins—the screams continued—they about-faced, running out of the storeroom, through the sewing-room, into Señora Mariana's bedroom, and, via the dining room and hall, out into the front patio (where the sole "patient" was listening with ears, eyes, and open mouth) and thence to the metal gate which separated it from the back one. Unfortunately, it was not only closed but stuck—this required that it be seized by main force and lifted up about two inches so as to clear the bottom sill. . . . Unfortunately, also, this had to be done quite carefully in order to avoid lifting it up about two and a quarter inches—which would bring it in contact with the electric wiring whose insulation had rubbed off in one or two places—the screams from the back patio were joined by screams from the front one—

The "patient", who had enjoyed it all tremendously, arose and carefully pushed the gate well shut again with a piece of wood. It clicked. She grinned a satisfied, snaggletoothed grin. She considered a moment, her disheveled head cocked to one side. Then she tiptoed into the kitchen and filled one

of the cups on the table from the coffeepot on the stove, added plenty of sugar—*white* sugar, not the stuff scraped from the coarse and sticky brown load of *piloncillo*—thrust some little cakes and some tortillas into her gaping bodice —gulped down the coffee and tiptoed out again. She decided not to bother waiting for anyone to return. Her hangover seemed quite cured. Coffee and white sugar . . . she made a mental note of that.

It was much nicer than herbs, too.

"Poor little Evans!" said Sarah, through her sobs. "He never hurt anyone."

"Terrible, terrible!" cried Sra. Josefa.

"What barbarity!" exclaimed her sister. They hugged Sarah and caressed her and patted her cheeks. "Poor little beast . . . *no tiene cuidado, Señora*—you can inter the poor little one over there in front of the rose bushes. Won't that be pretty? Oh, poor *señora!* Oh, what a shocking thing!"

And Jacob pointed out to her that the nature of the injury meant that Evans had died suddenly and therefore without pain. He got a shovel and dug a tiny grave in front of the denuded rose bushes, wrapped the little mangled body in two splendid new bandanas of scarlet and gold, and so the interment was accomplished. Señora Josefa then took Sarah to a remote corner of the patio where, behind the moldering ruins of the very last *diligencia* to ply the local roads, one small shrub forgotten in the previous day's excitement offered sprays of tiny blue blossoms. And while Sarah, still weeping, cut flowers for Evan's grave, Jacob knocked the earth from the shovel and said, bluntly, to his landlady, "Who did it and why?"

"Ah, Señor! Last night . . . how shall I explain it to you . . . last night there was a big fight among the drunken Indios in that bad *Barrio Occidental*. They tried to obtain the Holy Hermit, *ai de mi!*—possibly with the intention of holding an oratory service in their little chapel there, although the Lord God knows how they have always neglected it since the days of Don Porfirio Diaz until it is falling apart. But at any rate, there was a big fight: sacrilege—

simple sacrilege! And it was long before the Hermit was recovered, pray God that the Sainted One be not angry with us for not having taken better care—but without doubt this barbaric mutilation was done by those hoodlums in a state of intoxication. It is a disgrace for our *municipalidad*. I shall complain upon your behalf to the authorities, Señor, to guarantee that it will never happen again."

Her concern and indignation was obviously genuine. Jacob decided not to tell her of what he and his wife had seen during the night, there on the lower slopes of Ixta. "Many thanks for your offer to make such representations on our behalves, Señora. When do you intend to do so?"

"No tiene cuidado, Señor. Mañana, Señor. ¡Mañana!"

But at least Lupita came back.

Sarah, who had been trying a spiritual exercise of determining that she would see in her mind's eye only the image of the little heap of blue flowers and not the one of— Sarah was distracted by the sound of running water in the patio. She went to see . . . and saw Lupita washing the dishes. Most of the resentment melted in this infinitely welcome sight. Poor uneducated and downtrodden Lupita, washing greasy dishes so humbly and uncomplainingly in ice-cold water!

"Buenas dias, Señora."

"Buenas dias, Lupita. I to hope where your mother was much improvised in their infirmity?"

"Ah, yes, *alabada sea Dios.* The most of the malignness is terminated. Thanks."

"Of no one." Now that the dishes were clean, it was time to think about making lunch. But Sarah didn't want to think about making lunch. Making lunch was a grunch. People shouldn't have to think about such things when they were griefstricken. Of course, the fact that they were griefstricken didn't mean that they weren't *hungry.* People could be griefstricken and hungry at the same time. That was a well-known fact. "I am not sensing myself well today, Lupita. Dost thou plural thinking of to could tamales prepare whatsoever?"

"Excellently. How you will taste! Preparing tamales of

green chile, tamales of chicken fat, milled meat, and of *mole chocolado*. One little moment, terminating the utensils."

"Oh, yummy!" said Sarah, clapping her hands. And went to tell Jacob, who had returned from mailing his manuscript. He agreed it did indeed sound yummy. He went to his studio and stared a while at the pale yellow walls and the lithograph of Maximilian in its cracked frame. Lupita's head passed by, en route with the rest of her to get water for the nixtamal dough. He tapped on the window. She squinted, smiled, came to the door.

"Did I not hear singing last night, Lupita?"

"Securely, Señor. There was much singing. The fiera, you know."

"Ah, yes. The fiera. I went for a walk, also, last night . . ."

"Oh, was that indeed you, Señor? I thought I saw you, but I was unable to pause. I was seeking for the daughter of Don Esteban, she who used to be employed in the infirmary at Ameca, to ask her to come help my mother. Did you enjoy your walk, Señor?"

He looked at her, and she returned his look with her usual one of docile incomprehension. "Not very."

"Ah, no? It is insalubrious to walk much at night. The air of night is most unhealthy. Dispense me, Señor, I must mix the tamale dough in this little moment."

He said, gloomily, "Go with God."

Lupita went, but not with the God that Jacob had in mind. She mixed her dough and prepared the fillings and put the water on to boil after having made a little steam-bath in the pot, with a fire of twigs and torn newspapers. She was the servants of the gringos, and if she were not the servants of the gringos she would be the servants of others who were no better. All her life she had been someone's servant, someone else's servant, sweeping the dung from their stables and washing their floors and their dishes. Those who gave her orders wore shoes, but she had worn no shoes. Those sat in chairs while she, when she could snatch the time, squatted on the ground. They could read, she could not; they spoke the tongue of the *blanco* as a birthright, she had never fully mastered it. They spoke much of church, scorning

the poor Tenochas of the *Barrio Occidental* for paganism, but although many of them had lain with her none would ever marry her in church. And was not the church a thing of the *blanco*, anyway? What were all these others, *mestizos* in blood, but imitation-*blancos?*

And this had gone on for over four hundred years and for four hundred years a little handful among the Tenocha, the true Aztec blood, had preserved their faith that it would go on forever. Now this faith was being vindicated! The old Axteca gods were returning, had already established their base upon the sacred slopes of Ixta—Huitzilipochtli, Quetzalcoatl, Xiutecuhtli, Ometeucli, and Omecihuatl, Mictlanteuctli and Mictlancihuatl, Tezcatlipoca, and the others —she recited their potent names which hissed and writhed like serpents and clapped and roared like thunders! They were returning to reclaim their land and redeem their people, to drive out *blanco* and *güerro* and *mestizo* alike, put down the upstart and inferior tribes whose fathers the fathers of the Tenocha-Aztecas had conquered, and restore all things as before. . . . Resistance? Of course there would be resistance! All the better!

For resistance meant prisoners, hecatombs and hecatombs of them, and prisoners meant sacrifices, and sacrifices meant infinitely long and blessedly endless lines of bound forms being dragged up the steps of the pyramids and cast upon the altar-stones in such a manner as to arch their chests and make easier the task of the priests who with one stroke of the obsidian knife would part skin and flesh and with the other hand reach in and seize and rip out the beating heart and deposit it in the bloody basin as food for the gods— ah!—ah!

But not a gleam of this inner exultation disturbed the meek and stolid passivity of Lupita's face as she continued her work. She, humble and lame Lupita would nevertheless and at a near time become a priestess . . . a princess . . . a, perhaps, queen . . . She was uncertain of the precise title, but it was not important, not at all important. What was important was *blood*—blood from the pulsating, smoking heart, containing the essence of life, the source of the mystic power

of the gods, the benefits of which would accrue to all the gods' people: yes! And no more such trifling tidbits as the hearts of kids or of cats, but the hearts of *men!* Men of inferior Indian tribes, mestizo men, blanco men . . . A very faint gleam showed in her dull black eyes. She was thinking of how they would tremble and how they would plead and, finally, of how they would scream.

"Does the water now cook and steam, Señora?" she inquired.

"Yes, Lupita."

"Bueno . . ."

Soon, soon, she would serve the gods a proper godly food. Once again she recited their sonorous names. An almost imperceptible droop came to her lower lip. One god was still missing of the sacred company, and until he was present the re-Conquest could not be carried out. But this would not be long. It was known where he slumbered, and soon he, too, would be awakened.

Tlaloc! Tlaloc!

Luis rose slowly and delightfully from the depths of his slumber, drifting at leisure into waking. The vague lineaments of his recent dreams melted into golden mists. They had been greatly pleasant, that was enough. He was not totally awake as yet, but he knew that he was waking. So be it. All was well. In a moment . . . more or less . . . he would open his eyes . . .

It was a long moment, and he smiled to see that he didn't recall where he was. Some rustic shack. It would all come back to him in a moment, the name of the girl, the memory of her *pro forma* reluctance, and how without her little sighs and cries ceasing for more than a moment the nature and message of them had changed completely. . . . He sat up very suddenly and his mouth fell open. There was no girl and there had been no girl, not last night, he had been telescoping time and thinking of a rural amour of a month or so ago. What then *had* happened last night?

The delights of slumber and false memory ebbed fast, and, to his astonishment, he sobbed and was seized by a little

tremor of fright. His hand clutched something in a reflexive spasm, he opened his hand to see what it was—

—A piece of gold about as long as a cigarette and about as wide and thick as a small box of wax matches, but tapering at each end, with one end pierced and strung upon a cord of maguey fibre—

—The side facing him was smooth and blank; he turned it over and saw a spotted animal head, very stylized, with fangs bared: *ocelotl*: one of the puissant symbols of the Great Old Ones, They Who Had Ruled Before The Tenocha.

And it was They who had given it to him. He remembered all of this now and his fright vanished away. Once again he felt fine, excellently fine. *Take health and take rest* . . . His left leg, injured in a fight two years back, and which had begun to ache yesterday from all that climbing, no longer ached—in fact, his eyes and fingers now confirmed, the long dark dull scar itself was quite gone and the brown skin where it had been was glowed with health. Furthermore, one of his canines, always inclined to be a "bad" tooth, had lately seemed both loose and twinging: now it was neither.

Health and rest . . . He had received both, no doubt of that.

The hut he was in was unremarkable, a pile of mats and a sheepskin for a bed. Next to that on another and smaller mat was a small brown earthen mug of *atole*-gruel and the familiar small basket containing a napkin with warm tortillas and bean-paste. The gruel was still warm, too. So . . . He ate and sipped and reflected. They had said, the Great Old Ones, that they would see him and talk with him and answer his questions another time. But they had not named when that time would be. So . . . *entonces* . . . he, Luis, was going to decide that time. Now . . . or as near to now as it would take him to find them. True, he could not force them. If it was their pleasure to put him asleep again, he would be put to sleep again: *nada más*. And maybe again and again. But eventually they would tire of it and then the moment of true confrontation was bound to arise.

He went out of the hut and stopped to urinate and while

he was doing so he looked all around him. There, *there* was San Juan Moxtomí, not more than a quarter mile away as the hawk flies . . . but Luis, keenly aware that he was not a hawk, knew that it was a good hour's walk from where he now stood. Besides, he had no desire to go there now, it looked its usual sleepy self, with the woodsmoke escaping through the open eaves and the only sign of life the figure of a man who was doubtless engaged in the same simple necessity as he himself. Which necessity being concluded, Luis buttoned himself up and started to walk. He had two of the tortillas in his pocket and he might find something on or under the fruit and nut trees which were said to be still bearing (although not well or abundantly) around the ruins of the old hacienda which had been stormed and burned during the Revolution when the Zapatistas came pouring up from Cuautla. Possibly a corner of roof and wall were yet standing, and he just might shelter there if bad weather set in—

One never knew, so close to Popo, when squalls of snow might not descend. One *did* know, though, that beyond the ruins there was no human habitation in any condition on this side of the mountain. And it was thither that he was bound, up through the woods and up through the forests, over the fallen rocks and trees and over the gorges, up into the dominions of the wolf and the eagle and the bear, up into the black and barren volcanic sand which fringed Popocatapetl like a trailing mantle, up the snowy sides by narrow and twisting trails, over the flanks of ice, until—if need be, if he lived to get that far—over the frozen lips of the crater and down, down, down, into the slumbering, but still vulcanous, depths inside . . .

As far as he had to go, that far he would go; but he would find those he sought after.

If he lived.

Luis took the paths more or less as he found them, as long as they went in the general direction of his goal. Where there were no paths heading upwards he struck out across the unmarked land that was open. From time to time he saw the last settlement dwindle in size and finally vanish away

altogether. Once, looking down, he saw the shadows of the clouds pacing across a great valley, and, finally, he was able to look down upon clouds themselves; and at last he looked down upon the hawks and the eagles as they wheeled and circled and sought their meat from God.

The trees became fewer, the bare bones of the earth thrust up at him, the air grew thin and chill. He walked very close to the side of the rock-face now, and avoided further looks down into the deep gorge. And when he heard the growl and snarl of the beast and felt his male flesh shrink in upon itself and his heart swell in cold fear even before he, edging around a turn in the trail, saw the great golden eyes and the golden pelt spotted with black markings and the lips drawn back from the teeth—

He felt in his bones, cold fingers upon cold skin, and drew out the amulet, the sign of the Great Old Ones, and held it out as far as the cord would reach. The jaguar gazed at it, gold reflected into gold. The jaguar bowed his head down upon its paws. The jaguar retreated. When Luis made the next turn it was gone. It could have neither gone up nor down and even if it had gone back it would still be visible. But, of course, it was no ordinary jaguar, as he had known from the first, for this was not the natural habitat of such. It was the magic jaguar of the Olmec, it was a guardian beast . . .

Coming out upon a broad and bare plateau, he could not resist removing the loop from around his neck and fondling and admiring the amulet. It was gold, it was certainly gold, but it was not as heavy as gold should be, and he wondered if it was partly hollow—and why.

The first shout and shot startled him. He cried out, the object slipped, his lunge for it missed, he saw it fall and jumped for it. The second shot spun him around and spun the world around and he saw the darkness close in and the shouts became a roar. He crawled, with the weight of the whirling world upon him, seized and grasped the *ocelotl*, and surrendered to the clamoring dark.

VII

HE SMELLED the sour, stale stink of them . . . old sweat, old clothes, old pulque, and something else . . . worse than any of the others . . . his mind tried to identify this. Why, he could not say, particularly since part of his mind was aware that with some effort he could identify at least which puzzled him—and then recognition came: it was the evil, fishy reek of old blood, like a butcher who hasn't changed his apron for days. So.

That done, now to the voices. He did not know them well at all, but he did know them . . . that is, he knew that he had heard them. The memory was neither clear nor pleasant. He kept his eyes closed.

"A nice piece of venison," said one, poking a thick finger into Luis's ribs. An ordinary voice, this one.

"Not dead, I hope?" This one was hoarse and phlegmy, one of the familiar ones—and, whereas the first comment had been made in Spanish, this second was in Nahua. And now the first one spoke again, and in Nahua, too.

"I don't think so . . ." A hand was laid roughly on Luis's heart. "No . . . this is still good . . ." The all but imperceptible pause was succeeded by a sigh of genuine longing, such as one might hear from a mother awaiting her long-delayed child or a woman yearning for the arms of a distant lover. It was not at all the sort of sound which one might expect to hear from the man, whoever he was or whatever he was, with the ordinary voice.

And now a third voice spoke, a thin and whining-sort, this. "What is one? One is nothing, nothing at all. There must be hundreds, thousands!"

The hoarse one said, "Everything starts with one thing—

63

Vamanos!" he concluded, abruptly. They tied Luis hand and foot and one of them tossed him over a shoulder as though he were a sack of cobs, and jogged off, the others (as Luis could hear) trotting alongside. It was almost insufferably uncomfortable, but he would hardly expect that anyone would shoot at him with the intention of subsequently buying him a ride on a *primero claso* bus. Furthermore, he had something else to occupy his mind besides his discomfort.

It was the last word that had done it, supplied the key. What the man's name was, he didn't remember, perhaps had never known. But he knew now who he was—the barrel-shaped, frog-faced fellow who presided every Saturday and Sunday in the marketplace over a caldron of hog-*tripas* frying in dirty, viscid oil . . . and spent the rest of the week holding up the wall in one of the filthy pul-querias of the *Barrio Occidental*. Hardly anyone except his fellow slummy neighbors bought the evil-smelling chitter-lings, and it was his habit, as he slapped each leathery-looking portion, oozing oil, into a piece of paper, to shout, as though encouraging the next customer, *"¡Vamanos!"*— Let's go!" Ruiz. His name was Ruiz.

His going and the going of his comrades of course made a complete nothing of all of Luis's goings since he had started that morning. But his regret in this was swallowed up in the thudding of his blood in his ears—however far they were intending to take him, he might not be alive if he continued to be half upside-down as he was now. A genuine groan escaped his lips and he did not attempt to prevent it. The jogging stopped, abruptly, and he was dumped onto the ground.

"Come to, have you?" the gut-fryer asked. Luis nodded. *"Bueno.* Then you can walk by yourself . . ." He knelt with a grunt and loosened the cord at Luis's ankles. "Walk, that's what I said. Try running, and you'll get some lead sauce for your *tortas.*" He gestured towards the old rifle held in the arm of one of his friends, a rat-faced fellow.

"Let's kill him right now," said Rat Face—in Nahua. Luis just sighed and rubbed his head with his fists.

"Doesn't understand," Rat Face said.

The third, he of the ordinary voice and by his looks an ordinary *Barrio Occidental* lounger-around, probably supported by a washer-woman wife, said, "How would he understand the Tenocha-talk? Look at him—wears stockings—probably pretends he's a *blanco puro*—father is a landowner—grandmother was a dirty Moxtomí—"

The three of them spat. "*Vamanos*," said Hog Guts, giving Luis a kick in the fundament to emphasize his point. They started off once more, perhaps not so swiftly as before, for if Luis had tried to run his hobbles would have sent him flying. They were, it seemed, heading away from Popo . . . but not precisely downhill, either . . . towards Ixta . . . or at least in that general direction. Who were they? What did they want with him? Surely, despite it having been known to at least one of them that his father did own a *granja*, surely then it must also be known that it was a small one, only. If it was known, too, as much about his family that his grandmother was a Moxtomí, then wouldn't they also realize how very little favored he was by his father on this very account? That, even if his father could afford to pay a ransom, he was most unlikely to do so?

But he didn't ask. It was best to say nothing, for who knew what ideas it might put into their heads! And with that an idea came into his own head: perhaps these bravos were in some way connected with the alleged sulfur-stealers of the crater of Popo. . . . Frightened away, perhaps, by the presence of the Great Old Ones . . . it could be that they were for some reason afraid of his, Luis's—well, what? Betraying their presence to the authorities? The theory did not hang together well, but it was at the moment the only other one he could think of.

He was glad, though, that he hadn't revealed that he knew anything of the Nahua language—Tenocha, as they called it—Meshika, or Azteca, as others called it. The threat or proposal to kill him then was obviously only a ruse to find out if they could speak together in that tongue without his knowing what was being said. Keep your ears open, he told himself.

He couldn't think of anything else he could do for the moment, anyway.

"We should wear the skin for a week," Rat Face was saying, as they passed through a meadow wet with distilled mist. "Thus it was done, and was a thing of great honor, too. That is," he corrected himself, "*one* of us should wear it for a week."

The man whom Luis had come to think of an "Ordinario," in a very sharp voice demanded, "*Which* one of us?"

Rat Face scowled, and seemed to remember that he had the rifle. But Hog Guts, in his rough, mucousy voice, said, "Can't be done now. Whoever did it would stink like a dead dog . . . He'd have to hide out and there aren't enough of us. Wait. There is going to be plenty of time . . . and plenty of skins, too."

Ordinario grunted his agreement. Rat Face once again uttered his blissful sigh, and the look of one who sees a beatific vision settled on his face and almost made it good to look upon.

Luis was not sure what they were talking about. He knew that there were many pagan cult ceremonies involving in one way or another the wearing of animal skins—coyotes or deer, for example. But he had never heard of anyone wearing such a skin for a week, or why, even so, he would 'stink like a dead dog' . . . Unless the skin hadn't been well-tanned first. Nor could he imagine what kind of dance or ritual they could have in mind in speaking of 'plenty of skins' at some future date. It was a mystery. Perhaps he just didn't know Nahuatl well enough; there might be idioms and usages . . . for example, the curious phrase used by the man who had felt his heart to see if it was beating: *This is still a good one* . . .

But let it mean what it might; it all added up to something which he had felt for a long time, that no good thing ever came out of Aztec-land. The Tenochas had been barbarians in the beginning and they were still barbarians now. And bigots as well. "Dirty Moxtomí" indeed! As though the Moxtomí had not been partners in the grandeur and greatness

of the Olmecs and Toltecs at a time when the Tenocha-Aztecas had been naked snake-eaters in the remote and barbarous deserts of the north! *Pues* . . . they would see soon enough . . . the Great Old Ones had returned and soon would, he had no doubt, impose their victorious rule over all the land. And then—once those of *Hispanidad* had been expelled—then the Moxtomí would gain their rightful place as inevitably as water seeks its own level; the Tenocha-Azteca would remain as they were and deserved to be.

This sequence of thoughts comforted him all the way along to the *baranca*. This gorge twisted like a snake; Luis was totally unfamiliar with it, as he was with the small bowl-shaped valley to which it eventually led. And he was totally unprepared for what he saw.

He was, had been, of course, as familiar with pictures of Aztec temples and pyramids as a Greek is with the Acropolis or an Egyptian with the Pyramids. But this was no picture; this was no ruin. These walls, this temple, this pyramid, were—true—exceedingly old . . . they seemed to be older than the old church in Los Remedios . . . but they were in at least as good a state of preservation. He stood stock-still and stunned, and scarcely noticed when the cord around his ankles was removed and retied with almost no slack at all. The structures he saw now, here contained an unmistakable message: that in this place from a time before the Conquest of Mexico by the Spaniards, throughout the centuries of *blanco* rule, the centuries of Christian supremacy, this temple to the Aztec cult had been secretly and successfully maintained and preserved.

And when he reflected on that cult and all that it implied, his flesh turned cold and began to tremble.

His captors removed their clothes and dressed again in loincloths and mantles and headdresses of antique design. They drew water in a vessel of Aztec pattern and sprinkled it about the courtyard, chanting things in a form of High Nahuatl which he did not fully understand. Next they poured libations of pulque, then they built and kindled a fire, then they danced about it, singing, and in the course of this they drew embers from the fire into an incense burner

and cast beads of odorous copal-gum upon it. Back and forth, around and around, in a pattern which grew increasingly more intricate, the three men danced, their voices growing louder and louder:

"Tezcatlipoca-Titlacaoan: We are his slaves!
Shining Mirror, Smoking Mirror, Moon of the Night Sky,
Ruler of Darkness, Dreams, Phantoms, and the Coyotes of the Gloom . . .
Quetzalcoatl: Plumed Serpent, Sweeper of the Way!
Conqueror of The Sun, Supporter of the Sky . . .
Huitzilopochtli, Bright Hummingbird, Dragon's-head!
Drinker of the Rivers of Blood, Slayer of Enemies,
Lover of Many Hearts, Great Face, Burning Eyes . . .
Tonantzin-Cihuacoatl Our Mother, Woman of the Serpent!
Scatterer of Seeds, Feeder of Wild Beasts . . .
Tlaculteotl, Provoker of Passion and Lust!
All Ye Potent Ones, Guides of Our Fathers,
Delighters in the Sacrifices,
Attend to us,
Hearken,
Come!"

The three dancing men lifted up their heads, threw back their heads, howling like beasts, gashing their tongues and their earlobes till the blood ran. They threw themselves upon their knees and struck their heads upon the smooth pavingstones. From within the temple a horn of some sort sounded and blared. Luis, with staring eyes and trembling breath, saw a movement at the temple door. And then the great and terrible gods of the Aztecs appeared and then he screamed and screamed and screamed.

"All is prepared," the inhuman voice of Huitzilopochtli declared. "All, or almost all. The mirror is polished, the way has been swept, the weapons are prepared, the faithful await the summons, the cords are knotted and the knife is sharpened and the fire is prepared. The only thing which lacks is the Great Heart—"

The other gods brayed and groaned and clamored and stamped their feet and brandished their war clubs and their incense burners. Their eyes burned in the grotesque masks of their faces, their plumes waved, their tusks clashed.

"—the Great Heart of Tlaloctlamacazqui: Only this is lacking!"

The three men rose to their feet and resumed their dance and their chant.

> *Tlaloc-Tlamacazqui, Giver of Rain!*
> *Moistener of the Earth, Donor of Hail and Lightning,*
> *Sender of Storms and Perils on River and Sea,*
> *Dweller in Paradise,*
> *Attend to us,*
> *Hearken,*
> *Come!"*

But Huitzilopochtli and his fellows seemingly did not delight in this invocation; they advanced with menacing cries and gestures. The dancing and chanting stopped, the three worshippers crouched contritely, placing their palms upon the ground and raising them to their lips and kissing them. The ground round about them was stained with their blood.

"Have you not heard? Have you not understood? It is vain to invoke Our Brother Tlaloc! He is not here and he will not be here until that which we call his Great Heart is found and secured. It is in this region, Slaves of Tezcatlipoca! It is in this area, Servants of Quetzalcoatl! It is not far from here, Warriors of Huitzilopochtli! Sons of Holy Mother Tonantzin and Sacred Sister Tlaculteotl; we tell you that the mirror reveals that it is at no great distance, and we tell you that it must be found!"

The three men sat with their arms around their knees, their eyes cast down. And when Dragon-Headed Huitzilopochtli had finished and his distorted voice was silent, the heavy one said, "O Drinker of the Rivers of Blood, when it is found, this Puissant Object, then will all proceed as planned?"

"All! All!"

The thin one asked, "Slayer of Enemies, when it is found,

then shall the Tenocha rule over all of Anahuac, all of the Valley of Mexico, as before?"

"All! All!"

He sighed his same blissful, yearning sigh. And Ordinario, in turn: "Dragon-Head, Great Hummingbird, when it is found, then will the gods be pleased to accept all of our sacrifices and grant us all their benefits as before?"

And for the third and final time, the great beaked muzzle of the Huitzilopochtli parted and the utterly alien voice declared, "All! All!"

"Why, then, do you tarry?" it brayed.

They leaped to their feet. "The Great Heart of Tlaloc, we will find it! And in the meanwhile, O our father's gods, be pleased to accept the finest fruit of the first of our offerings!" Two of them turned and seized hold of Luis and tore his clothes from him; while he screamed and struggled, the third mounted the pyramid. Luis was borne, kicking and twisting, up the stone steps and thrown and held upon the altar, his pleas and shrieks never ceasing. A stone with a convex surface was under him, so that his chest was thrust up. The thin Tenocha, his face transformed, leaned over and lightly stroked the sweating skin as though to mark the place, then lifted the knife with its blade of curved black obsidian.

"Stay! Hold!"

The Huitzilopochtli itself mounted the steps. Something gleamed in its paw. It seemed simultaneously vexed and puzzled. "We had anticipated the joy and pleasure of tasting heart and of being strengthened by the fluid of life," it said. "But—see—." It was the golden ocelotl, just now fallen from Luis's suddenly spastic fingers. "This is a sigil of the so-called Great Old Ones and it is in some way connected and in communion with them. And even though we have often defeated them and driven them away from this and other worlds, and even though it is true that they are indescribably far from this world at present . . ." He brooded, emitting small squawking sounds from time to time; then the great grotesque head bobbed abruptly, nodded.

"Release him; do not choose him again. Where he obtained a sigil, how many fives of centuries old it may be,

I do not know. But inasmuch as our total plans embrace the ultimate and absolute defeat of those Great Old Ones, it is far from our desire that they be made aware of our presence for now. So. Go!" It flung out its hand and stalked stiffly away.

The three men gazed at each other, blinking. They seemed to have awakened from a dream. Then the one with the knife severed Luis's bonds. Another helped him to his feet, and the third restrung the cord with its gleaming symbol about his neck. "The gods have exempted you from sacrifice," they said to him, softly, awed, without resentment. "How you have been honored!" And after a ceremonial leavetaking, they helped him rearrange his tattered clothing and conducted him respectfully back out of the hidden valley, down the gorge, and far, far down the escarpments of Ixtaccihuatl, until at last their feet touched a much-trodden trail.

"*Con permiso,*" he said, irony upheld by belatedly-returned courage.

They looked at him with sober eyes, sarcasm having totally passed them by. "*Pase Vd.,*" they said. And they watched him go, faces only faintly regretful, and totally drained of anger.

There were many things in the mind of Luis as he picked his way down the path. Not smallest of the wonders was the difference between these men as he had known them in their outer appearances, boors and buffoons, dwellers in a despised quarter; and as he saw them now in their innerness, heritors of an antique trust and an ancient, unbounded faith.

But the improvement was one which he felt that he and his fellow-countrymen could well afford to do without.

VIII

TATA SANTIAGO TUC, his nephew Domingo Deuh, and others of the council of the pueblo of San Juan Bautista Moxtomí, sat at the feet of the Great Old Ones. The vast and benign countenances of the latter gazed upon the calm and trusting faces of the Indians.

"It was not by our own wish," explained the Elder Old One, first among equals in their own councils, "that we should leave you. True, that we were pleased to return to our home in the most distant stars, my sons. But we traveled, even then, between here and there with little more difficulty than any of you might travel between Chalco and Cuautla. Often we went, often we returned. We knew the Olmec, we knew the Toltec and the Mixtec and the Maya, as well as the Moxtomí and others. We loved them as our children, they loved us as their fathers; we taught them, they were apt, and learned. And so the maize grew and was harvested, and so the ages passed.

"When the Tenocha, whom some call the Azteca, came down from the north, what were they?"

Tuc answered, his seamed face split by a bitter and contemptuous smile. "A handful of savages, lizard-eaters, knowing nothing of agriculture or of any other of the arts of civilized men. War was all that they knew—only war!"

But as the Aztecs were descending from the north, fighting and butchering as they went; at about this same time the Huitzili were descending on the land from their own home-world among the distant, distant Evil Stars. Few were their own numbers and, at first, small their own resources. But with the cleverness of the wicked they had recognized that the Aztecs were a people designed, as it were, by nature to be their tools and the means of their own advancement.

Far, far different was their appearance from the appearance of men, unlike the appearance of the Great Old Ones whose form was like that of giant, exalted men. But the Huitzili were grotesque, horrid, ungainly, distorted . . . Mete and suited to impress the rude minds and coarse fantasies of the Aztecs, who at once elevated the Huitzili to the status of gods—

And then, under their guidance and with their aid, proceeded to conquer as they came, until all the lovely land of Anahuac was theirs, and then the adjacent lands, even unto the sea.

The price was, of course, great, for the Huitzili loved the hearts and blood of man-flesh, and literally rivers of it flowed upon their altars. War, which had first been made to gain land and then to get tribute, continued after both land and tribute was guaranteed . . . *had* to continue, for only from the multitudes of prisoners, could come the requisite number of human sacrifices. And thus, as the power of the Aztecs increased, so did the power of their gods, their allies, the Huitzili.

"War was not our own talent," said the Elder Old One. "And after each encounter we continued in our previous ways, expecting each time that life would be as it was before, that now at last the Huitzili would menace no more. But, by the time we had realized that the Huitzili would always menace because it was a structural part of their nature to do so, events in and around our own world prevented us from full-scale resistance here on this world. But we did what we could . . .

"We lured them away . . .

"To assure our children here of at least some continued benefits, we hid that goodly thing which has been called the Great Heart of Tlaloc, we set an appointed guardian and watcher over it—"

Domingo Deuh said in a low and breathy voice, "*El Hermito Sagrado . . .*"

"The Guardian was in the shape of an ordinary man, the humble custodian of a humble Indian shrine located over and above the cavern where the Tlaloc-which-contained-the-

Great-Heart-of-Tlaloc was located. The presumption was that none would look for it in so obvious a place, and this presumption had proved correct. The Great Old Ones fled, luring the Huitzili with them. For long ages chase, pursuit, encounter, fight, between the two forces continued. Meanwhile, here in Anahuac, the unforeseen had happened. The Azteca-Tenocha, did not—deprived of Huitzili guidance—crumble and fall apart. Their momentum carried them on to further conquests; unable to offer human blood and human hearts to their actual and present "gods," they continued nonetheless to offer them up before the idols and the images. And the butchery and bloodbath continued. . . .

"Then came the Spaniards, who, with the aid of many of the subject tribes and nations of Mexico, destroyed the Aztec power forever. True, they introduced a new bondage, but it had not the same stench of rotten blood about it as the old one had. And the Guardian appraised this new situation and he met it well; he himself embraced the new faith and under his influence most of the other local Indians embraced it as well. As a result, he was able to remain where he had been; eventually he 'died' . . . But, as he had foreseen, even in his 'death' he was able to continue on guard. The legends which grew up around him, of course, helped in his task. If he rose from his bier in the night to inspect the cavern where the object was concealed, the whisper went around that he had miraculously been transported to Rome to serve the Pope at mass. . . .

"But one group of local Indians had never trusted him, never accepted him, loved nor venerated him; and these were the descendants of the local Aztec priests of the bloody sacrifices, who—decayed and downtrodden, sullen and suspicious—still lived in the *Barrio Occidental*."

Old Santiago Tuc nodded his head. "*Si, Viejo Poderoso* . . . it is true. That is why they would try to capture his catafalque during the procession each year. They believed that this would help them to find where the Great Heart was hidden. And then they would have the key to open and to close the rain and then they would make all of Anahuac to do their bidding." He sighed and groaned. "It is known

and revealed how we Moxtomí have suffered since the Spaniards came. Generation after generation we have lost some of our communal lands—confiscation, sequestration, rectification of boundaries, taxation—what names haven't they used! They have eaten our lands like a child eats *gomitas*. The King, the Viceroy, the First Republic, the First Emperor, then Santa Anna, then our good Juarez, the Second Emperor, again Juarez, Diaz, revolution, revolution . . . Now and then we regained a little *milpita* here or there, but mostly it has been loss. . . .

"Still, *Viejo Poderoso,* though we hold only a handful of our *ejido* lands, it is better than being flung upon the altars of the vile Tenochas, to have our hearts cut out and our skins flayed off! *Ai!* I do not know what powers the Huitzili still may have, or how such power may compare to the military and air force and the armada of Mexico. I have heard it said, though, that it matters but little to the pitcher whether it is dropped upon the stone or if the stone is dropped upon the pitcher. We do not want war, we do not want sacrifices, we do not want drought. We want only our old *ejido* lands—and if we cannot have them back, then let us at least have peace. We look to you, Great Old One, to save us from this present threat."

A faint and infinitely patient smile passed across the massy features of the Elder Old One. "We hope you do not look in vain . . . There is, we must tell you, more at stake here besides Anahuac. In the Great Heart of Tlaloc—and need I tell you that it is not indeed a real heart—that it is, how shall I compare it, an engine, a device of infinite power and infinite potency, such as our own much reduced capacities are no longer capable of replacing . . . dwindled as we are from centuries of combat—in the Great Heart of Tlaloc lies more than the ability to insure rain. In it lies the means of turning life to death, matter to not-matter. Should the Huitzili succeed in capturing and mastering it, not Anahuac alone, but the entire universe may well be helpless before them. The struggle between us has been costly to them as well as to us. The few of them who are here once again,

once again masquerading as gods, are all of them that are anywhere.

"This is their last chance!"

Some of the men spoke in favor of proceeding at once, then, to seize and remove the Great Heart from where it had so long lain concealed. But others counseled caution. "It is not the Huitzili alone who are sniffing like dogs," Domingo Deuh pointed out. "They know that the Great Heart exists, but they do not—*yet*—know that it is hidden inside the Tlaloc under the Monte Sagrado.

"But the government has sent troops—the government is going to remove the Tlaloc and take it to the new Big House of Old Things in 'Mexico'—but the government and the military does not know—*yet*—that anything is inside of it. Many of the people in the district are very uneasy, and say that if Tlaloc is moved then there will be no more rain within the whole land of Ahahuac, that is, the Valley of Mexico. And, they, too, stirred up as they are without fully realizing the whole of the matter, may prove a danger."

The huge head of the Elder Old One slowly went down and as slowly came up again. "Then we must move," he said, "not only as swiftly as possible, but as secretly as possible." His great golden eyes sought those of his fellows, and, as slowly and deliberately, they nodded as well.

A wind, chill and pure from the heights of the snowy mountains, came through the village and shook the cedar trees until the air was filled with their rustling.

"Let it be done. Let it be done. *Let it be done.*"

Jacob Clay nibbled at his pipe and stared at his typewriter. Truthfully, he had no inspiration for writing anything at all at the moment and the long hours he had put in on the manuscript just completed had depleted his nervous energy to the point where he felt in need of rest. How nice it would be to throw a few things into a *bolsa* and take off for a few days in, say, Cuautla, or Cuernavaca! But this dream died a-borning. They were too broke. And even though nothing he could begin writing now could possibly bring in any money soon enough to take the vacation while he was feeling the

need of it, still, conscience would not allow him just to say "The Hell with it!" and have Sarah pack a picnic lunch which they could eat in the arcadian beauty alongside one of the little rivers. In short, the time would just go for nothing—unless, most unlikely, the Paraclete would be pleased to descend after all, with an Idea clasped in its bill like an olive branch.

"*Bienvenida,* Luis," he called out, thankful for an excuse, as he saw the young man hesitating in the patio. "Come on in . . . sit down. . . ."

"Jacobo, you are not too busy?"

"No, no. All the time in the world."

"But I think maybe you are too busy. I was rudely bothering you the last occasions."

Jacob winced. "No . . . I'm afraid that I was the rude one then. But then I was busy and now I'm really not. Take a chair, please."

They looked at each, smiled a trifle constrainedly, said nothing. Finally, Jacob, to break the ice, said, almost without considering, "Luis, have you ever heard of any kind of club or cult or something which meets in the woods up there and then some of them dress up in coyote-skins and the others dress up like the old Aztec gods? Have you ever heard of—" He broke off. Then he said, "Oh. You have. Well. I see. I'm sorry I mentioned it. I see by your face that I shouldn't have. *Dispenseme.*"

Luis touched his tongue to his lips, swallowed. "No. No, Jacobo, it isn't that you—Jacobo, Jacobo! They do not dress up like. No, ah, no— They *are* the old Aztec gods! Very terrible! *Ai de mi!*"

"You've seen them, too, then? But you're not one of the, mmm, worshippers, then? No. Good . . . 'Terrible'? Christ, yes! Gave me the creeping meemies. But, now, Luis, when you say that those characters really *are* the old Aztec gods, well, come on now! You know better than that, for crying out loud. You've been to school."

Luis stretched out his hands, automatically beginning to gesticulate, and Jacob's eyes saw the marks on his wrists. Luis saw that he saw, and exposed his ankles as well. Jacob

grunted. "Ah, these are nothing, the marks are already fading and will be soon gone, thanks to the power of the *sigilo* of the Great Old Ones, *Los Viejos Poderosos*. They gave me this, you see?" He opened his shirt, and there against the tan skin of his chest was the golden object with the ocelot's head.

Jacob peered at it. "This sure looks old," he said. "I'm no judge of such things, really, but it does look very old . . . Toltec, maybe . . . or maybe even Olmec . . . Where did you get it, Luis?"

And Luis, talking more rapidly than quite coherently, told him of the Great Old Ones who were now returned and had their place on, or in, or perhaps only very, very near Popo —and of the also latterly-returned Aztec gods, and what they had tried to do and almost did do to him a while back that day. "They fear the power of the Great Old Ones, Jacob! They fear them, but they do not yet know that the Great Old Ones are already here."

Jacob got up. "Well . . . Something is sure as hell going on that's not strictly kosher. Tell you what. Let's go talk about this to Macauley. What do you say?"

Luis's face lit up. "Bueno! Excellent. Don Roberto is a very good person to consult. He knows much of all the *costumbres* of the countryside, and of our history as well. Good, good!" He almost danced in his excitement.

Jacob knocked on the window of the living room to attract Sarah's attention. She looked up, her face tear-stained and abstract. She was engaged in painting a picture from memory of poor sweet-tootsie-little Evans.

"Luis and I are going over to Mac to see him about that business of last night."

"Oh . . . All right, dear. . . ."

"We may not be back till quite late, I don't know. Be sure to lock and bolt all the doors, particularly the back one into our patio. I'll get in from the front patio. Okay?"

"Oh . . . All right, dear. . . ."

She had forgotten all about him by the time the door to the front patio had closed. How fortunate that she had thought to bring these paints and papers with her. And that

78

she'd gotten the idea to do this picture while his little memory was still fresh in her mind—not that it could ever possibly fade!—but still . . . She brushed her hair back, absentmindedly smearing her face with paint. Then she smiled fondly as she looked at the outlined figure on the paper. Perhaps a black background, to show off his white markings? No . . . that would never do . . . it would fail to show off his *black* markings. Blue, perhaps . . . or red . . . Blue would go best with his poor little golden eyes.

Sarah bent over her portrait.

Sometime later she looked up, aware of being faintly disturbed by something. What was it? Hunger, that was it. The tamales had been very good. Perhaps some of them were still left. But would Jacob want some? No, Jacob had gone to Mac's place and he said he'd be there quite late, which meant that he would eat as well as talk. Sarah got up slowly, considering. Heat up some tamales . . . and what else? Not much, of course . . . Maybe a few tostados. Nothing heavy. Cheese, perhaps. And a little salad on the side. A cup of tea. And a *pastelito*, if there were any. Perhaps a piece of fruit.

People had to *eat;* they had to keep their strength up, even if their hearts were just *breaking.* Look at all those rich, yummy recipes Martha Washington was always working on. She probably had cried *buckets* while George and those tootsie soldiers were freezing their toes at Valley Forge, but *that* didn't prevent her from trying out a new way to make poundcake, did it? Although, when you come right down to it— Sarah moved into the kitchen—what it was that George *saw* in her, well, really. "*She's* nothing to look at, wouldn't you agree?" Sarah asked aloud of no one in particular.

Certainly of no one in the kitchen, for there *was* no one in the kitchen. Oh, well. She would toss up her little meal by herself. She looked around for pots and pans and utensils and dishes. There were none. "Hasn't Lupita finished washing them *yet?*" she exclaimed. And went, frowning, out into the patio. The dishes and pots and other utensils were there all right, grease and all, in the concrete sink by the water barrel. Only Lupita was not there.

79

"La Lupita?" repeated the landlady, looking a bit displeased. Yes, Lupita had been seen. First, *el joven* Luis had gone into the *oficina* of Don Jacobo. Then, la Lupita, the without-shame, had been perceived to listen at the door. Then she had left the patio—"going very, very rapidly"—and the house, and disappeared into the streets. *Donde?* "Ah, where indeed? Who knows? The Señora would be well-advised to examine well among her own possessions, to see if la Lupita did not have 'little hands.' "

The usually most pleasant landlady struggled with her feelings, finally admitted, "She is neither amiable nor sympathetic, that girl."

Saran gave a small moan. "Do thou was knowing also possibly to have another girl for employer more responsible?" she inquired.

Señora Mariana shrugged, threw out her hands. "Ah, poor lady! But these girls today prefer to go to 'Mexico' to seek employment, because there they can obtain more pesos." She quirked her mouth and made a circle with thumb and forefinger to indicate the roundness of the peso. But more than this she was unable to do.

Sarah returned, slowly, and lugubriously. She reheated the tamales and ate them, somberly. Then she went out and looked at the pile of dirty, greasy dishes and pots again. She tested the water with her little finger. It was very, very cold.

Mac, advised in English that a matter of the gravest importance was to be discussed, had sent his lady friend and her ancient aunt out to buy pulque, and grilled *carnitas*. "Be sure to hurry there and back," he had told them.

The lady scowled. "Securely, we will sprout wings like the birds and fly," she said. "With the gringos it is always, *pronto, pronto, pronto!*"

As they left, twitching their rebozos indignantly, he smiled at his guests. "That should insure us at least an hour . . . So. What's up, Doc?"

Jacob sighed. "Well . . . It doesn't sound as crazy to me as it would have yesterday. But . . . well . . . Luis claims

that those oddballs in the boondocks, the Aztec-god ones, I mean . . . he claims that they captured him early today and tried to turn him into a human sacrifice. The cardiectomy clinic—just like you said."

Macauley pursed his lips and let out his breath in a near-whistle, so that his golden moustache floated up. "Well, well," he murmured. Then he turned to face Luis. *"Digame,"* he ordered.

Luis, after hesitations and stumbling starts, began by re-capitulating the various rumors sweeping the town on the eve of the fiera of the Holy Hermit: that lights had been seen on both Popo and Ixta, that the government was going to take away the Tlaloc from under the Monte Sagrado, that smoke had been seen rising from Popo, that soldiers were in town on an unholy mission, that there would be trouble with the procession, that the abominable *naguales,* or were-coyotes had been seen once more, and so on.

He described his visit to the Moxtomí pueblo, San Juan Bautista, in hopes of discussing these rumors—how he found them in an uproar, how they put him off. He described the fight, the genuine and not symbolic attempt to seize the catafalque as it passed through the *Barrio Occidental,* and then: "And then, *hombre!* My word of honor! The catafalque fell and the Hermit tumbled out and then he walked away—*he walked away!"*

And so all the other details came out, how the Hermit was really the long-time Guardian of the Entrusted Object and how the Entrusted Object was the Heart of Tlaloc, only it was not really a heart; how the true or false "Aztec gods," the Huitzili, were, like the pseudo-gods of the old Olmec and Toltec days, really denizens of other and distant worlds . . . detail by incredible detail, the story emerged.

Macauley chewed the ends of his long moustaches. "Wow, boy," he said. "Well, Jake, I think we've got two choices, count 'em, two. The first is that Luis's story is the real Mc-Coy, the clean quill, weird and way-out as it is. And the other is that *some*body out there"—his hand gestured toward the wild uplands crowned by the snowy sierra of Ixtaccihuatl and the shining cone of Popocatapetl—"has (a) been read-

ing one hell of a lot of science fiction, and (b) been spending one hell of a lot of time and money and effort . . .

"On the whole," he said, thoughtfully reaching for his gigantic moustache-cup of coffee, "on the whole, I tend to think that the first one proposes far fewer problems."

Jacob asked, "What's to do about it, then?"

Macauley smiled. "Find out about it! I wouldn't go near that pseudo-Aztec crowd with a ten-foot ack-ack gun. But Luis seems impressed with the good will of the pseudo-Olmec/Toltec boys. I vote that we take a nice hike up in the general direction of Uncle Popo and see what we can see."

The vote went with *aye*.

Jacob, afterwards, was not sure that it should not have been *ail*

Huitzilopochtli blared and brayed his rage and his delight. "You have done well, you have done well, woman!" His Dragon-Head and blunt-beaked muzzle darted up and down. "We have returned to reward you all and we will reward you all, but we have also returned in that we are necessitous of obtaining once and for all the Great Heart of Tlaloc. And now that we know that the Great Old Ones, our enemies, have returned as well, it is certain that we know that they, too, seek this Puissant Object. They know where it is—they must know! For it is they who malignantly concealed it in the first place!"

And his fellows stamped and howled and it was agreed by all of them that they would go up to Popo and espy out all there was to espy, and then decide on what was to be done.

And thus it was Jacob and Macauley and Luis were observed as they climbed. And were followed, as the sun sank and the shadows grew.

IX

THE IMMENSE golden-bronze-bell voice of the Elder Old One was raised but a single note, yet it seemed that all the sounds of the forest and the night fell silent and hearkened to it. "We have not been here long," he said, "nevertheless, we have been here long enough. Both the lights and the smokes of our vessel have been seen on Popo. There has been talk, suspicion must follow, eventually attempts to investigate will be made. I believe it would not be well for our star-ship to be seen where it is concealed within the upper crater of the mountain which once smoked itself."

The lids of his benign eyes lifted but a trifle more, the golden and glowing pupils flashed a message to his fellows and to the Moxtomí. "The synchronism of events is disturbing. It cannot be helped that both the Huitzili-things and the forces of the present government of this land are both now intent upon the same mission as we are, though for far different reasons. The alien and evil enemy may begin at any time to proceed against the hidden Object. We know what time the military intends to begin: tomorrow.

"I say that we have, accordingly, only this single night in which to accomplish our intention. If any have reason to gainsay me: speak. I wait. I listen."

The night was silent, the fire glowed, reflecting glowing sparks in both the golden eyes and the brown ones. Old Santiago Tuc said at length, "I know of nothing that we Moxtomí, your servants, can say against your words. Go, *Viejos Poderosos*—go, Lords, and we will follow."

The lips of the Great Old Ones moved in mild smiles and their eyes exchanged consent. Their senior said, gently, "It will be in this way, younger brothers: let the Moxtomí go

before, as befits their position of prime dwellers in this land. And *we* will follow."

Old Tuc rose from his haunches and fell upon his knees. "It is too much honor," he murmured. Then he got to his feet and gave crisp orders, pointing with his finger and naming names. In a very few moments only, the pueblo of San Juan Bautista Moxtomí was left in the charge of its women and children and patron saint. And the silent night was penetrated by the slight but sustained sounds of marching feet. Domingo Deuh went before, with a torch in one hand and a spear, formed of a knife lashed to a pole, in the other. Behind him came *Tata* Tuc, holding a censer of burning coals of the old pre-Spanish fashion in one piece, and a pouch of beads of copal-gum, from which he, from time to time, took a pinch and cast it on the embers. Behind him came a man with the pueblo's single shotgun, then the other men, armed with clubs, knives, improvised but, nonetheless, deadly spears.

And behind them, carrying nothing which the Moxtomí knew to be weapons, but serene and utterly self-confident, huge bodies and massive limbs, towering so high that they now and then were obliged to lift their hands and push away thick and overhanging limbs as though they were mere twigs, came the Great Old Ones.

They wore only what seemed to be the lightest of garments and the Indians were swathed from chin to calf in thick, blue-black sarapes; but neither appeared in the least bothered by the bitter-cold mists which wreathed the trees and paths like wraiths and parted only before the chill winds which now and again blew gustily down from the snowy mountains behind them.

The group did not always take the best-known and most-worn paths, those which followed at an easy slope to avoid difficulties of the terrain; but frequently they availed themselves of shortcuts of the most precipitate kind. Yet not so much as a pebble was dislodged, and all difficulties vanished before their feet as though magically smoothed away.

By and by the intense cold grew less and the descent of the land less abrupt. They halted. The Indians consulted

among themselves a moment. Then old Tuc turned to the towering figure of the Elder Old One.

"Lord, here we can take one of two paths," he said. "This, to the left, is unavoidably longer than this, to the right. But the one to the right connects with the old road from Ixta, and—"

"And there the evil Huitzili-things are encamped. I understand. It would be well to avoid them. They have often defeated us. They may defeat us again. It is possible. It is possible that we may defeat them. Or we may miss them or they miss us altogether. Indeed, all things are possible, except that none may miss Time and none may hope to defeat Him.

"Therefore: the path to the right."

In a moment all had passed: torch, censer, Indians, aliens. Nothing remained to mark their passage but a fallen and trampled leaf and on the still, chill air the fragrant smell of copal-gum.

The Huitzilopochtli paused, lowered its monstrous head. Behind him . . . well behind him . . . one of its men-priests said, "Dragon-Head, Drinker of Blood, the path to Moxtomí-town and thence to Popo lies in the other direction. Pardon your slave: pardon, pardon—"

"It is neither the town as a place nor the mountain as a place which concerns us," the Huitzili said, subduing its terrible voice to a muted murmur. "We are concerned with the creatures called the Great Old Ones: principally concerned with them: and I smell that they have passed along this way and that they have turned down that way. More: many men have passed with them, and their bodies contain beating hearts and their bodies contain the essence of life, which is blood . . . which is blood . . ."

The voice died away to a drone, the fearful head wagged as it turned. Its fellows droned their understanding and their acceptance, they turned, too. And the men-priests and the women, too, understood, turned . . . shivered with more than the cold wind and the freezing mists and icy dews . . . shivered with anticipation and exultation.

"Blood . . ."
"Blood . . ."
They turned, swung about, followed the lead figure. Its monstrous snout, which only the monstrous imagination of the Aztecs could have likened to that of a hummingbird, swung from side to side, snuffing up the wind, gathering information from the lingering scents along earth and air. From time to time it muttered, ". . . *men* . . ." and from time to time it mumbled, ". . . *hearts* . . ." and from time to time it droned, ". . . *blood* . . . *blood* . . ."

Gorgeous in glittering embossment and plumage, hideous in mask-like visage, the other Aztec "gods" went clinking and clattering, stumbling-dancing, swaying-stamping, flapping-prancing, bawling and braying reduced to a minimum —stopped abruptly as the chief Huitzili-thing stopped in front where it had been smelling as it ran, like a dog.

"Other men were here," it grunted, half-pleased, half-annoyed. "Three other men . . . All paused a while but not a great while . . . Odd. No anger. I smell no anger. Different men, quite different, but no anger between them. How perverted. Enough!" The great head swung up once more. "Onward and after them! For we seek the Puissant Object called the Great Heart of Tlaloc and it may be that they will lead us to it, after which, if so, we will accept their hearts and drink their blood and nourish our needs. But let us be wary of both entrapments and willful resistance, never forgetting how perversion engenders a disposition towards both."

In another moment all had passed in the darkness, leaving behind a trampled leaf and an odor of rotting blood, of hatred hot as fire, of stale sweats engendered by alien suns and ancient lusts, and of hungers long unappeased by never so loathsome feasts under never so distant moons.

Far away, far down the valley, a dog sleeping behind a heap of corn raised its muzzle and widened its nostrils. For a moment it stayed quite rigid. Then it shivered violently, a deep growl muted in its chest; and then it lifted its head and it howled.

Luis moved as fast as any of them, but he heard scarcely a word which was said. His eyes were glazed with bliss and his face wore an expression of frozen joy. A song sang in his heart and in his head, and its words were of the true old gods, the veritable angels, the return of the proper patron saints of the Moxtomí-Toltec-Olmec peoples, older than either the god or angels or saints of Mexican Christendom. Its words were of the terribly long delayed, but now about to be realized, return of the great days, with all things to be as they were, not only before the Spanish conquest but before the Aztec conquest as well. Sometimes his words passed his lips and sometimes they did not, but he was scarcely aware of this, either.

The Elder Old One said, "You are called Roberto?"

"Yes, Your Reverence," Macauley answered, feeling more than a little confused, but desiring very much to be polite, at all events.

"What is that, Roberto, which you have with you?"

Ahead, tight, tiny, the few lights of Los Remedios had begun to gleam an uncertain welcome in the black velvet fabric of the night.

"Why, it's called *dynamite*, Your Honor . . . I used to be a miner, that's to say—but I guess you know. Anyway, more or less out of habit, I generally have some on hand in case of who-knows-what. These are sticks of dynamite, these are detonation caps, fuses—" He explained the uses and applications as they proceeded on towards the town.

The Elder Old One nodded. "Crude, but effective in a limited way. We will hope its use will not be necessary. Perceive: that light which appears to be burning in the middle of the air: it is on top of the hill now called Monte Sagrado?"

Macauley nodded. "Yes . . . And the entrance I suggest is on the other side of the hill. For that reason as well as the obvious one of secrecy, I suggest that we go around the town instead of trying to go through it." He took out a Cuautla *puro* and lit it and let a mouthful of smoke billow out.

He had scarcely taken a second puff when a dog howled

somewhere off in the distance and one of the Moxtomí gave a fearful exclamation. They halted, on one leg, so to speak, turned behind them without precisely knowing why. The wind veered about and struck them in the face and they recoiled. "The Huitzili! They are following us!" a Moxtomí cried, as the telltale air brought its message.

Macauley grunted. "Come on, then," he said. "Double-time!"

The ground along the rough semi-circle which they had to cover in turning the town was broken up by fields and gulleys, hills and hummocks, the narrow-gage railroad tracks of both the main line and the spurs. It was not smooth going. Once they had to veer to avoid the unfinished walls of the bullring, and once Jacob slid and would have fallen into the gaping foundation of a grain elevator if Macauley had not caught him. Already behind them they could hear the *thumpthump-thumpthump* of the pursuing feet, and the not-quite-describable sound of voices, both human and quasi-human, allowing excitement and fury to unbridle the restraints of caution.

The troops of the first Montezuma had passed this way, doing a deadly work of execution with those war clubs inset with small blades of obsidian along the sides. Cortez had passed on the same path, with mounted men in armor upon armored horses, the Indians, at first and for long, assuming the two to be one creature, like a centaur. The swarming rebel forces of patriot-priest Morelos; the gaudily-uniformed cavalry of the supreme military mountebank, His Serene Highness General Santa Anna; the red-bloomered zouaves of the French Foreign Legion; the shabby but deadly-determined Constitutionalist troops of President Juarez; the beautifully-tailored, efficiently tyrannical *rurales* of President Diaz; every conceivable kind and type of revolutionary band and army—all had come this way and gone this way, and the town had been in its place and remained in its place, had sometimes watched and sometimes (in the person of its people) fled and sometimes resisted and sometimes surrendered—

But never had the hills and fields observed any stranger

sight than they did now, and yet the town stayed still and silent, the town slumbered and the town slept.

Always those who mounted the wide and shallow steps leading up around the *Monte Sagrado* had mounted slowly and gravely and in reverence . . . but not now. No one climbed slowly and painfully and penitentially upon hands and knees, no one paused to genuflect before the Stations of the Cross, not a hair was torn out nor a garment rent to supply an offering to the *ahuehuete* trees. The steps were leaped by twos and threes and then the formal steps were left behind and the running feet raced along a tiny dirt path. A time-stained picture behind cracked glass showed the painting of the Virgin of Guadalupe, as painted miraculously upon the mantle of Juan Diego, in the fitful light of the tinest of lamps . . . the niche was beside a door ancient and massive of wood, reenforced with wrought-iron and locked with an enormous and elaborate lock to which there was no key.

Jacob Clay had ceased to think anything much except, *What in God's Name am I doing here? and why don't I just stop running and go home, for God's sake?* He watched, dumbly, numbly, as they all came to a halt before the great gate sunken below the level of the worn stone threshhold. The giant who (he was dimly aware) was known as the Elder Old One, with no sign of haste or strain, put his fingers to the lock and turned them as though they held a key. He heard the key, the nonexistent key, he heard it turn the protesting mechanism of the lock, heard the click-clack-clock, saw the door swing open upon loud-lamenting hinges. They entered. The door was swung shut and locked again. Echo, echo, echo . . .

Probably few of the multitudes had, throughout the course of pagan and Christian and secular centuries, been even dimly cognizant that the so-seeming solid bulk of the Sacred Mountain concealed within it a sort of maze or labyrinth, hall after hall, cave after cave, catacombs and chambers and vaults. Old statuary in rich dim gilt leaned against the roughhewn walls, hands in stiff benediction raised. Grills barred ways to neat heaps of monkish bones. The splendid

embroidered palls covering the Holy Hermit next engaged their eyes in the gorgeous gloom, but little dispelled by the huge dripping candles of brown beeswax on iron stands before the cracked catafalque.

"Guardian, arise!" the Great Old One as he spoke strode forward and touched the head and hands, the only visible parts. The dark and sunken eyelids rose and the candles glittered upon the dull eyes. The hands moved, groped, found those of the Great Old Ones, the covers were lifted and set aside, the figure which Luis had seen move before, moved now.

The Hermit set his feet upon the stone-flagged floors and moved, trance-like, down the dark and mazy corridors; the footsteps glowed and glimmered briefly before vanishing; they followed, followed, followed. Down winding passages, down flights of deep-cut steps.

Above, far above, muffled but audible, something crashed and battered at something. Something gave way. Monstrous feet trampled.

Door opened after door, door after door was closed. And the last door of all revealed a passage in the rock, a cleft—

"We cannot pass through," the Elder Old One said. The Guardian, seeming to awake more from its trance, spoke briefly. The noise from above increased. Jacob never afterward was clear as to what was said, he recalled the Great Old Ones departing along the level to an unknown destination, recalled slipping, squeezing, getting through the orifice in the rock, recalled wet and darkness and then a kindled torch and resinous smoke and flaring, spurting light and the great stone head in the falling spray and the old Moxtomí swinging his one-piece censer before and murmuring chanting prayers through the clouds of odorous smoke. Smoke which increased the dimness. Heard the increasing clamor behind him, recognized the chanting and the hooting . . . braying . . . blaring . . . the combination of human and inhuman voices he had encountered in the woods the night of the procession, a century or two ago—

—all happening very quickly—

—stones falling from the wall of the cave—

—the Great Old Ones thrusting their way through the new-made opening—

—the Elder Old One standing beside the great carven head with the enigmatic smile, something in his hands which glittered and shimmered and moved. *"Tlaloc, Tlaloc, Tlaloctlamacazui . . ."* Did the great carven eyes move? Did the great carven lips tremble? What hideous sounds of clamor and rage behind them! "Tlaloc, Tlaloc, Tlaloctlamacazui, give us your Puissant Heart . . ." And something moved, for certain and for sure, something came swimming through the surface of the stone, something not unlike the thing held against the stone by the hands of the Elder Old One, a something which also glittered and shimmered and moved. The two met, the two became one, then as deliberately and inexplicably as before, something retreated back into the stone as a stone sinks into ice, but swiftly. And the Elder Old One, that which he held in his hands now increased in size and light and weight, walked . . . slowly . . . slowly . . . walked away.

But not very far away.

He turned, a look of regret briefly resting upon his majestic and massive face, before giving way once more to its expression of infinite calm. He turned, he gestured. Jacob, Mac, Luis, the Moxtomí, found themselves having gathered behind him. Saw the other Great Old Ones moving forward with deliberate speed so as to form a shielding semi-circle around their Elder. And saw, too, and heard, too (and felt, up through the floor—and smelled, as well—) the rushing onslaught of those who had pursued them.

Hideous muzzles stretched forward, inhuman eyes flashing redly, the Huitzili surged in upon them. And their allies from the debased Techoma of the *Barrio Occidental* followed behind. Noise shouted and roared and echoed. It echoed still another endless second as all action ceased.

Then Huitzilopochtli spoke. "The Heart of Tlaloc!" it said.

Silence. A calmly resisting, a speaking silence.

"Old Ones, the Heart of Tlaloc! Let us have it, and you may then depart."

From his guarded position, the Elder spoke. "You may not have it. You may not have it because it is not yours. You may not have it because you would misuse it. It is not for you to say we may depart and it is not for you to say that we may not."

No shout followed on this, but from the gathered enemy came a low, guttering growl which was more chilling than any clamoring noise. Then the voice of Huitzilopochtli spoke up, low and intense and hideously grinding and echoing within itself. "Old Ones, our patience is short. Do not further abuse it. It is ours, the Heart of Tlaloc, because we defeated you before it was placed here. Surrender it and depart! Surrender it and flee once more to enjoy that peace which your perverted natures crave! Refuse, and we will destroy you forever. Now! At once! Relinquish the Object!"

The figures of the Great Old Ones did not move. But from them a Voice composed of all their voices said, "If we are to be destroyed, we will not alone be destroyed. Better for us all here to perish here than for us to escape and leave you with the means of making millions perish."

Warm and golden, like the tolling of great golden-bronze bells, was that Voice, yet Jacob felt himself shivering faintly. The enemy spoke no word. The Great Old Ones spoke no word. The confrontation, delayed such endless centuries, was now upon them all. Jacob tried to still his shivering; he could not. It became a quiver, then a tremble. The coldness of fear and the fear of death, he thought . . . so it was like this. The coldness of fear and the fear of death. The coldness of death, now and here, before he was already dead. He compressed his lips, but a soundless sigh escaped him anyway, and he saw his breath smoke and vapor on the still, chill air.

It took a moment for him to realize what this meant, and what it meant made no sense. It was no chill that lay only within himself, arising from his own human fears and weaknesses. The cold he had been feeling was from outside. And it was not, and it could not have been, affecting him alone. He saw that Macauley's breath, and Luis's too, was visible . . . and, slowly, slowly, at first like a mere haze upon the

air, those of the Great Old Ones as well. Their metabolisms were different, then. That was to be expected. Less water-vapor in their lungs? He dismissed the fruitless speculation. He wondered if some sudden cold front of the sort which American television meteorologists were always announcing as "coming down from Canada" had come all the way this far down.

Something disturbed his ear. A noise? A sound? He cast his eyes around. The great Head of Tlaloc sparkled and shone and it glittered with an icy mantle. Ice! No wonder he was so cold! So terribly, terribly cold . . . It was not sound but the absence of sound which had disturbed him: the soft sound of seeping water falling like a spray of rain upon the Head of Tlaloc below the spring. Jacob saw the newly-formed stalactites. Icicles. It was unnatural. Uncanny. Frost was now appearing on the walls, spreading like a leprous-white fungus. The air cut his nostrils, he breathed through his mouth, his throat and lungs hurt, he thrust his hands between his legs.

Listen, stranger: snow and ice, and it grew wondrous cold . . . He moved his icy-burning feet and heard the rime crackling under his feet.

He heard Luis draw in his breath, followed his glance, all but shrieked at what he saw. There, motionless as a frieze across the cavern, the Huitzili stood, burning red as fire. Heat rippled the air where they were, and he saw sweat rolling down the faces of the men and women beside them . . . among them he recognized Lupita, but he deliberately put this aside: he would wonder about this later . . . Heat. Heat. Heat . . .

It was evident what was happening. They were locked in silent struggle, a battle raging nonetheless on the level, perhaps, of the flux of subatomic particles. The Huitzili, deliberately, were sucking the warmth and heat from the air of the cave and from the still-living bodies of their enemies, drawing the warmth and the heat as a magnet draws iron filings, drawing it unto themselves and into themselves . . .

Suddenly, almost shockingly suddenly, three things happened: the cold fled, the warmth returned; the Elder Old

One had thrust his hand into the Heart of Tlaloc . . . one hand . . . the other he placed upon the shoulder of the Old One next him . . . who extended his hand to another . . . who did the same . . . it was Luis's hand which lay so warmly upon Jacob's . . . Warmth from the glowing engine called the Heart of Tlaloc. Thus, two of the things: and simultaneously and horribly, the Huitzili began the *Noise*.

It could not have come from their mouths and throats and lungs alone, it was too great, too dreadful. Sound upon sound, wave upon wave, and Jacob sobbed and fell on his knees and pressed his hands over his ears. But still the Noise clamored and echoed and rang and every cell in his body seemed stricken with a deadly vertigo and he screamed and screamed and—

"This must be the last for now," the Great Old One said, his voice coming pained and painfully through the sudden silence. Something like a wavering shield, transparent but not utterly clear, had fallen (or risen) between the two groups. "We must begin to leave now, seek time—I do not yet know how long we may have—" The other group beat upon the rippling panel, assailed and assaulted and were held back by it. "This must be the last for now. We cannot, we do not dare continue using the Heart of Tlaloc this way." He went on to speak, but Jacob was no longer intent on listening.

He was watching Macauley, he was listening to Macauley. "I'm not sure about the amount of the charge," Macauley was saying, preparing his dynamite and thrusting it deep into an opening in the cavern. "I don't want to bring the whole mountain down on top of us, if I can help it—" He grunted. His hands moved. They seemed, to Jacob, to be moving slowly. But he said nothing, realizing that of this he knew as near to nothing as made no difference.

Again the voice of the Great Old One broke in upon his mind's ear. "—if I can somehow fix this barrier to remain a while, then it may be that we can destroy their ship. They will still be dangerous, but less dangerous; if they emerge from here—"

Mac said, companionably, puffing his cigar as though they

were seated at ease over a bottle of gin, "Now, there's the matter of the fuse, too. Over-long, I may blow up an empty cave. Over-short, I may blow up a corridor full of . . . well . . . *me!* And, of course, you. Read much Kipling? His politics left much to be desired"—another grunt. He cut the fuse. —"but he could turn a neat phrase. *The widow-maker.* Always liked that one . . . Okay. The fire goes," he gestured, *"here—"*

And then the Great Old One made a sound they had never heard from him before. Slowly, slowly, he began to withdraw the hand from within the alien engine called the Heart of Tlaloc. They all began to retreat. The shield, the barrier, rippled violently.

But not so violently as the beating of Jacob's heart as he began to move.

That moment, however bewildering, however confusing, had yet had some element of clarity. Confusion worse confounded succeeded it. The barrier gave way in one place . . . in another . . . Hideous muzzles thrust forward. Knives. Struggle. Stench. Mac falling. Jacob seizing him, somehow grasping and pulling. Screams. Smoke. Luis, calmly bending to pick up the still burning cigar which had fallen from Macauley's lips. Crush. Trampling, dragging, dreadful noise, concussion, falling rock. Above, the stars.

X

From the hills above Los Remedios, the town and countryside, the Monte Sagrado itself, all looked the same. Slowly the mists rolled away, slowly the sun came toiling up from behind the two mighty mountains, slowly the morning cook-fires sent their thin wreaths of smoke upward to be slowly dissolved upon the winds. Heaps of big brown adobe bricks stood curing in the air, cattle lowed and slowly moved along

the roads towards pasture. Burros laden down with fire-wood passed them on their way. A thin and melancholy scream announced an eagle in the air. A thin and melancholy scream announced the *mas o menos* coiling its way up along the narrow tracks towards town. The bells of the three churches broke into voice as they had each morning for hundreds of years, the great wheels turning, the bells revolving, falling, falling back, the tongues resounding against the sides, the sextons bending to the ropes, rising, releasing, grasping, bending. The old women in black picking their way along the unpaved streets, the middle-aged women setting up their breakfast-stalls in the market. And from every house, the sound, immemorial, older than the bells, older than any sound of human kind except the sleepy human voices themselves, the sound of the pat-pat-pat of women's hands shaping the dough for the tortillas.

"Where now?"

The Great Old Ones lifted their great hands. "Some of us to our own vessel, hidden in Popo. Some of us to the vessel of the Huitzili-things, hidden in the crags of Ixta. We will destroy it. And thence, we hope, barring Time and Chance and the Unforeseen—things which no one and nothing can bar—thence to our own world."

The Indians, listening, burst into tears. "*Viejos Poderosos*, do not leave us! Stay with us and restore the days of old, for we have waited for them as we have waited for you!"

The smile of the Elder Old One was something less than, something more than, melancholy. Something akin to, something other than: "No one and nothing, younger brothers, can restore the days of old. Can one restore the melted snows? Can the bird return to the egg? And yet, younger brothers, new snows will fall, much like the old; and new birds will hatch from new eggs. Think no more, or at least think not much, of the days of old which may have been good. Think instead of the new days to come which may be good." The Elder One gestured. Another of his kind moved forward, holding in his arms a great chest. He set it down and regarded, first it, then the weeping and now beginning

to murmur Moxtomí with gentle wonder not unmixed with mild pleasure. "Here is something which we had almost forgotten, for it is not a thing we value. *The sweat of the sun, the tears of the moon.* What are they called in more modern words?"

Old Santiago Tuc, tears still wet upon his face, but even more than a mystic disappointed, a hunter and a farmer and a man more familiar with facts than with dreams; Santiago Tuc looked up with quickening excitement and said. "Gold? Silver?"

"Some silver. More gold. Yes . . . The years which were yards of lost labor because of your lost lands, younger brothers, ah . . . gone forever. But the land remains, the earth abides. Take it, then, tokens that we are not false altogether. It will regain the lost lands for you, and one will hope that new years and good years will grow therefrom for you."

Macauley and Clay shook their heads when asked about Luis's family. He had had no hopes in that family; that family had had no hopes in him. All of his hopes had been with the Moxtomí, and in their now-realizable hopes of reclaiming through purchase the lost Moxtomí communal, *ejido,* lands, the Moxtomí were fulfilling all of his dreams which were worthy of fulfillment.

Mac said, "I didn't even think he was listening when I explained about the dynamite. I didn't even think he was paying attention when the balloon started going up, down there inside of the *Monte.* But he had been and he was, sure enough . . ."

Jacob Clay winced, nodded. "It didn't occur to *me.* Not to do what he did, not even to realize what he was doing when he was doing it." But the memory of the young man came back strongly and clearly as he spoke: Luis, face no longer blissful and enchanted, but a strong and totally calm male face. Luis bending to pick up Macauley's still lit, still burning *puro,* waiting until all the others—Great Old Ones, Moxtomí, and Jacob (with the help of young Deuh) carrying Macauley—had gotten out of the cave, then himself moving with deliberate haste and lighting the fuses from the cigar and tossing the sticks of dynamite—one against the

opening through which most had entered, one against the larger opening the Old Ones had made for themselves—then moving purposefully against the third opening, the doorway of escape, and standing there with the burning charge in his hand so that none others might pass:

Until it, too, had gone off.

Side by side the two Americans walked down towards the town. "We might have asked them for, oh, I don't know—some sort of a souvenir, maybe," Macauley said. "What do you think? Hey?"

Jacob didn't think so. "No one would believe us, anyway," he said. "Unless we turned up with that whatever-it-was that they had. That machine or engine or . . ." He waved his hand, at a loss for words. "And from what they tell us about that, the sooner it gets lost, the better."

A passing herd-boy paused a moment as he came up to them.

"Did you feel the *temblor*, Señors?" he asked.

"What *temblor*, young one?"

"Ah, you did not feel it, then. During the night, Señores, a *temblor* in the town. It cracked several of the steps upon the Monte Sagrado, and overthrew that old archway on the edge of the town. Other than that, no damage—" He broke off to lope after his cattle.

Macauley grunted. "As I understand it, though, after the exchange . . . or the transformation . . . whatever you want to call it—*you* saw it! Damn it! Did those things slide between the subatomic particles coming in and out and back again, or *what*? Hell . . . But anyway, it's my impression from what they were telling us that neither remaining . . . what's the word I want? 'Device', there . . . that neither remaining device is harmful.

"Oh, well. You're probably right, though. Nobody would believe us. Unless maybe the Saucer Cultists, and I guess we can do without that . . . What do you suppose the devices are good for, *now*?"

Jacob shrugged. "Making rain, maybe," he said. They both laughed.

Neither could resist going back to the Monte Sagrado and joining the crowd which stood and examined the cracked steps. "Securely, it was nothing more than a minor earthquake, such as has happened time after time here in the Valley," someone was saying; (Jacob recognized him—the merchant Lopez, member of the Constitutional *Ayuntamiendo* of the town) "possibly because of the proximity of *los volcanes.*"

But not everyone agreed with him. And one old man, so agitated that he removed his enormous old-style sombrero and struck it with his hand, cried, "And I tell you, Don Procopio, that, securely, it is nothing of the sort! It is the work of *el Tlaloc!* A warning that he is not to be molested—"

Don Procopio Lopez scoffed. "Do you call yourself a Christian?" he demanded.

The old man wagged his head. "I do, I do, and I tell you what every child knows: that *el Tlaloc* is himself a Christian, converted, *probablemente*, by the blessed Apostle Señor Thomas himself when *el santo* visited Mexico after the death of Our Lord—as witness that the emblem of the Tlaloc is a cross." The crowd murmured. "Can anyone deny this?" the old man demanded.

A market-woman, one of those who knelt hour after hour, usually, alongside a pile of produce, without visible show of weariness, now nodded her head vigorously.

"*Mira*, Don Procopio, he has reason, this old one," she said, emphatically. "The Tlaloc is very well where he is. It is said that he is himself a quality of saint—the saint of rain. How is it otherwise that the Holy Hermit made his home above the Tlaloc? Have the priests been molested by our Tlaloc? Has the bishop? No! Why then should the government and the military molest him?"

Don Procopio began to perspire very slightly. On the one hand, he was a member of the government and obliged to defend its doings; on the other hand, he was a businessman, and his customers were right here in the crowd and not among *los burocraticos* in the Federal District. "You also have reason, Señora Veronica," he declared. "I can assure you that is not the motive of our institutional and revolution-

ary government to molest el Señor Tlaloc, no, no—on the contrary—it is nothing more than the intention, without embargo, to remove him from his present obscure position in which he faces danger of destruction by earthquake and thus to bestow him with the utmost respect to a position of equal honor and greater salubrity—"

Macauley tugged at Jacob's sleeve and muttered in his ear, "Let's get on up and see what's doing." Jacob nodded. They gently slid through the crowd, which was already beginning to evince a degree of persuasion.

"The time is past," they heard Don Procopio orating, "when our national treasures and patrimonial heritages can be suffered to molder in the darkness. Does not the work of The Revolution still continue? Are not new schools, new centers of health and maternal care—"

Macauley murmured that he would not be surprised if Don Procopio did not eventually rise to the position of Alternate Member of the Chamber of Deputies, or something equally commensurate with his talents. "He's wasting them peddling galvanized nails here in Los Remedios—hello! *soldados.*"

Sure enough, the entire cavalry troop seemed to be engaged on something quite important on and inside of the Monte Sagrado—not, to be sure, on horseback, though. There was much running back and forth, excited shoutings, and—as a sort of double-take—their way was barred by an armed guard. "Damn," Mac said, low-voiced. "Look—picks, shovels, pit-props . . . They're going to excavate! I suppose that we might have known that they'd excavate! We should have realized! The *militario* was sent here to secure the Tlaloc . . . and they are damned well going to *secure* the Tlaloc! . . . or know the reason why. Damn, damn, damn."

The guard continued to face them with a sort of this-is-merely-me-in-my-official-capacity attitude, without menace or resentment. *Orders, Señores, are orders,* his face said . . . *another time, and you can buy me a drink . . . but just don't come any further or I shall be obligated to fusilade you.*

Jacob said, "I just thought of something. You suppose there's anything *left* of the Tlaloc?".

His friend sighed and shrugged and winced. "*I* just

100

thought of something. You suppose there could be anything still *alive* in there?"

"Ugg. Christ. Yes, I mean, I hope *no*. You mean—"

"I mean." They faced each other. "Of course, there aren't—weren't—many of them . . ."

"Who knows how they reproduce? Or what they might do? Just suppose that any of them are alive and say just enough to alert, say, the Air Force, to reconnoiter around the tops of Popo and Ixta before the Good Guys take off . . . ?"

There was then, in the indeterminate distance, a muffled scream. A shout. Many shouts. Another, or perhaps the same, scream. Less muffled. Growing louder. Feet running, trampling, stumbling. Voice shouting. The guard moved warily so that he was able to cover with his weapon both the two foreigners and what until that second had been his rear. And another soldier came into sight, face insane with fear. "¿Joven, que pasa?" the guard cried.

"Ah—ah—ah—not masks—not masks—no hearts—no hearts!" the fleeing one screamed and babbled. "Ai, Jesusmaria, men whose hearts were torn out!—things of night-mares—ai!—ai!" He clawed at his eyes, staggered, slumped to the ground in a faint.

"I guess that there *was* something still alive in there," said Macauley, looking rather sick.

Jacob swallowed. "And I guess we can guess what they've been up—" He stopped abruptly. His eyes, Mac's eyes, the eyes of the guard, all swung around to the opened gate which led into the depths of the Sacred Mountain. The sound was ragged and prolonged. It was repeated. And again. Jacob said, "Three volleys . . ."

The guard had begun to tremble. "Oh, my mother," he muttered. "What has this poor one seen? What are they shooting at in there?"

They never knew if he ever found an answer. Very shortly a file of soldiers appeared at port arms, eyes staring and mouths sagging; at their head, their commanding officer. ". . . don't know and don't want to know," he was saying in

101

a high, tight voice only kept by great self-control from being a shout. "Wall them up, what's left, forever, and—" He stopped short on seeing the two foreigners.

Macauley asked, crisply respectful, "Are all dead, colonel?"

"Securely, they are all dead, and pray God they all remain so!" Something seemed to click behind the eyes of *Coronel* Benito Alvarez Diaz. He drew himself up. "I do not know exactly or even approximately what you may think you may be referring to, Sir Macauley," he said. "But this I *can* assure you: the United Mexican States constitute a secular, a totally secular Republic; and as an educated man and a freemason I not only do not fear, I indeed totally defy all superstition, whether Christian or pagan!"

His eyes blazed at them. Macauley made a gesture in between a salute and a bow. "I understand, Colonel, and I respect infinitely both your motives and the compliment of your confidence."

"It's well . . . Now, for the love of God, get out of here, say nothing, and let us all have a good, stiff drink!"

It was quite a good while later before Jacob got back to his own patio, walking with exaggerated care, and smelling strongly of *Oso Negro* gin. He found Sarah in so deep a mood of self-sorrow that she barely bothered to scream, "Where have you been all night, you son-of-a-bitch?" at him, as he, breathing heavily, pulled off his shoes with all four hands and needing every one of them, too.

"Dispense, dispense," he muttered. "Work of utmost importance to peace and happiness of future generations. Elder gods. Bad guys. Smelled real bad. Foreign names. Can't pronounce. Don't get wrong idea," he cautioned, crawling onto the bed. "Some are all right. Best friends. But not in same neighborhood."

Sarah began to weep. It was all too much. Not alone that he had been gone all night and now had come home stinking drunk. But Lupita, evil and wicked and faithless Lupita, had yet again and yet once more failed to show up. And so once more and yet again she, lovable and put-upon

Sarah, was left with a pile of dirty dishes and greasy pots and nothing to wash them in, or with, but ice-cold water. "You bastard," she sobbed. "A lot you care!"

From halfway along the bed Jacob opened one bloodshot eye. "Let one in," he cautioned, "first thing you know: brings in his whole family." He closed his eye, was instantly and catatonically unconscious, and began to snore like a demented lumber mill.

Señora Mariana, the landlady, and her sister, Señora Josefa, were properly sympathetic. "Ah, the poor pretty norte-americaness!" they sighed to her. "Yes, yes, we have sent to inquire, and the response is that la Lupita is not encountered at all today; no, no, Señora, she is not to be found. What barbarity!"

"But why?" Sarah demanded. "Where can she have *gone?*"

They shrugged. They shook their heads. "Thus it is, Señora. One takes the troubles to teach these girls the proper management of a household, and as soon as they have learned, what passes? Always, but always, Señora, they go off to 'Mexico,' where they can make more pesos. Thus it today, Señora, but it was not thus when we were young. You are well off without that cruel Lupita. Very well off," they nodded, seriously.

Sarah thought that they might well be right. But . . . still . . . What was she going to *do?* How would she manage, up here so high that water scarcely boiled, no O-cello sponge mops, no Campbell's soups, no Comet cleanser, no detergents—and now: no maid?

They did not entirely understand her, but they were sympathetic nevertheless. "Do not weep, poor pretty Señora," they urged. "All men become drunk, but observe in how much more civilized a manner become drunk los norteamericanos! And as for a girl, *pues*, Señora, have no concern: my sister and I will inquire, we will seek, we will securely find you another girl to aid you."

Sarah smiled a wobby but already-begun-to-be-reassured smile. "You *will?*"

"Oh, without doubt, Señora!"

"Absolutely, Señora!"

"Oh, good! That's all right, then . . . *When?*"

"Mañana, Señora!"

"Mañana!"

Partly as a result of the eloquence of Don Procopio in pointing out that active noncooperation might well result in peril to the basic Revolutionary principals of Effective Universal Suffrage and No Reelection of Presidents, and partly as a result of rumors that Colonel Alvarez Diaz had already shot a large number of resisters and interred their bodies up within the Monte Sagrado, further resistance to the removal of Tlaloc melted like snow in the summer sunshine.

Further troops arrived, archaeologists arrived, engineers arrived, gigantic machinery of all sorts arrived, a special railroad spur was constructed; and so, little by little, and with infinite pains, the Tlaloc was slowly removed through a new-made opening in the side of Monte Sagrado, gently eased down the slope, hoisted aboard the flatcar, and conveyed and convoyed by day and by night slowly and carefully the entire length of the *mas o menos* line to its terminus in the ancient Estacion San Lazaro in the City of Mexico. Here it was placed with equally painstaking care onto the specially constructed, specially reenforced bed of the most powerful truck in the Federal District: and, slowly, slowly, slowly, under constant military and civil escort, conveyed along its route to its new home in the new Museum of National Antiquities and Patrimonial Treasures.

Tlaloc's fame had gone before him, as such things have a way of doing. By the time the truck was underway it was well past midnight. Nevertheless, the route, which passed by a total of twenty-seven churches and the cathedral, was lined with what traffic experts calculated must be at least two million of the five million inhabitants of the City of Mexico. As the truck bearing the gigantic stone head, its eyes half-closed, on its full lips an expression of infinite majesty and calm, passed on its slow way through the throng, not a sound was heard.

Not a sound, that is, except the continual sound of the pouring down of what all observers and all records agreed was by far the heaviest cloudburst of rain ever seen on that date in any year in the entire Valley of Mexico.